Praise for *Jamaica Tough*

"Mrs. Stack has written a compelling novel exposing the dark underpinnings of a vacation island often called paradise. She brings to our vision the horrors of a brave young woman who grew up in poverty. This book draws the reader in from the first page. "

Jon Michael Miller.

JAMAICA TOUGH

This book is a work of fiction. Names, characters, places, and incidents are either the product of the author's imagination or are used fictitiously.

For more information contact: Natalee Stack
natcole876@aol.com

Language Note

The official language of Jamaica is English, but the spoken language of Jamaicans among themselves is a dialect called *Patois* (Pat-wa). Some call it broken-English. *Patois* is a French term without a precise linguistic definition. Most people in Jamaica speak both English and *Patois*, but there are people who only speak *Patois*. The Jamaican language is fast, fun and creative. Jamaican Standard English is grammatically similar to British Standard English. In this novel, there are very mild *Patois* passages in dialogue. Here are some examples—instead of saying *him*, Jamaicans would say *im*. *Im* is also used for *his*. Instead of saying *I*, Jamaicans say *me*. Also regarding pronouns, the personal form is used as well for the possessive: *me* = *my*, etc.

Acknowledgements

With heartfelt thanks to my husband and daughter, Kevin and Kailee Stack,
for their patience & support.

To a lifelong friend, John Oceretko.
My literary guide, Jon Michael Miller.
For my mother, Patricia Dunwell.
And my late brother, Michael Jr.

Prologue

Rape, so she heard say, is not a matter of sex but of power. His eyes showed her this truth. They told her who was in control. He made sure she knew he could do what he wanted, that she counted for nothing. He used and tossed her in the gutter, flicked her away like a cigarette. No need to kill her; she'd never tell. Not for his pleasure at all, but his cruel satisfaction only, squalid victory. With each brutal thrust he stole her freedom — not a thought of bother in his vicious mind.

Chapter One

Jones Town, Kingston, Jamaica, 1986

In a red and white plaid uniform dress, Mishka Campbell was anxious about her first day of school. Like many Jamaican girls, her hair was styled in pigtails, braided at the end and tied with red ribbons that matched her uniform. She had the most angelic features a little girl could ever possess—the darkest of skin, almond- shaped eyes framed by thick lashes, and a small determined nose. The arch of her brows gave a look of continuous interest, and the slight indentation on her cheeks formed a glowing smile.

Draped on her shoulder was an oversized backpack which made her look as though she was going hiking, but contained only a soft cover notebook and a pencil. She held on tight to her mother's hand as they approached the entrance of her new school. It was a chaotic scene.

Jamaica Tough

Watching the other students, a wave of fear overwhelmed Mishka. Her excitement about starting school suddenly dwindled. She squeezed her mother's hand tighter. Other students were waving goodbye to their parents, some crying, not wanting to stay. An elderly, grey haired gentleman with thick eyeglasses met Mishka and her mother at the doorway.

"Morning, Sophie," he said pleasantly, making way for them to step inside.

"Mornin', Mister Raymond," Mishka's mother said.

Hands in his pockets, he stood firmly and looked down at Mishka.

"How you do this morning, sunshine?"

With hands behind her back, Mishka slowly began to speak.

"Me fine, sir."

"Good, good," he said. "You know, since you were old enough to talk, every-single-day that you walk past here with Sophie, you always want to know when you can come to my school. Now, I hope you don't cry after Sophie leave."

She looked up at her mother. “You soon come back for me?”

Sophia laughed and patted the top of Mishka’s head.

“Marlene will come for you after school. Behave yourself for Mister Raymond, you hear?”

Sophia gave her a kiss on the cheek and waved goodbye.

Mr. Raymond was a retired teacher who devoted his golden years giving back to his community. His school was located only three doors down from Mishka’s home. After retirement he built a small classroom on his property that accommodated thirty or so students from the neighborhood, most of whom were indigent. His wife, also a teacher, worked as his assistant and prepared lunch for the children. Everyone in the community respected Mr. Raymond. Nearby neighbors didn’t seem bothered by the voices of precious preschoolers repeating their A-B-C’s and 1-2-3’s.

Hot and sweaty, Mishka sat quietly at a small wooden table observing everything and everyone around her. When Marlene, her mother’s friend and next door neighbor, finally strolled in to pick her up, Mishka gave her an earful about her first experience in a classroom.

Jamaica Tough

"Me don't cry after Mommy leave me this mornin," she said with a girlish voice. "Me behave meself too, and learn to spell *cat*, then Mister Raymon' tell everybody to say grace and eat lunch."

Everyone in the neighborhood knew Mishka's family. They lived on a small compound at the corner of a narrow street which spoke silently of desertion and a legacy of lost hope. Colorful murals of Bob Marley blanketed walls up and down the road, attributed to the man who took reggae music from the slums of Kingston to the world. Mishka's three-bedroom, shanty-like cottage was made of plywood and zinc. The unpainted outdoor bathroom was concrete, the shower separated from the restroom by a wall, no bathtub, just a cement floor and a rusted shower head, a door on both for privacy. At the back of the house, lines were strung along the fence for laundry after hand-washing. A cistern sat in the front of the yard, used for fetching water.

Although their house was sparsely furnished there was much warmth and vigor. The family spent most of their time in the sitting room, where an eighteen-inch color television sat atop a homemade shelf. Facing the TV was a ragged red sofa decorated with large teddy bears. In the center of the room stood a coffee table overwhelmed by artificial flowers of every kind. Mishka's little bedroom was only a footstep away; her bed, dresser, and laundry basket left just enough space for her to move freely.

After school each day, Mishka stayed with Marlene and her children until Sophia came home from work. Mishka loved her mother dearly, but was often puzzled by her seemingly pessimistic outlook at their world. She supposed Sophia was either emotionally worn-out from life or simply tired from working long hours. Sophia was tall and had a dumpy figure. Though relatively young, she appeared much older and dressed the part. She merely wore long, loose clothing and a black, flappy hat.

Mishka's father having gone to America left a strain on her mother, but she managed to do what many single mothers did each day—struggle fiercely and make sacrifices. Her situation wasn't unique; a vast majority of Jamaican women raised their children alone with minimal resources. Luckily, Sophia had Marlene to fill the babysitting gap. Mishka was aware of her father's absence and didn't seem troubled by it. Once in a while she asked Sophia, "When Calvin come back to look for me?"

Sophia's response was always the same. "Me don't know, Mishka."

On Saturdays, Mishka and her little brother Ricardo sometimes went with their Aunt Tracy to church up the road from home. Although Mishka didn't comprehend the fundamentals of Adventism, she enjoyed being among children her own age during Sabbath classes, and singing hymns along with the congregation.

After dinner on Sunday Sophia and Marlene took the children to Devon House for ice cream. They walked out on the main road and squeezed into a crowded route minivan. Mishka didn't get outside of Jones Town often and was always happy to be with Marlene's daughter Roxanne, her best friend. Marlene was also a single mother of three, the father of her children having left her. She made a menial living by vending at local street bashes at nights, selling cold beer, cigarettes, and such.

Mishka thought that Devon House was the most beautiful place she'd ever seen. Although Sophia didn't have much education, she liked explaining childlike things to Mishka. Strolling through the gift shop, Sophia told her that Devon House was one of Jamaica's most celebrated historical landmarks.

"What is *celebrated*, Mommy?"

"Means everybody know bout it," Sophia said. "Jamaica first black millionaire build this place long, long before you born."

"What is *millionaire*, Mommy?"

"Somebody with more money than you will live to spend," Sophia said, laughing.

"Im eat ice cream too?"

The children rolled around on the lush green lawn having the time of their life. For Mishka, this was anything but her Jones Town shack. They stared in amusement at a wedding couple who posed for professional photos.

"Her dress look pretty, Mishka said, "like a princess. Me want to wear one like it."

"That mean you mus' get married." "Why people get married?"

"Cause them want to live together with kids."

"But my mother an' father live together when me an' Ricardo was baby. Them never married."

"You want me to ask Mommy why people get married?"

"No. She will say, *we too out of order*. Only big people mus' know bout them things."

They hopped over to a nearby picnic area where some other children played. Sophia and Marlene sat and talked about the neighbors.

Chapter Two

One year later …

Awakened by the usual sound of cocks crowing, Mishka and Ricardo had to rise for their new schools. Now six, Mishka was to be enrolled into primary school and Ricardo, five, into Mr. Raymond's school. Sophia made porridge and prepared the children for the school term. Mishka stood in front of the mirror admiring the detail of her new, navy blue, pleated uniform.

"Mishka!" Sophia said. "Go sit down and eat-up your breakfast. Me don't want to be late for work."

Mishka hustled over to the table and joined her brother.

After dropping off Ricardo, Sophia walked Mishka to school and gave her a peck on the cheek.

"You don't have to kiss me, Mommy. Me a big girl now."

"You still me baby."

Jamaica Tough

Sophia reached into her bag and handed Mishka some coins.

"This no much, but it can buy something for lunch. Marlene will pick up Ricardo and then pick you up later, you hear?"

Jones Town Primary School contained grades one through six, a lot larger than what she'd imagined. She joined the other students in the courtyard for morning devotion. She listened intently as the students and teachers recited the national anthem and school motto. In class, she was happy to sit next to Roxanne. Most of the basic school students she graduated with were now going to this school.

At lunchtime, the older students raved about the school principal and the belt he whipped them with if they misbehaved.

"We call it the scorpion," said one of the second graders.

At the end of the day, Mishka and Roxanne waited outside to be picked up by Marlene.

"Miss Marlene," Mishka said. "You know principal can beat we at school?"

"If im have to beat you that mean you do something bad. Make sure it don't happen, cause me know Sophia will beat you on top of it. Same thing go for you, Roxanne."

The girls exchanged glances.

Marlene brought the children home and made dinner, after which Sophia ambled in from work. Sophia andMarlene was best friends. Marlene, however, was rather eccentric in appearance. Her choice in clothing was often revealing, her hairstyles outrageously colorful, and she wore lots of gold jewelry. Mishka always knew when Marlene was approaching because she could hear the jangle of her bangles. Mishka hugged Sophia and told about her day at school, without mentioning the principal.

"Take Ricardo an' wash im hand," Sophia said.

After washing their hands the children came back and sat on the floor of the verandah. Marlene placed the children's meals between their legs. She and Sophia sat on chairs with plates on their laps.

"The Chinese people them soon close the factory," Sophia said, chewing. "Next week."

"Next week!"

"People start to walk off the job already. Some hold up sign an' protest outside, say the Chinese treat we unfair an' shouldn't give such a short notice bout the layoff."

"But why them close?"

"All them say is that them have to bring business back to China. We have over three-hundred women who work there. Nobody will have a job after next week. Me so stress, don't know which way to turn now cause work so damn hard to find."

"Even harder when you come from roun here."

"Yes me sis. People don't think we good enough for decent work."

"That's why me don't bother to look. Paul give me a good start with the little money im give me other day, that is how me buy-up all them goods you see me sell."

"Mus' be true when them say bein'poor is a crime."

"So wha' bout Calvin? Im can help with the children till you find work."

Digging around in her plate, Sophia shook her head hastily.

"Don't talk to me bout Calvin, Marlene. You know the situation already."

"When last you hear from im?"

"Out of the clear blue last week, im call me phone, say im come to look for the children."

Marlene stopped eating and fixed her eyes on Sophia. "You lie!"

"Same thing me tell im too. Im been sayin' that for five years now."

Mishka stopped eating and focused on Sophia.

"Im bring me go to foreign with im, Mommy?"

"Not as far as me know, darlin'."

"So why im come for then?" Ricardo said.

They shrieked with laughter.

"You never ask a better question, child," Marlene said.

The children went back to their meal.

Marlene leaned closer to Sophia. "You better hope that im come, treat im real good, and make im want to carry you back to America with im."

Sophia rolled her eyes. "As you well know, me used to treat im good, real good, but all me get out of it is two children me can hardly feed."

"Never too late."

"Calvin don't want me, Marlene. Im married to

American woman now."

"That don't mean a thing—old stick catch good fire."

"Well, that's all me is now, old stick. As me say, Calvin married now, to American."

The children left their dishes on the floor and went outside to play in the yard. Marlene chased away the mongrels as they moved toward the children's scraps. They cleaned up after the children and chatted before Sophia gathered her pair and went home.

Mishka didn't know anyone who had a father. She wanted to know more about what he had said to Sophia regarding his return, so she went into Sophia's bedroom and lay across the bed.

"Go get me a glass of water an' come back," Sophia said.

"You can ask Ricardo to follow me? Me fraid."

"Fraid for what?"

"Too dark out there. The bulb blow."

"Me put one in tomorrow. Tell Ricardo me say to follow you."

Ricardo accompanied Mishka outside to the cistern to fetch Sophia's water. She came back and handed it to Sophia.

"You believe Calvin will come back, Mommy?"

"We will have to wait an' see. Im never want me to tell you and Ricardo, say im want to surprise you."

"What me mus' say to im if im come?"

"You say whatever you want. Long as you not out of order."

"Me mus' call im *Daddy*?"

"What else you want to call im?"

"Calvin."

"An' why is that?"

"Cause me never call im *Daddy* yet."

"You used to, but that was so long ago you don't remember."

Mishka had difficulty falling asleep. In the grand scheme of things the word father was meaningless, but after hearing that Calvin might finally return to Jamaica, she began to feel a sense of joy. Not because she missed him, but because deep down inside, she held out hope that he would someday return. She took a Polaroid photo of her family from the sitting room and brought it back to her bedroom. She held it under the lamp. Her eyes squinted as she studied it. They stood outside a hutted restaurant at the beach. Calvin held Mishka between him and Sophia who was undoubtedly expecting a baby. Mishka might have been two, had on a two piece swimsuit and what appeared to be a black flappy hat, Sophia's most prized possession. She couldn't recall that long-ago moment, but anxiously counted down the days until Calvin's arrival.

Friday afternoon on the way home she saw a strange car parked at her gate. No one ever came to visit them in a car. She hurried inside to see who it was. When she walked through the door, a nicely dressed gentleman sat on the sofa talking to Sophia and Ricardo. Mishka stood there and looked at him. He resembled the man in the photo, but a little older.

"Mishka!" he said, rising slowly from his seat.

He walked toward her and extended his arms. She reluctantly fell into them and wrapped her arms around his waist. He squeezed and kissed her on the forehead. She felt overwhelmed and unsure how to respond. This was the first time a man hugged and kissed her. He took a step back, held her by the shoulders and glared down at her without speaking. She hung her head, waiting for him remove his hands from her shoulders. The room was quiet.

"This is your father," Sophia finally said.

"How you do, Mishka?" Calvin said, still holding Mishka's shoulders.

She looked up at him. "Fine, thank you, sir."

He kissed her on the forehead again before walking back to his seat.

"She grow tall," Calvin told Sophia. "An' she resemble me too. Me can tell you take good care of them."

"Go change your uniform, Mishka," Sophia said, her face turning into a frown. She pointed at Ricardo. "Go with your sister so me can talk to your father."

Mishka walked slowly so she could hear what they talked about.

"Me *take good care of them*?" Sophia said. "Me alone them have! You leave me here with them an' don't try to help me feed an' put them through school. Me don't have no work now, so me hope you plan to do something."

"Now is not the time to argue with me, Sophie," he said calmly.

"Me no argue, me tell you as it is. Look like you forgot how hard it is to survive out here. All these years, me alone suffer with them till now. Bout, *me take good care of them*."

She rose and shut the front door. He quickly moved his feet back as she made her way past him to sit.

"Me have papers now," he said. "When me go back home me apply to bring the children to live there with me. Them will get through fast now that me have papers. Me give you me address before me leave so that you can mail them birth paper whenever me ready for it."

She lifted her hat and placed it beside her, then glared at him.

"Oh, so that's why you come back here, to tell me you take away me children. Last month make five years, five years! since you leave Jamaica. You say you go to America for better life, for all of we, but you go there an' through stone behind you, find new woman, get married. Now you want to come here an' take me children from me, leave me here with nothing?"

"Me don't come here to fight with you. This is about the children, not what happen five years ago."

"Me talk bout the children, yes—five years ago you left them here an' forget bout them. Plenty nights me go to bed hungry, jus' so them can eat, yes, that's how me *take good care of them.*"

"America's the best place for them. Them have a better chance at life there."

"Maybe so, but what is my life without them? After you leave me here all me ever have is me children. You think it so easy to give them up?"

"Wasn't easy for me to leave them behind either, live without them for all the years you talk bout, but it was for the best. See, now me can give them a better life with more opportunity. If you love them give them a chance to leave here. Me send them back to you every holiday for visit."

Mishka changed her clothes and went back out where her parents now sat quietly. Ricardo walked out behind her. Calvin rose and walked toward the children.

"Me come back tomorrow," he said. "We spend the weekend together."

Mishka hung her head and nodded. They followed Calvin to his car and watched as he drove away. Mishka hugged Sophia around the waist. “Me don’t want to move to America with im.”

“Me stay here with you, Mommy,” Ricardo said.

“Don’t fret.” Sophia said. “Me don’t think me let you go anyway.” She stopped. “You listen to what me say to your father?”

The children looked at each other.

“The house small, Mommy,” Mishka said. “You never whisper.”

Calvin came back to pick up his children. Gazing out the window, Mishka sat quietly in the passenger seat.

“Sophie tell you guys why me come here?” Calvin said.

Neither of the children responded. He glanced at Mishka.

“Look,” he said, “me know it’s been a long time, but me tell Sophie that me want you an’ Ricardo to come live with me in American. You will get to see Disneyworl’ an’ all them other nice place. Me send you back here every summer for visit with Sophie.”

“Why you wait so long to come back?” Mishka said.

“Lotta reasons why. You wouldn’t understand them now. One day me explain it all to you. To say the least me didn’t have proper travel document but now that everything worked out me here."

When they arrived at the hotel, Mishka got out and held her brother's hand. She admired the nicely decorated lobby as they walked through. Whenever she rode past here in buses with Sophia, she always wondered what it looked like inside. Now that she was here it felt as though she didn't belong. She followed Calvin to the swimming pool where a petite, middle-aged woman wearing sunglasses floated about. Calvin waved and caught her attention. She climbed out, dried herself and walked to where Calvin and the children stood waiting. She wrapped the towel around her waist and hurried toward them, smiling.

"This is me wife, Jackie," Calvin said.

She reached out and shook the children's hands, her nails nicely manicured.

"I've heard a lot about you both," she said. She touched Mishka's cheek. "Aren't you pretty, and a clone of your father."

Mishka didn't know what the word *clone* meant, but *pretty* sounded familiar. She looked up and smiled with a tinge of embarrassment. Calvin led the children to his suite where Jackie showed them the gifts she brought.

When it came time for Calvin to leave Jamaica, he brought the children back to Sophia and kissed them goodbye.

"Me come back for you guys soon, hear?"

They nodded. Sophia gave him a look of disapproval. He handed her a piece of paper.

"Me address on there," he said. "Me call and let you know when to send the birth certificates."

Without looking at the piece of paper, Sophia jammed it in the pocket of her dress. He slipped her some American dollars and went on his way. Mishka went inside and showed Sophia the gifts Calvin gave her.

"Im wife say me pretty," she said. "We eat at big restaurant, an' go beach." She held up a bag. "Look, me an' Ricardo get a whole heap of nice things—game, clothes, shoes, cellular phone, book, an' pencil."

Sophia smiled and picked up the cell phone. "When you old enough me let you use it."

"You send the birth paper to im, Mommy?"

"Go put away your things."

There was a knock at the door. Mishka stepped out to talk to Roxanne.

"Miss Sophia tell me yesterday that you gone with your father for the weeken'."

"Yeh, me jus' come back."

"You have nice time?"

"Yeh, me get foreign things too—pretty clothes, shoe, cellular phone. We drive all over the place and im wife take picture. Me an' Ricardo stay at hotel with them, name Wyndham."

"You show me what you get from foreign?"

"Come to me room. Me give you some book an' pencil for school."

Sophia walked next door to Marlene's while Mishka showed Roxanne what Calvin gave her.

Chapter Three

Four years later ...

Mishka went home excited about her first major class outing. She hadn't been on the outskirts of Kingston in her life. Her last outing was the weekend she spent with Calvin and Jackie in New Kingston. She rushed home to tell her mother.

"Evenin', Mommy," she said, strolling in.

"Come here, darling," Sophia's voice sounded from the kitchen.

Mishka kicked off her shoes at the doorway and later found Sophia standing by the stove stirring stew.

"Good evenin', Mommy."

"Afternoon, darlin'."

Mishka reached into her backpack and handed Sophia some papers. "Permission slip for me Rose Hall trip."

"Which Rose Hall?"

"The Rose hall Great House down by Montego Bay. We goin' to see the house where the white witch live when she was alive."

Sophia wiped her hands on her top and took a seat on a kitchen chair. She read carefully.

"First let me see if we can afford to send you. House cleanin' don't pay anything."

She handed the papers back to Mishka who folded and stuffed them in her backpack, losing hope about attending. She walked to her bedroom and changed out of her uniform, thinking about how much it would suck to miss her first school outing. Everyone in her class was excited about it. She later went back to talk to Sophia.

"You ask Calvin to help pay for me trip?"

Sophia wiped her hands on the front of her dress and placed them on her hips, her eyes now on Mishka.

"You ever see me beg anybody for anything?"

"But Calvin is me father."

"As much as me broke, you know me would never ask people for anything, especially money. Me don't want you to pick up bad habit to beg people for anything. Whatever we don't have, you do without. Nobody mus' know when you in need, hear me?"

"Calvin isn't just anybody. You always do everything for me. This is the first time me ever ask im for anything."

Sophia walked back to the stove and tended to the pot.

"You right," she said, conceding. "Me call im an' see bout it."

On the morning of the outing, Mishka rose at dawn and helped Sophia prepare lunch, which she packed in a small cooler for Mishka. She kissed Sophia goodbye and went next door to wait for Roxanne. They walked to school together filled with joy.

"Me so glad we get to go to Montego Bay together," Roxanne said.

"Me almost didn't get to go. Mommy don't have the money to pay but she ask Calvin an' im send some."

"Me glad we can go together. Me always think bout what the rest of Jamaica look like."

At school, a minibus waited for the chaperones to do their count and load the students on board. Mishka sat next to Roxanne and sang along with her favorite songs playing on the radio. The farther away she was from Kingston, the nicer the view. Finally in Montego Bay, she sat back and took in the nicely manicured golf courses, strips of lavish hotels, and tanned-bodied tourists walking along the streets. It almost felt like a new planet compared to the wooden houses and zinc fences in Kingston.

When they approached the Rose Hall Great House, a male guard rose from his chair and opened the double gate. They drove past a gift shop and up a paved driveway to the entrance of the mansion. They were greeted by a young woman who wore a long plaid skirt with matching head-wrap. She introduced herself as the tour guide and then led the class inside. Roxanne and Mishka held hands as they walked through. The shiny wooden floors were immaculate, antique furniture and portraits everywhere. Mishka listened carefully to the history of the Great House, especially about Annie Palmer's ghostly presence after her death. At that moment, the room became tense. No one spoke, except for the tour guide. The curtains in Annie's bedroom rustled with the wind through the door leading onto her ocean view terrace. Mishka was reluctant to continue the tour with the group into the dungeon of the mansion. The tour ended at the graveside of "The White

Witch of Rose Hall," as Jamaicans referred to her. Mishka sat on the lawn and ate lunch with her group before boarding the bus back to Kingston. Although the stories were atrocious, it didn't take away from the beauty of the plantation.

Back in Kingston, Mishka's mood suddenly changed. The scene in Montego Bay was breathtaking. She wished she had a chance to talk to the tourists, listen to their accents, and ask questions about their country. She wondered why they came to see Jamaica, and why they wore sunglasses. At home, she waved goodbye to Roxanne and went inside.

"Evenin', Mommy," she said walking in.

"How come you look so tired?"

She settled into the sofa and dropped her bag to the floor.

"Long drive."

"How was the trip?"

"Good, but the witch was a very wicked woman."

"Wha' you mean she *wicked*?"

"She was a slave-driver, come here from a place name Haiti. Murder her own husbands, poison an' kill them all then go out late at night to ride horse-back. Them say that the people who buil' her grave never buil' it strong enough so her spirit still roam the place. That's why no one ever live there after she die."

"Me hear all them story bout that witch since me was a little girl. Me mus' go see for meself one day."

"Me wish we can live in a nice house like some me see down Mo Bay."

"Sure you can live in a lovely house one day. The only way is to take in your education. If you turn out to be a bright young woman maybe one day you will get good payin' work and take your poor mother to live in a big house with you. Me want to give you more out of life, but me couldn't afford university. If you have good education and brilliance you can do anything you want. Your children won't have to want for a nice, big house; you will already have it to give them. Me can't give you the world, but me here for you as a mother who love and will show you the right way through life, so take heed to what me tell you an' make me proud one day, hear?"

During class, Mishka noticed Roxanne had a very hard look on her face and wasn't as talkative as always.

Jamaica Tough

"Why you look out in space so?" Mishka said.

Roxanne opened her textbook and picked up her pencil as if her thoughts were interrupted.

"Me tell you lunchtime," she said.

While having lunch alone inside their classroom, Mishka studied Roxanne from across the table.

"Why you don't eat, Roxanne? Everything alright?"

"You mus' promise not to tell no one."

"You know me wouldn't tell."

"Promise."

"Alright. Me promise."

Roxanne pushed her plate aside and leaned closer. "Last night Paul feel me up."

"Feel you up?"

Roxanne pointed between her legs. "Touch me with im finger."

Mishka pressed her hand tightly against her mouth. Her eyes widened.

"Me beg im to stop," Roxanne said, her voice quivering.

"Why im do something so nasty?"

"Don't know. Late last night me feel somebody wake me. Me open me eye an' see Paul, im say me mus' come to Mommy room. Me think something wrong with her, but when me go, me see she don't come home yet. Im lock the door and tell me to lie down, lift up me nighty. Spit on im finger and touch me private. Me tell im to stop but im push im finger all the way an' hurt me."

"You tell Miss Marlene?"

"Im say me mustn't tell."

"But Miss Marlene will bring you to the police station an'…"

Roxanne interrupted. "Im have gun."

"How you know?"

"Im take it from under the bed an' show me. Say if me tell im kill an' bury me."

Mishka knew Paul, a man who rode a bicycle to visit Marlene. He had severe features, a hideous scar along the left side of his face. He often had a marijuana joint hanging from the corner of his lips, never smiled, and carried himself discreetly. He was a self-proclaimed *Don* in the area who surrounded himself with young, poker-faced thugs. No one crossed Paul.

"Me feel really sorry this happen to you," Mishka said.

Roxanne wiped her tears on the sleeve of her blouse and emerged with a look of vengeance in her eyes, one that could kill.

"Me make im sorry im ever touch me," she said.

"Wha' you mean?"

"You will see."

"Why you can't tell me?"

"You will see."

Mishka's face formed a question mark. "You jus' tell me the worst thing that can happen, but now you can't tell nothing else?"

Roxanne hesitated. "No matter what happen, no matter how bad, you can't say anything to no one, not even miss Sophia."

Mishka's brows drew together. "What you goin' to do to Paul, Roxanne?"

"Me goin' to poison im this evening."

"Poison im?"

"Make im drop dead. Same like wha' the white witch do to her husban'."

"You serious?"

"Dead serious."

"You won't get away with that. Miss Marlene bound to find out."

"Nobody will know if you don't say anything."

"How you think you will get away with it?"

"Mommy always ask me to bring dinner to Paul. This evening after she share im food, me put poison in there before me bring it to im. Im won't know it."

"But where you get poison from?"

"Mommy keep rat poison inside the house. She use it to keep out the mice."

"Rat poison! That's for rat, not people."

"If it work for rat, it will work for Paul. You will see."

Mishka leaned across the table. "Look, me know you vex bout what Paul do, but you shouldn't poison im. If im find out something worse might happen."

"Im can't hurt me no more than what im already do."

"Don't do it!" Mishka said, her eyes pleading. "You know Paul a gun man. You will only make things worse!"

"After what im do last night, me want to see im drop dead."

Roxanne cautiously reached into her pocket and took out a tiny black bottle and held it up.

"See it here. Me get up early this mornin' an' mix it with water. Me ask Mommy wha' she cook for dinner this evenin', she say soup. Later on she will ask me to bring Paul im dinner. All me have to do is drop some of this in there an' watch im eat."

Mishka recalled watching Sophia setup overnight traps for the rats. By morning it would lay stiff. Sophia would then take it outside and dispose it. Mishka rose and gave Roxanne a steady glare, sending an unspoken rebuke to her plot. Two girls carrying boxes walked into the classroom behind their teacher.

"Me want to talk to you outside," Mishka said.

Roxanne placed the bottle back into her pocket and followed Mishka to the back of the school yard.

"Why you so stubborn, Roxanne?" Mishka said. "You don't see you out to get yourself in a big trouble with Paul?"

Roxanne folded her arms and looked down at her feet, her back against the trunk of a mango tree. Mishka waited for an answer.

Roxanne finally looked up at Mishka. "Me never ask im to touch me."

"But you say im have gun, right?"

"Im won't know who do it."

"But if this thing don't work only you an' Paul know that im touch you. Who else you think im will believe try to poison im?"

"Paul always have trouble with people, that is why im carry gun. Nobody will know it's me."

The two had an intimate friendship, but a conversation with this level of intensity had never come into play. They leaned against the tree side by side without speaking, Mishka contemplating a way to get through to Roxanne. The sudden ring of the school bell shook Mishka from her meditation. She peered around the corner and saw the school principal telling a group of boys who were hunched over marbles to get to class. She turned back to Roxanne.

"You have to try an' forget bout what Paul do."

Roxanne moved slowly toward Mishka. "Forget bout it? How can anybody forget bout this?" "It's bes' you forget bout it. It will serve you better."

"Bet if it happen to you it wouldn't be so easy to forget."

Mishka held Roxanne's hands in an apologetic manner. "Don't talk like that. You know me always on your side. Me only say that cause me don't want Paul to hurt you again."

Roxanne started up the corridor. "Im won't hurt me again."

Back inside their classroom, Mishka kept looking over at Roxanne. She didn't want to imagine the outcome of Roxanne's plot, and she certainly didn't want to see Roxanne in trouble if she were to go through with it. She opened her book and wrote a note to Roxanne. The teacher stood at the front of the classroom lecturing, her eyes all around the room. Mishka folded the note and dropped it on the floor. She kicked it toward Roxanne. Roxanne picked it up.

Later that evening, Mishka went home and maintained her composure. She wanted to tell Sophia, but she'd sworn secrecy and could not betray her friend. After completing her homework, Mishka walked outside and peeked through a hole in the fence. Paul sat on Marlene's verandah smoking a joint. She quietly went back inside, hoping that Roxanne had given up on her crazy idea. But what if she hadn't? Mishka was startled by Sophia's voice yelling out from the kitchen that supper was ready.

It began to get dark. In the midst of gathering her things for school, Mishka heard the sound of Marlene's bracelets urgently jingling past her window, and then a loud bang on the front door. She went out and saw Marlene and her children standing there, Roxanne among them. Marlene hurried inside.

"Quick, go get Sophia."

Mishka called out for Sophia who came out from the kitchen.

"What is it, Marlene?" Sophia said.

"Me have to carry Paul go hospital, now! Im sick bad over there, spit up blood. Let them children stay with you till me come back."

Sophia pointed the kids toward the sofa, her eyes still fixed on Marlene. "Wha happen to Paul?"

Marlene exited the house and rushed toward the gate. "If me don't come back early, let them children sleep here till mornin'!"

Roxanne and Mishka exchanged glances, but shifted their eyes away from each other when Sophia turned to sit. Through the corner of her eyes, Mishka saw Roxanne's look of terror, sweat on her nose. She stood in the corner of the room.

"Wha' wrong with Paul, Roxanne?" Sophia said harshly.

"Me don't know, mam. Im only say that im don't feel good an' cry out for im belly. Im fall down on the floor an' start to spit up blood."

"But me never know of Paul havin' belly problem. You sure?"

"That's what im say, that im belly hurt im bad."

"Me hope them reach hospital quick. You all hungry?"

"No mam. We eat already."

Mishka woke up the following morning and noticed that Roxanne and her sisters were gone. She hadn't had the chance to speak with Roxanne about what she'd done. But she imagined Roxanne's plan had prevailed, and she'd have to live with the guilt of knowing that she did nothing to stop her friend from poisoning her mother's lover. She rose and walked to the kitchen. Ricardo waited at the kitchen table with a slice of bread in one hand and an enamel cup in the other.

"Mornin', Mommy," she said.

Sophia raised her eyes from the kettle. "Mornin."

"Roxanne them gone home?" Mishka said.

"Marlene come for them bout five o'clock this mornin'."

"Everything alright with Paul now?"

"Doctor keep Paul to run more tests. Them think somebody poison im."

Chapter Four

Three years later ...

Before dawn, neighbors' voices coming from outside woke Mishka. She remembered it was the last day of school before summer break, and today she would sit for the high school entrance exam. The voices continued. Mishka wondered what the commotion was about so early in the morning. She rose and saw her family awake.

"Wha' go on outside, Mommy?" Mishka said.

Sophia walked to the front door. "Me go out there to see."

They walked outside in time to see the new boy who lived across the street surrounded by neighbors as he told a story. He looked upset. Mishka's family walked over to listen.

"Two man with black mask kick off the door and ask for Harold. One of them tell me to get up an' lead im to where Harold sleep. When we reach in there im wake up

Harold. Harold beg for im life, but the man put a pillow on Harold head and shot im dead!"

Mishka was terrified! She'd heard about similar incidents in the neighborhood but never this close to home. Neighbors were walking in and out of Harold's house to look at his body.

The cops finally came and took a statement from the boy.

"How old are you?" the cop asked the boy.

"Seventeen, officer."

"What are you to the dead man?"

"Me uncle."

"You live here?"

"Me move here from country bout a month now to stay work with me uncle at cement factory, but me go back home to country day."

"Good move," the cop said, walking away.

Another police officer waded through the crowd, pushing Mishka aside.

"Leave the scene!" he said. "This is not the first dead body you people see."

Residents spoke quietly among themselves about what might've triggered the murder. Still dressed for bed, Marlene and her children came over to where Mishka's family stood, Marlene next to Sophia.

"Me did know something go on out here," Marlene said. "When me come in off the road roun three o'clock, the dawg them wouldn't stop bark. Them bark whole night. Scratch up the fence. Little after that Paul come in an' tell me, say man dead out here."

"Me never hear a thing till this mornin'," Sophia said. "The noise out here wake me."

Sophia later took Mishka and Ricardo by the arm. "You two mus' get ready for school now."

Inside, no one spoke. Mishka sat across from her brother at the kitchen table, a look of terror in his eyes. Sophia prepared breakfast and showed no emotion.

"Can't believe people so wicked to kill Harold like that, Mommy," Mishka said.

Sophia brought breakfast to the table. "Not another word bout wha happen out there this mornin'. Learn to keep your mouth shut roun here. It will save your life. How an' why Harold dead is for the police to fret bout. Now, eat an' go put on your clothes for school."

Baffled about her deceased neighbor, Mishka walked to school with Roxanne without speaking about Harold. Mishka was upset, and wondered why Sophia appeared so unmoved by what had happened. She couldn't shake the fear of something so awful happening almost at her doorstep. All she'd ever seen of Harold was his going and coming from work in his dusty clothes. He hadn't seemed like a bad guy. She went to class and pretended as if nothing happened.

After lunch, Mishka's teacher introduced a middle-aged woman by the name of Jenny, who wore a yellow T-shirt with the words *Hope for Children's Development Company* across the front. Jenny waved at the students and began to speak.

"HCDC is a community-based organization. We try to enhance the well-being of children of our inner cities. We provide assistance through skills-training, summer camps, after-school programs, and community advocacy. I know that today is the last day of school and I wanted to drop by and tell you about our upcoming summer camp."

Mishka raised her hand. "Where will the camp be, miss?"

"Ocho Rios. We're going to be there for one month. Last year, we went to Port Antonio and had over one-hundred campers. The goal is to give you a break from the community and get you involved in everything Camp Hope has to offer. It will be fun."

After a one-on-one conversation with Jenny, Mishka liked her. Jenny reminded Mishka of her Aunt Tracy. She was nurturing and had kind words to say. Thinking about Harold's death only made Mishka want nothing more than to get away from home.

She and Roxanne walked home that evening with a plan to talk their parents into allowing them to attend summer camp. Mishka knew that it would take some persuading for Sophia to give her consent.

"One month!" Sophia said. "Next thing you know me can't find you."

"No, Mommy, Miss Jenny a nice lady. She give me her phone number and say she will come here and talk to you or we can go to the office to meet her. Please, me really want to go."

"Give me the number. Me want to see her in person first and hear more bout this camp you pressure me so much to go to."

Mishka kissed Sophia's cheek.

"Me don't say you can go yet," Sophia said.

Mishka ran next door to see how it went for Roxanne.

Entering the front gate, she saw Paul leaving. Without making eye contact, she stepped aside and gave way. Roxanne sat on the steps of her house. They spoke together away from
Marlene.

"She say me can go," Roxanne told Mishka.

Now at summer camp in the countryside, Ocho Rios seemed a world away from Jones Town. Mishka missed her family but was happy Roxanne was there with her. They were camping at a prominent high school in the district. Jenny gathered her group for their first meeting. They sat in a circle under a tree.

"This is Mister Allen," Jenny said, pointing to a man who stood beside her. "He's been one of our counselors since the beginning of our organization. He'll be my sidekick, keep you all grounded."

Mr. Allen smiled.

"I'm going to give everyone what's called a journal," Jenny said, digging through her bag. "You're to make note of every day that you spend here. We'll do this session once a week. It will give us a chance to get to know one another."

She handed a journal to each camper.

"So," she said, sitting in the center of the circle. "It has been two days. What does everyone think about Camp Hope so far?"

A boy from Mishka's school raised his hand.

"Say your name, age, and the community you're from," Mr. Allen said.

"Kemar McDonald, Sir, twelve years old, me come from Jones Town."

"Welcome, Kemar," Jenny said. "Tell us what you think about being here."

"Me like it, miss."

"Can you name something specific that you like?"

"Yes, miss. Me like that we near to the beach. Me never go hikin' before so me like that too, we pick some sweet,

sweet mango yesterday. Me like the dorm room them, an' the food we eat here taste good."

Everyone laughed.

"What would you be doing this summer, Kemar, if you weren't here?"

"Sell at the market downtown with me mother."

"Do you miss helping your mother at the market?"

"No, but me do it to help her still."

"I understand. Where's your father?"

"Im dead, miss. Police kill im."

As the conversation progressed, Mishka wanted to join in, but Sophia's warning about keeping her mouth closed caused her to remain silent. She sat close to Roxanne and listened to what others had to say. No one seemed happy about their living condition at home, Mishka included. Jenny didn't offer a perfect solution, but her words of encouragement minimized Mishka's fear about going back home to the memory of Harold's sudden death. She hadn't imagined camp would be such an engaging experience. After the meeting, Jenny suggested that Mishka should enter for the annual beauty pageant.

"Me don't think me can win, mam" Mishka said.

"But you're a beautiful girl, Mishka."

Mishka hung her head. "Me don't think so."

"No one's ever told you that?"

"Only me father wife from America."

Jenny placed her hands on Mishka's cheeks and raised her head.

"You're a beautiful young lady, Mishka. You can win."

Leading up to the event, Jenny and Mishka spent their evenings together rehearsing.

"There will be a talent segment," Jenny said. "I'm going to teach you Folk dance, ever heard of it?"

"No, mam."

"It's demonstrated through art, influenced by the Africans who were brought to Jamaica as slaves. Over the decades Jamaicans have added their own flavor to the original dance."

Mishka wasn't a great dancer, but she was surprised to see that Jenny had better moves, elegant.

"Before walking out there," Jenny said, "take a deep breath, stand straight, and keep a smile. When it's time to dance you can't be shy. Remember everything you've learned. It's a beauty contest so you will have to model a formal dress."

"Me don't have formal dress, mam."

"We have some from last year. I'll find one for you."

Mishka had no idea what she was getting into, but the more she practiced the more self-assured she felt.

The night of the competition, she felt intimidated by the audience and had a brief moment of stage fright. After taking a deep breath she glided gracefully across the stage. The applause made her feel proud. She saw Roxanne cheering her on. When the judges finally announced that Mishka Campbell was the new queen of Camp Hope, mouth wide open, she ran into Jenny's arms and gave her a hug and kiss. At the end of the evening, she had her very first dance with the camp king. She anxiously waited for her mother to visit to tell her all about it. Camp coming to an end was bittersweet. She scanned through her journal and recalled all the fun times that she had. Camp having been home away from home, she was already thinking about returning next year.

Back at home, Sophia informed Mishka that she passed the National Common Entrance Exam to attend an elite

Catholic high school for girls. Sophia beamed with pride as she handed Mishka the local newspaper.

"See your name there," Sophia said proudly.

Mishka used her finger to find her name among the many Campbells listed.

"Me?" Mishka said. "Alpha?"

"Me don't know how we will pay for you to go to that kind of school, but by the help of God you will go."

"Let me use your phone to call Calvin, Mommy."

She dialed his number and waited for an answer.

"Me pass me exam for Alpha Academy," she told him.

"Good," he said. "Keep it up. You have to be bright before comin' to America. Me send some school supplies for you before school start."

He was closer to being called *Dad* but not quite there yet.

For the rest of summer she and Roxanne walked to see friends they'd met at camp. She sometimes went to local soccer games, but Sophia insisted she be home at an appropriate time. By now, Sophia seemed well aware that Mishka was no longer a little girl, but rather a young lady whose body was fully developed. Mishka understood why her mother became strict. On her strolls with Roxanne to and from the soccer games she noticed a young man who stood by a shop at the corner near the ball field. His stares made it apparent he noticed her too.

"You know that boy over there?" she said.

"Im name Nathan," Roxanne said. "Why you want to know?"

"Nothing."

Roxanne laughed. "You like im."

"Me don't like im."

"Im tell me that im like you."

"Stop lie."

"No, true."

"What im say?"

"That im like me frien'."

At fifteen-years-old, she took high school seriously. On the first day, she looked as sharp as can be. The seamstress did an awesome job with her uniform. Sophia had sent her to the hairdresser to have her hair relaxed, which she pulled back in a sleek ponytail, accentuating her facial features. She rode the bus with other students going to her school, looked around at them and noticed that all were attired for the school's dress code. She missed walking to school with Roxanne, who didn't pass her exam but enrolled in a comprehensive high school. The term "*Comprehensive High*" was adapted from England. These schools were affordable even for families living in squatter communities such as Jones Town. They didn't select their intake of students based on academic performance or aptitude. Mishka's school, Alpha, was the total opposite.

Several weeks later with nothing having happened between her and Nathan except exchanges of looks, after getting off the bus from school she decided to take a different route home. She walked past his house but on the opposite side of the street, and it just so happened Nathan, apparently with the same idea, was standing on the opposite side than usual. They made their eye contact and smiled at their mutual plan.

"Ey," he said. "Me can have a minute of your time?"

She stopped as he sauntered toward her, nicely dressed in his khaki uniform and several inches taller than her.

"What's your name?" he said politely, still smiling, his teeth perfect.

"Mishka. Why?"

"Cause me see you walk past with Roxanne all the time and me like you. Me want to get to know you. Next time, we can talk again?"

"Sure, as long as you not out of order."

He laughed. "Me never out of order. Me mother teach me good manners."

They both laughed. "Alright," she said. "Me have to go now so next time."

Eager to inform Roxanne about her conversation with Nathan, Mishka stopped by to see her before going home. Roxanne and her sisters were sitting on the verandah when Mishka walked through the gate. Roxanne rose and met Mishka half way.

"Come with me to ball field," Roxanne said. "Me have to talk to you."

"Why all the way to ball field?"

"Me tell you when we reach there."

No Man's Land, the huge open field that bordered the next community, was where boys and men practiced and competed in soccer games whenever the community was peaceful. No one lingered by the border when the gangs were in conflict. When they arrived at the field it was empty. Mishka sat on the grass and waited to hear what Roxanne wanted to talk about.

"Remember when we were in primary school an' Paul touch me?"

"Yeh."

"Last night im rape me."

Mishka held Roxanne as she sobbed quietly in her chest.

"Im hurt you bad, Roxanne?"

Roxanne wiped her eyes. "Me want to cry out from pain but im tell me to shut up."

"You see doctor yet?"

"No. Me cry whole day."

"You talk to guidance counselor at school today?"

"Don't go to school today."

"So how come you have on uniform?"

"Me take the bus to Devon House this mornin' an' sit there alone till two-thirty."

"Oh Lord, Roxanne. What you think we should do now?"

"Don't know."

"Want to talk to the police bout it this time? Me go with you to the station."

"Me tell you before, Mishka, Paul have gun. Best if me leave an' go stay with me father."

"Maybe that's the best thing. But you think Miss Marlene will let you go?"

"Me will tell me father to ask her first."

"Paul is a wicked, nasty, dawg for doin' that to you."

"Me want to cut off im balls, make dawg eat them. Wish im did drop dead when me poison im."

Mishka fell back on the grass and covered her face with her hands.

"Me want to move an' go live with me father as soon as me can."

Mishka sat up. "You want me to ask Mommy if you can sleep at my house until then so that Paul won't trouble you?"

"Me can't do that. Mommy will ask why me don't want to sleep home. An' then Paul will think me don't shut me mouth."

They walked back home in complete silence, Mishka's arm around Roxanne's waist protectively.

Chapter Five

One month later …

Roxanne moved to live with her father in nearby Denham Town, fifteen-minutes away. Mishka missed Roxanne terribly, but she felt some consolation knowing she was safe and away from Paul. Roxanne hadn't gone back to Jones Town after her move. On her way to visit Roxanne, Mishka looked across the ball field and saw Paul standing with a group of men watching the soccer game. She proceeded across the border into Roxanne's community. Roxanne was waiting outside. They rushed into each other's arm and hugged tightly.

"How you like it here?" Mishka said.

"Better than to go back where dirty Paul is."

"Miss Marlene say when you leave'?"

"She say me only leave to make her look bad."

They later said their goodbyes. Mishka hurried across the soccer field. Up the street, she saw Nathan sitting on a bench in front of his house. He reached out and touched her hand when she walked by.

"Where you come from jus' now?" he said. "You go look for your boyfrien'?"

"Me don't have no boyfrien', Nathan. Me go to see Roxanne. She don't live roun here no more."

"So since you don't have no boyfrien' me can fill that gap?"

She smiled. "Can't answer that right now. Have to think bout it."

Alone in the privacy of her bedroom, she reminisced and wrote in her diary about her feelings for Nathan. It brought her a sense of excitement and comfort. She logged their every encounter, and sometimes wrote until her fingers went numb. She imagined them holding hands, hugging, kissing. She wondered if he felt the same. She knew that eventually, the topic of sex would arise and it scared her. Most girls her age were doing it. Roxanne had spoken about how much Paul hurt her, so Mishka asked herself some questions she hoped to find answers to sooner or later—was Nathan a gentle guy? If she decided not to do it with him, would he still like her? She knew that most girls who had a boyfriend were happy, but would it be that way for her too.

At the bus stop after school, she saw Nathan standing there in his school uniform. She thought that he'd get on the bus, but instead, he stood there and watched as she stepped off the bus. They greeted each other.

"You see how much me like you?" he said. "Even walk you home like a real man."

"Thanks, but me know the way home."

"You don't have to act feisty. All me want to do is show you me care." Walking close next to her, he held her hand. "You think bout bein' me girl?"

"A little."

"Me see how you smile every time you see me. Me know you love me."

"Love!" she said, laughing. "Keep on dreamin'."

"Tell me the truth," he said, his arm around her shoulder, "how much time a day you think bout me?"

She laughed even harder. "You don't need to know *what* me think bout. Me don't ask what you think bout."

"You don't have to ask. Me always think bout you—roun the clock—every day."

"You only say that to try an' make me feel good. For all me know you might be jus' like them other boys roun here who only want one thing. If that's all you want look somewhere else."

"Me want you for me girl, not a one night stand. You think me walk an' hold your hand if that is all me want? Even meet you at the bus stop?"

"Don't all boys play nice when them want something from a girl?"

"Me can't talk for all boys. Can only tell you bout me. An' me don't have to preten' or play nice for you. Me keep it real with you cause me like you. You the only girl roun here me like."

With his reassurance, she agreed to be his girlfriend. She went home and hastily completed her homework and chores, after which she closed her door and began writing in her journal.

His meeting her at the bus stop became a routine. She often walked past his house just to see his delightful smile. On the weekends after visiting Roxanne, Mishka stopped at by to talk to Nathan. They sat on a bench at his gate and talked about school, and events around the community.

Jamaica Tough

With Christmas only a few days away, Mishka and Roxanne planned to attend the annual fest together to be held at the community center, a blocks away from where Mishka's home. When the event came, she wore a green mini-skirt, white blouse, and wedged sandals. Nathan smiled at Mishka when she and Roxanne strolled past him on their way to the fest.

"Why Nathan look at you like that?" Roxanne said.

"We together now."

"Miss Sophia know?"

"No. She always talk bout pregnancy and disease. Me already know bout it."

"You an' im do it?"

"We only kiss."

Mishka saw Nathan walking up the street with his cohorts. As they walked by, he stepped away from them and stopped where Mishka and Roxanne were standing. They greeted each other. Clear that Nathan wanted to speak with Mishka alone, Roxanne excused herself.

"Mommy sell out here tonight," she said. "Me go get free drinks an' come back."

Nathan hugged Mishka around her waist and whispered in her ear, "You look good tonight."

She caught a whiff of his cologne. "You smell nice."

"You don't want no moldy-arm man for your boyfrien'?"

She smiled.

"Me want to spend some time with you," he said. "Over me yard."

She was glad that her Romeo had the opportunity to see her dolled up, but such an invitation caught her off guard. They hadn't been alone except for when they sat together in front of his house.

"What we do there?" she said.

"Nothing you don't want to. Me only want to spend some time with you."

She thought about it for a moment and couldn't find a reason to decline. She wanted to be with him just as much.

"After the party we can go," she said.

"Me want you to come now. Me don't care bout the party, rather spend time with you."

"But if we leave together now gossip will start. Miss Marlene jus' cross the street. She might see and tell me mother."

"Stop worry bout wha' people will say. Me gone now, wait for you home."

He walked away into the celebration. Roxanne came back empty handed.

"Wha' happen to the drinks?" Mishka said.

"Paul come to talk to Mommy soon as me get there. Me can't stan' im so me leave."

"Im say anything to you?"

"Im smile an' ask how me do. Me don't answer cause im know that me don't like im."

Mishka chatted with Roxanne for a while longer, and then told her she was going to be with Nathan.

"Me think you stay here a little later," Roxanne said.

"Nathan say im rather spend time with me."

Roxanne rolled her eyes and smiled.

"Where Grieg?" Mishka said.

"Up the street. Me go to tell im to walk with me home now. No need to stay here if you leave anyway."

"Go get im. Me wait here so we can all leave together."

When Mishka walked up the block with Grieg and Roxanne, Nathan stood in front of his house watching her as she approached. She said goodbye to Roxanne and walked toward Nathan. He hugged her tightly. They held hands and went inside to his bedroom at the back of the house.

"Where's everybody?" Mishka said.

"Them still at the party. Jus' me an' you here."

His room was spick-and-span, his bed nicely made. There was an entertainment center with a television, stereo, and video games.

"Your mother clean your room?" She said.

"Me always do it. What, you think me a dirty boy?"

"No, jus' didn't think men can clean this good."

He turned on his video game and sat down to play. She walked over to his dresser, looked at all the photos, and spoke casually, trying to make polite conversation. She was relieved he wasn't rushing things. Perhaps she would run away.

"Come over here," he said, handing her a control. "Me teach you how to play Super Mario."

She got comfortable on the floor next to him and began to play. It turned out to be fun.

"Am I any good at this or you only bein' a gentleman and let me win?"

"Me bein' a gentleman."

"Hey, me kinda thirsty."

"The shop lock but me have a key. Me go out there now an' get you something."

"Soda is jus' fine."

They lounged on his bed with their sodas watching television. He later turned her toward him so they were facing each other.

"Me glad you here with me," he said.

Before she was able to respond he leaned in and kissed her deeply and intimately, more than he ever had. He used his hands to embrace her. She didn't resist. A few minutes of kissing led to his touching and caressing her breasts.

He stopped. "This your first time?"

She nodded. "Sorry, don't know what to do."

"You fraid?"

She shook her head no.

"Me won't hurt you."

He removed his shirt and shorts, and then undressed her slowly. He admired every curve of her body. She felt awkward being naked in front of a boy. The sight of his abs and strong arms made her shiver. His chest didn't look like the little boys who walked around shirtless. He looked almost like a man. Then she became nervous.

"We mus' use condom so that me don't get pregnant."

He smiled the warmest smile. "Don't worry, me have one."

"Me don't want to be a teenage mother like most girls roun here."

"We can't let that happen. Miss Sophia would crucify you an' leave me lonely."

He reached into his drawer. She lay on the bed and watched as he cautiously slipped on the condom. Obviously, this wasn't his first time. He climbed on top of her, kissing and touching her again, but more passionately. She could feel him up against her belly. He was ready.

By now, she felt a strange sense of excitement, one that she hadn't experience before. Gently, he parted her legs and entered. When she recoiled, he reassured her that he was almost there. Before she knew it they were moving together harmoniously. She held his face and kissed him as he had her. She was lost in delight, her legs securely wrapped around him. After a while he began to sweat profusely and made some eerie sounds, causing her to wonder if he was okay. His breathing became rapid, and then he stopped thrusting. He pressed down on her chest. She felt his heart thumping against her.

.

Chapter Six

One week later …

Thinking about her special night, she became a slave to the memories. No matter where she was or what she was doing, Nathan was the only one on her mind. Being in his company was the best feeling she'd ever had. He held her, kissed her, and more. He told her that she was the most beautiful girl God created. She felt loved, wanted. She trusted Sophia and wanted to tell her about Nathan, but this part of her world was something she wasn't ready to share with her mother. Instead, she wrote about it in her journal and slid it underneath her mattress afterwards.

New Year's Eve, Sophia was in the kitchen cleaning up after cooking and baking all day. Mishka helped herself to a slice of fruit cake.

"Don't eat such a big piece," Sophia said. "Me use Red Label Wine with the recipe."

"Me can't taste the wine. The cake taste sweet though. Save some for me and Roxanne before Ricardo eat it all."

"Ricardo won't eat any, im is Adventist now. Them don't eat nor drink anything with alcohol. Me and Marlene walk to church later to watch im baptize."

"Ha! Baptize?"

"Yeh, baptize, the best way for young people nowadays."

"Oh boy," Mishka said comically. "Me brother soon turn big pastor."

"You need to follow im footstep. See your Auntie Tracy, if it wasn't for the church me don't know wha' would happen to her roun here."

"When the time is right me get baptize, Mommy. By the way, me and Roxanne go out tonight."

"Where?"

"To see fireworks, downtown."

"Make sure you find your roost when it over. Christmas, you walk in here after twelve o'clock like you a night owl. Me warn you before, when man see young gal roam street late at night, them think you look for something out there, drag you in a bush and rape you."

"But tonight the fireworks downtown go off at twelve. Me come back here by twelve-thirty, the latest."

"One minute later and me come find you."

"Alright, Mommy."

"So wait, how you an' Roxanne get there? An' where is Roxanne now?"

"She meet me at the bus stop. We take taxi downtown an' back. Don't forget that bus an' taxi run all through the night for the holiday."

"Let me ask you something."

"Wha'?"

"Why Roxanne move to live with her father?"

"Me don't know."

"You and her friends all these years, why she up an' move so sudden?"

"You ask Miss Marlene?"

"She say she don't think Roxanne like Paul. You know anything bout Roxanne an' Paul fallin' out?"

"Mommy, when it comes to Paul you should have nothing to say."

"Wha' you mean by that?"

"Me don't know why Roxanne move. She only say that she move to live with her father. That is all me know."

"Hm. Me know jus' how to live roun here. Make sure you always remember wha' me tell you. Keep your mouth shut, nobody will ever trouble you." She reached into her bag and took out an envelope. "Here, Calvin send letter with U.S. dollah for you and Ricardo for Christmas."

Mishka put a twenty in the back pocket of her shorts and left.

She found it peculiar that Sophia would mention Roxanne not liking Paul, and marveled at why Marlene would even say that. She met Roxanne up the street. On their way to the bus stop, Nathan pulled up next to them in a car, Roxanne's boyfriend Grieg in the passenger's seat.

"Where you two walk to?" Nathan said.

"To see the fireworks, downtown," Mishka said.

"Let me drive you downtown," he said. "Me don't want you to go too far dress so sexy."

Mishka and Roxanne got into the back seat.

"Me an' Grieg go beach tomorrow," Nathan said. "You and Roxanne want to come?"

"You wouldn't go without me?" Mishka said.

Everyone laughed.

Nathan dropped them off and drove away with Grieg. Downtown, Kingston was teeming, bumper to bumper traffic and people everywhere. There were vending booths and stalls along Kingston's waterfront. Mishka stopped and bought cotton candy for her and Roxanne. It was a cool, still night; the sky dark and the stars stood out against it. The girls found a quiet spot where they were alone and away from the crowd.

"Roxanne," Mishka said. "You tell Miss Marlene that you don't like Paul?"

"No. She say that?"

"Mommy ask me tonight why you move. Me don't tell her why but she say Miss Marlene don't think you like Paul."

"Me mother right. Me hate im. But me never tell her that."

"So why she tell Mommy that?"

"Before leavin' there me always try an' avoid im. She notice it an' ask why me want to mash up her life."

The popping sound of fireworks above their heads interrupted their conversation. Mishka leaned against the parapet and looked up at the sky, mesmerized by the magic that lit up the night.

"Remember the first time we come here?" she asked.

Roxanne smiled. "Yeh. We used to play dolly-house back then. Feel like yesterday."

When the show was over they pushed through the crowd and squeezed into a taxi.

Home, Mishka handed Roxanne a nightgown to sleep in. Sophia and Ricardo came home as the girls were preparing for bed. Sophia opened Mishka's door and poked her head in.

"You come back quick," she told Mishka.

"Happy New Year, Mommy."

"Same to you, baby." Sophia looked at Roxanne. "Hello stranger. Long time no see."

"Hello, Miss Sophia. Happy New Year."

There was a knock at the door. The girls walked out with Sophia to see who was at the door.

"Who that?" Sophia said.

"Marlene."

Sophia opened the door and Marlene stepped inside. She saw Roxanne sitting on the sofa.

"Me didn't know you up here," Marlene told Roxanne.

"Me stay with Mishka tonight," Roxanne said, "We go beach tomorrow."

Marlene rolled her eyes at Roxanne and turned to Sophia. "Lend me your phone charger. Me can't find mine an' me phone dead. Me have to call Paul an' tell im to find somebody to fix the water. The pipe burst an' wet up the front yard."

Sophia went for the charger and later walked outside with Marlene. The girls closed the door and climbed into bed.

"Miss Marlene don't look happy with you at all," Mishka said.

"She must still believe me want to mash up her life with Paul."

"You don't live there no more so don't fret bout it."

"Anyway, what's new with you an' Nathan? Me see im really like you."

"We do it."

Roxanne sat up. "Lie! When?"

"Shh!"

Roxanne's voice lowered. "When?"

"Christmas."

"How it feel?"

"Me miss Nathan more an' more, want im every time."

Roxanne's mood changed.

"What?" Mishka said.

"My first time wasn't like yours."

Next morning, they woke up and prepared for the beach. Sophia was awake and making breakfast. The girls gathered their things and waited to eat.

"Who you two go beach with?" Sophia said.

"Me frien," Mishka said.

"Which frien?"

"Nathan. Im live roun' the street where the supermarket is."

"Don't get in any trouble out there."

They finished breakfast and met Nathan at home where he and Greig waited for the girls in a car. They greeted and later took off, Mishka sitting up front with Nathan.

"You have license?" Mishka asked Nathan.

"You try to be funny?" Nathan said, smiling.

"No. Me only want to know."

"Me father take me to get license soon as me turn eighteen."

"Maybe she ask cause she see wha' me always try to tell you," Grieg said. "You drive like you buy your license."

"Wha' the fuck you know bout drivin'?" Nathan said, giggling.

At their destination, Mishka surveyed the surroundings and realized that her hopes of taking a long walk on the sand with Nathan were dashed by the horde of people that occupied the beach. It appeared as though the entire population had descended on the deep-blue shimmering sea. People set up sunshades and picked out picnic spots wherever there was space. They laid out towels as if to mark their territory. The whole beach was taken up. A little boy screamed as a man tried to coax him into taking a dip. Children buried each other neck deep in the sand while others took turn building sandcastles. They chased each other playfully, and scurried toward the ocean to avoid getting caught. People move to the music coming from loud speakers while men sold horseback ride up and down the beach.

Mishka and Nathan walked hand in hand until they found an empty wooded chair at the secluded end of the beach. She placed a towel on the sand and lay her beach bag on top. Nathan hugged her around the waist as they strolled toward the water.

"Me like how the bath suit fit you," he said.

She climbed on his back and wrapped her legs around his waist as he walked out into the deep.

"Me miss you," she said.

"Miss you too. You come look for me later?"

"Yeh but jus' for a little while. Mommy don't know we together an' she don't want me out late."

"Wha you think she will say if you tell her bout me?"

"First thing she will tell you is don't get me pregnant."

Nathan laughed. "Me wouldn't want that to happen now."

They hugged and kissed as if there were no one else around. After much fun in the sun, Mishka's tummy began to grumble. She treated her friends to lunch with the U.S. dollars Calvin sent for her.

Jamaica Tough

Home from the beach, Mishka showered and walked with Roxanne across the soccer field toward her home.

"Today was so nice," Mishka said. "Me hate that you have to go home."

"Me would invite you to stay here one weeken' but Miss Sophia won't have it."

"Yeh she too protective sometimes."

They later said their goodbyes.

At the corner of the street where she lived, Mishka saw a car speeding down the road toward her. She hurried onto the sidewalk to avoid being hit and fell. A man who was standing there helped her back to her feet. Suddenly, the car tires came to a quick halt, Mishka looked up and saw the back window rolling down. A gun pointed at her. She let out a scream and ran toward home as fast as she could.

Breathless, she slammed the door behind her. Sophia rushed from the kitchen.

"Why you shut the door like that an' frighten me, gal?"

"Somebody shot Jimmy!"

"Say wha'?"

"Yeh! Right outside!"

Sophia sat next to her on the bed. “Take your time an’ talk. You say somebody shot Jimmy jus’ now?”

“Yeh! One man in a car. Me fall down an’ Jimmy help me up, then me see the car stop, an’ the gun … me think im come to kill me but when Jimmy get the shot an’ fall down me run!”

Mishka’s thighs were shaking. Sophia placed her hands on Mishka’s knees.

“Settle down,” she said. “You see who do it?”

“Yeh, an’…”

Sophia raised a finger. “Make sure you forget seein’ anything, hear me?”

Mishka nodded frantically.

“Me tell you before, if you want to live long roun’ here you mus’ keep your mouth. Gun man don’t like people who chatty-chatty. Them come for Jimmy, not you. You never see anything, understan’ me?”

Mishka was horrified and realized she’d urinated on herself. She changed out of her wet clothing. Sophia peeked through a window that faced the street.

“People out there,” she said.

Soon she went outside too, and cautiously Mishka followed. A crowd had gathered at Jimmy's home, Marlene and Roxanne's younger sisters among them. Neighbors stood in groups as they buzzed and gawked. Jimmy lay face down in a pool of blood on the sidewalk. His children and their mother knelt by his lifeless body wailing hysterically.

"Me can't believe them come roun' here an' kill innocent people in a broad daylight," Marlene said.

"Only God knows," Sophia said. "If me have somewhere else to go, me take me children an' leave from roun' here."

She finally noticed Mishka behind her and grabbed her by the arm.

"Come," she said. "We go inside."

Mishka followed Sophia's lead through the gathering. "See why me tell you to stay inside? If you listen to me you wouldn't see anything. Make sure you keep your beak shut. Me don't want anybody say me harbor informer, kick off me door an' kill me."

The incident led to an ongoing feud between gangs in the community. People hurried along through their daily lives to hunker down early and braced for the sounds of gun battle among neighborhood ruffians throughout the night. Women and children became victims of the violent uproar, most of which were accidental deaths. Some were in the wrong place at the wrong time, while others died as a way of revenge. Nearing the general election for the country's next prime minister, the violence escalated. Besides cautioning the children, Sophia didn't discuss what was happening, and by now Mishka had learned not to ask.

Late one night there was a knock at the front door long after her family had gone to bed. Mishka thought that she was dreaming until she heard Sophia's voice asked who was there. A dominant voice came from outside telling Sophia to open the door. Mishka heard Sophia unlocking the bolt. The inside of the house was dark, but Mishka quietly walked into the living area to see who was there. A young man stood by the doorway talking to Sophia. Mishka stopped and took a good look. She recognized him—the man who killed Jimmy! She panicked, wondered why he'd show up at her door in the middle of the night. Perhaps he knew that she saw what he had done and wanted to speak with her about it. She tiptoed back to her bedroom without being noticed and crawled under her bed, hoping the man wouldn't come looking for her. Her heart racing, she lay there and listened.

"The don want every woman roun here to go out an'vote tomorrow," he told Sophia.

"Me don't normally vote, you know."

"Me say," he said, "Make sure you vote, PNP."

"Alright." Sophia said.

Mishka heard the door slam shut, and the man walked past her window. She heard Sophia walk back to her bedroom and close the door. She slid from beneath the bed and knocked softly on Sophia's door.

"Who was that, Mommy?"

"One of them gun-boy from roun here, say me mus' go vote tomorrow."

"Why im tell you to vote?"

"Them work for politician, Mishka," Sophia said, whispering. "That's how this place here run an' that's why people call it politricks. Me never yet vote a day in me life, but like it or not, me do what im say. Politics cause serious problem in a place like Jones Town. Me don't want anybody to call me sell out. That boy don't look much older than Ricardo, im probably just ol' enough to be me son. Me pray all the time that one day, one blessed day, me can move from here cause this is pure fuckry."

Mishka went back to bed.

Chapter Seven

One month later …

She hadn't seen Nathan or Roxanne since the unrest began but she spoke with them over the telephone. Finally, she was relieved after watching the nightly news, Jones Town caught national attention and a curfew would be imposed in the area. After many lost lives, the vendetta finally came to a standstill. Armed forces in tanks increased their presence forcing some of the bad guys to flee the area. It was still tense, but people were able to go cautiously about their business. Public transportation resumed their route in and out of Jones Town. Mishka stood outside of her home and watched police officers on foot stop and search boys and men. The news media were there to get their take on what had happened. They sought comments from anyone willing to speak.

"Police kick off me door this mornin'!" a woman said, an infant hanging at her hip. "Them take me baby-father from me bed, carry im go jail, say im a person of interes'. Im never kill nobody! We want justice roun here!"

A female reporter with a cameraman just behind her made their way toward Mishka.

"Can you tell me what it felt like here with the place under siege?"

"Me don't have anything to say, mam."

The reporter walked away, still in pursuit of answers. She went from person to person asking the same question. No one gave an answer. Directly across the street from Mishka's home, she saw what appeared to be bullet holes through a concrete wall. To her, it spoke volume. She glanced up the street and saw Paul riding his bicycle in her direction. She was stunned that he stuck around while the police were still present. He didn't seem concerned. Approaching Marlene's home, he nodded at the officers, parked his bicycle, and went inside without being stopped.

One day the police barged into Mishka's home.

"Get out of me fridge!" Sophia said. "Wha' you look in there for?"

"Guns," the officer said.

"Me don't have no gun in here! When we really need help from police you come after everything finish happen an' harass innocent people."

"That's because you people don't tell anything. The gun-men you cover for, them same one kill off your children an' fuck up your community. What you expect the police to do if people don't want to cooperate?"

"People roun here don't trust police!" Sophia said. "Look how much people dead an' you don't do nothing to stop it. If you don't protect we now, you protect we after we turn informer, or cooperate as you call it? Weeks now me children can't go to school cause of this war, where was police all the time?"

The cop moved to Sophia's bedroom with an M-16 hanging from his shoulder. Sophia and Mishka stood by and watched as he picked up the mattress, all the time casting furtive glances all around.

"Why you ransack me damn house so?" Sophia said. "You come look for gun, you have search permit?"

He gave a loud chuckle. "Permit? Where you think this is, Beverly Hills?"

"Oh, so that mean a poor woman like me not supposed to ask bout permit? See why people roun here hate police?"

"Shut up before me cuff an' carry you to the station."

He walked to Ricardo's bedroom. Sophia followed. "Carry me go station," she said. "Lock me up over the truth." She turned to Mishka. "See why me always tell you to take in your education? Poor people here don't have no rights."

The cop stopped, turned. "You chat too much," he told Sophia. "Step outside till me finish."

"Leave you alone in here with me son for you to kill im, an' then lie, say you find gun?"

The officer shoved Ricardo's door open. Ricardo lay across his bed playing a handheld Gameboy that Calvin gave him years ago.

"Get up." the cop said. "Turn aroun' an' put up your hands."

Ricardo followed the officer's order. He emptied Ricardo's pockets and patted around his waist.

"Where them boy hide the big guns?"

"Me don't know, sir."

"Me son is neither gunman nor informer. Don't ask im bout no gun."

"What you mus' do to be police?" Ricardo said.

"What you mus' do?" the officer said. "Don't have time to joke with worthless kids. Jones Town boy like you only become criminal, not constable. Majority of you don't finish high school. You pick up guns instead, an' end up in the cemetery before the age a twenty."

The election came to an end and so did the curfew. The gunmen returned to their respective territories and called for a meeting between rival gangs. After coming to an agreement to suspend the hostility, word circulated that an official celebration for peace would be held at the corner of the street where Mishka lived. A few young men stacked large speakers on the sidewalk before the event began. It was Friday evening and the neighborhood was vibrant once more. Folks sat comfortably in front of their homes and watched children dance in the streets. Mishka stood outside of her home and observed the scene, surprised to see people from across the border in attendance. Only weeks ago, no one walked these streets after dark. Everyone's spirit was lifted again. She asked Sophia's permission to leave the house.

"See the time?" Sophia said, pointing at the wall. "Five-thirty. Get back here before dark."

"Me go look for Roxanne and then say hi to me other frien', Nathan."

"Come back before dark."

With good will in the air, Mishka walked to nearby Denham Town to visit Roxanne. Denham Town was the same as Mishka's *garrison* and the others surrounding it. These communities were called *garrisons* because of their high rate of crime and level of poverty.

Mishka had been bound to her home for over two weeks. It felt great getting out. To reach her destination she had to walk across the soccer field. Several streets beyond was Roxanne's house. Closer, Mishka saw Roxanne standing out front waiting. They rushed into each other's arms as if it had been years since they met.

"Me see you live and direct on TV other day," Roxanne said.

"See me?"

"You tell the newswoman you don't have nothing to say when she ask you bout the war."

They laughed hilariously.

"You turn superstar."

"But me never say anything to make news. Oh Lord, maybe Nathan see me too, people at school. What a shame."

"Me so glad everything over now cause me think bout you and Mommy them every time me hear the gunshot start to fire up there."

Roxanne sat on the sidewalk. "Me have something to tell you."

Mishka sat next to her.

"Me pregnant."

"You know for sure?"

"Every mornin' me wake up sick, vomit. This mornin' me go to the clinic, doctor say me pregnant."

"So wha' you do now?"

"Abortion. If me father know me pregnant im will throw me out. Me can't stay with Grieg."

"You know abortion illegal?"

"Some doctor still do it, but me don't have big money for doctor. Me talk to me Auntie an' she say me can boil and drink herbal bush name Rivina Humilis."

"Wha' name so?"

"People call it dog blood. It good for flush out baby. Auntie tell me bout one pill too, name Quinine. She say me can take it with Pepsi, it will flush out the baby faster."

"No, no, Roxanne. Me don't like how that soun'. Where you get this pill from?"

"Town, pharmacy."

"You tell Grieg im breed you?"

"For wha? Im can't help me."

"Dammit, Roxanne. Why you don't make im use condom?"

"Im say it don't feel good, pull out every time im cum. No worry, me go stay with Auntie tomorrow for one week so she can help me take care of it."

"But you sure it safe?"

"Me trust Auntie, she a ol' woman. Anytime she sick she always use bush tea. Never yet see doctor."

"Alright, me gone now, Mommy don't want me outside after dark. Can't even stop to see Nathan now."

They held each other tightly before walking away.

Mishka hurried home. Half way across the soccer field she heard a rattling sound, turned, and was startled by a man riding up behind her on a bicycle. It was Paul. He caught up and stopped beside her.

"Wha go on, girl?" he said, smiling. "Where you come from?

"Me go look for Roxanne."

He rode beside her as she quickened her pace.

"Why you move so fast?" he said.

"Me mother don't want me outside after dark."

"You walk with me, nothing won't happen to you."

"Thanks."

"Me always eyes you, Mishka" he said, "Me like how you sexy. Pretty little girl. Me want you."

"Me always see you come look for Miss Marlene."

"Yeh." His tone turned stern. "But me don't talk bout Marlene now. Me talk bout me an' you. Me want you."

"Me have a boyfrien'. An' me don't want anybody to say me take away Miss Marlene man."

"Me will leave her for you. Don't mus' come see her again. Nobody will know, only me an' you."

"Me don't want to hurt me boyfrien'."

He stopped his bicycle and parked it in front of her, blocking her path, still sitting on it. By now it was totally dark out. They were still on the soccer field, no street lights, and the ball players long gone. They were alone in No Man's Land.

"Me try to talk to you nice," he said, "tell you me like you. But since you want to give me trouble, hear this, me want to fuck you."

It was clearly not a joke. He was serious.

"Give me some time to think bout it. Please, let me get home to me mother."

He leaned over his handlebars. "We go to my place, me want you now, tonight!"

"But me only sixteen-years-ol'. You a big man for me."

"Me don't care bout age. You look ripe an' me want to pick you."

He drew a machete from a sheath hidden beneath the seat of his bicycle, held it up and glared at her.

"See this," he said. "Me an' you alone out here. If you try anything me cut your fuckin throat. Nobody will hear. Know wha' me mean?"

"Me on me period."

"If you lie me make you sorry. Lift up your skirt an' draw down the panty."

"What if somebody past an' see?"

"Do wha' me say!"

Will she succumb or will someone stumble upon her corpse when the sun comes up?

She ran. He jumped off the bicycle and chased her. She tripped over a rock. He snatched her by the back of her blouse.

"You think me let you get way?" he said. "Get up!"

Still gripping her top, he led her back to his bicycle. "Now, me say you mus' draw down the panty."

Tears in her eyes she stood quietly, hoping someone would walk across the field or that he would feel sorry for her and let her walk home. She needed to make a decision, and fast.

She lifted her skirt and removed her underwear. He smacked her across the face. She fell to the ground. He reached down and grabbed her by her throat, choking her and yanking her back to her feet.

"Why you tell me lie?" he said.

He dropped the machete to the ground, spit on his finger and touched between her legs.

"Please!" she cried, tears streaming down her cheeks and onto her blouse.

"Shut up!"

He put his finger to his nose and inhaled. Sheathing the machete back beneath the bicycle seat, he looked at her.

"Hop on," he said. "Me bring you back to me ends."

When he rode past Roxanne's home, Mishka looked inside. The lights were on. The gate shut. Residents were going about their business, sitting idly in front of their home, talking, laughing— for them, a normal night. Still riding along, neither of them spoke. A block away, Mishka saw a pair of bright headlights moving slowly toward them, a blue light-bar atop the vehicle. It was a police patrol car. Finally, this could be her chance to get away. As the car approached, she thought of the safest way to draw the police's attention. She needed to think fast. If she were to flag down the car and fail at getting a response, Paul would be livid! She may never make it home alive. Then another idea hit her—jump off the bicycle and in front of the patrol car before it would get close enough to hit her. Paul continued pedaling. The patrol car came closer. She surveyed the distance between the bicycle and the car and waited for the opportunity.

He poked her side with his finger. "Don't do anything foolish or else me push me cutlass straight through you."

Her heart sank. The car cruised by and one of the officers nodded at Paul. Mishka said nothing. He turned onto a dim street and stopped the bicycle at a dilapidated duplex. Next door, a group of women sat outside. He nudged Mishka toward the door. The women glanced at them and went back to their conversation. He unlocked the door, moving aside for Mishka to step in, absurdly like a gentleman. He followed and locked the door behind him.

It was pitch black. He walked over and turned on a television. Mishka found herself in a large room, with a bed, table, and a stand-up lamp. By a firm grip on her wrist, he tugged her toward the bed where she sat staring at the TV, not noticing what was on. He removed a firearm from the front of his waist and placed it on the table. She began crying again, quietly, not accepting what was about to happen to her. The thought of him on top of her turned Mishka's stomach inside out. He pulled his shirt over his head. By his cold confidence, she was more certain than before that he had done it to Roxanne, and she imagined that Marlene would knock at the door any moment.

"Take off your clothes," he said, undoing his belt.

He attempted to help unhook her bra. She rose and reached behind her back, releasing it. She sat back on the bed, saw him checking her out. He reached for her breast but pushed his hand away. He smiled naughtily.

"Please," she said getting up. "Let me go home to me mother. Me won't say nothing to no one bout this."

He shoved her back on the bed. Naked, he was coming toward her. She leaped off the bed and ran for the door, struggling to unlock it. He caught her by her hair and threw her to the floor. She saw the firearm lying on the table and lunged herself at it, knocking over the table. They scuffled before he overpowered her, pointed the pistol at her. She crouched in a corner with her hands pressed tightly on her face.

"You want me shoot you bomboclaat!"

"No!" she said. "Don't shoot me!"

"Get up."

She crawled across the room and climbed onto the bed. He put the table back in its place and lay the firearm on it. He picked up his pants and searched the pockets.

"Use a condom," she said.

"Of course, me don't want no disease from you. Me know you fuck Nathan."

He rolled it on and forced her legs open and climbed on top He tried to kiss her. She covered her mouth and began crying harder, telling herself to endure the torture by not resisting. He forced his way in and exhaled. Her body became numb, motionless. His teeth clenched as he pounded without cessation, not saying a word, growling, as though he wanted to injure her. His sweat dripped on her neck, her cheek, marijuana and beer on his breath. Still glaring at her, he grumbled and discharged. Not as if he was having pleasure, but as though he was murdering her. She narrowed her eyes and through the blur of her tears she saw his eyes, reddened, burning her with cruelty.

Finally, he pulled out, chuckled, smiled nastily, and lay next to her, sweaty, breathing heavily.

"Finish?" she said.

"For now. You a good fuck."

She quickly put her clothes on, hoping another guy wouldn't come in. When his breathing slowed down, he walked to the bathroom. The door was partially open and Mishka had her eyes on him. He pulled off the condom and tossed it in the toilet, flushed it. Back in the room he put his clothes on. She sat on the bed, waiting for his permission to go home.

He took a cellphone from his pocket and told someone to come over. He didn't say a name and the conversation was short. She became nervous again and thought she wouldn't let him win, but he had. She was under his complete control. He reached back into his pocket, took out some bills and handed it toward her. She shook her head no. He tossed them on the bed. He lit a joint and settled himself next to her. She moved to the far end of the bed and away from him. He smiled at her and lit his joint. Smoke bellowed from his mouth and nose. The smoke-filled room caused her to cough uncontrollably. She rushed to the bathroom and drank water from the faucet. After a while, her cough was contained. She went back to where they sat without speaking, until there was a knock. He rose, stepped outside, and closed the door.

He came back inside. "Me brethren will take you home."

She slipped on her sandals, left the money on the bed and stumbled outside to see a black car waiting. She opened the door and sat in her seat. A young man, maybe early-twenties wearing a baseball hat sat behind the wheel. She recognized him—the man who'd shot Jimmy! Her fear heightened. She began to fumble with the door. Before she could push it open he reached across her and enforced the lock, using his elbow to push her back against her seat.

"The boss say me mus' bring you home."

She nodded. They took off.

"You know me?" he said. "No."

"Sure?"

"Positive."

On the way, they rode in complete silence. She wanted to open the door and jump out of the car, but he knew where she lived. When he drove past Nathan's house,

Mishka saw him sitting outside with Grieg. She was shattered.

He dropped her off and drove away. She ran inside and to the cistern where she scrubbed her face with cold water. She dried with the front of her blouse and went inside. Ricardo's legs slumped over the arm of the sofa, his hands behind his head. He appeared engrossed in the sports report on television.

"Mommy here?" Mishka asked.

He looked up at her. "She gone next door to Marlene. You jus' now come back from Roxanne?"

"Yeh."

"Why your jaw look so swell?"

"Me teeth hurt me."

He sat up and studied her for a moment. "You smoke now?"

She peered back at him, a question in her eyes. "Me look like me smoke?"

"No, but you stink a weed."

"Oh. Me frien'. im give me a ride jus' now. Im smoke weed in the car."

"Make sure Mommy don't smell it."

She walked back to her room and lay across her bed. She felt filthy, and thought that if Nathan found out he wouldn't like her anymore.

She went to the outdoor shower and cleaned up, got his crud off her body. Under the spray of the cool water, she tried to convince herself that it didn't happen, but suddenly recalled his frightening words—*for now*. Could they mean anything other than he wasn't through with her? What if he came back to see Marlene and daunt Mishka with his presence to make sure she didn't say anything?

She dressed and looked at her face in the mirror. The side of her cheek where Paul slapped her was swollen, reddened. She closed her bedroom door, slipped into her nightgown, and reached under her mattress for her journal, her only way to express what had happened to her. She wept quietly. Tears dripped off her nose as she wrote with great fervor. She wiped her face on her pillow and turned off the light. Lying in the dark, she wondered how many other girls were raped. How long would it be before she finally forgot about it? How would she ever face Nathan again? The only conclusion was that awful people lived around her and she shouldn't trust anyone, ever. She would have to stay close to home and never go away alone. She would be a prisoner in her own home. She pulled a sheet over her, head to toe, like a corpse.

She heard the front door open, then Sophia's voice. Sophia's footsteps approached. She opened the door and flicked on the lamp.

"Oy!" she said.

Mishka removed the sheet from her head, her back turned.

"Wha' me tell you before you leave here?"

"Come back before night."

"So where the fuck you was?"

"Me stay an' talk to Roxanne."

"Turn roun when me talk to you!"

She turned and faced Sophia.

"Wha' happen to your face?" Sophia said.

"Me teeth hurt me."

"Listen, an' listen to me good. If you can't follow me rule an' find your yard when night come, don't ask me to leave this house again, hear me?"

"Yes, Mommy."

"If Roxanne or any other frien' want to see you, let them come here. Me give you one inch, you take a mile. Me ask you to come back before night, look, nine-thirty, an' you jus' now walk in here. Don't ask me to leave this house again."

Chapter Eight

One week later ...

No longer did she have a shred of self-confidence. She felt demoralized and found herself saturated in grief. Whenever Sophia opened her door and asked if everything was okay, Mishka gave up no information. She was learning to suppress her emotions. She would have to be good at it if she ever decided to see Nathan again. She withdrew from the world to the inner compartment of her mind where she spent most of her time. It was the only place where she felt safe, where she'd have to pick up the pieces and try to restore herself. When Roxanne told about Paul raping her, Mishka felt sorry for her, but now that she too fell victim, feeling sorry was an understatement. She never thought that it would happen to her too.

She secretly went to the local clinic. She looked around to make sure that a neighbor wouldn't see her and tell Sophia. After a while, finally, she was moved to a waiting room. A nurse came in and asked Mishka why she wanted to be seen.

"Guidance counselor," Mishka said. "She tell all girls to get regular check-up."

"So I can assume you're sexually active?"

"Two times, mam, with me boyfrien'."

"Are you having any symptoms I should know about?"

"No, none."

"What are you testing for?"

"Everything."

The nurse led Mishka to an examination room.

"Pee in this cup," she said. "Undress from the waist down and wait for the doctor."

Lying on the table, Mishka waited. She heard a knock. An older man wearing a white lab coat walked in and shut the door behind him.

"How're you today, ah, Campbell?"

"Fine, sir."

He walked to the sink, washed and dried his hands, then slipped on a pair of latex gloves.

"Alright, let's see here," he said. "Open up."

"Any woman doctor here, sir?"

He stopped. "Not today. I'm the only one. Is there a problem?"

"Never have a man doctor before."

He smiled. “I usually have a female nurse come in with me, but they’re all busy, it’s Monday.”

“It’s alright then.”

“Sure?”

“Yes, sir.”

“Open up.”

She flinched at the touch of his hands.

“Relax.” he said.

Paul’s face flashed across her mind, but she remained calm and silent.

At the end of the examination she dressed and walked back to see the nurse.

“Here,” the nurse said. “Birth control samples and condoms.”

“Me don’t need them, miss.”

“Are you sure, Mishka?”

“Yeh.”

“Suit yourself.” She placed them back in the drawer. “Come back for your results next Monday.”

When she arrived home, Roxanne met her at the gate.

“Why you don’t answer your phone?”

“Nothing. Have a lot on me mind.”

"Why me get the feelin' you don't want to be me frien' now cause me pregnant?"

"Don't have anything to do with your pregnancy."

"So wha' it have to do with then?"

"Me sorry, don't want to talk bout it."

"Alright, keep your secret. Me jus' now see Nathan an' im ask me for you. You an' im not together?"

"Why you keep on ask me so much question? Me tell you, me need time alone, will deal with Nathan later."

"Why you bite off me head so?"

"Sorry. When me feel better me tell you."

"Me see you later then."

"Wait."

Roxanne stopped.

"Wha' happen with the abortion?"

"Auntie do it tonight."

Mishka began to look at every female closely, the nuns at her school, her own classmates, or those passing on the street as possible victims hiding their past. Was rape a national secret?

Sophia knocked on Mishka's door, and walked in with a sheet of paper in her hand. She held it up.

"Why you hide this from me?" she said.

"Nothing."

"You always get A for everything, never C. What's the problem?"

"Don't know."

"Me see you don't talk to Roxanne no more. Wha' happen, you an' her fall out?"

"We still talk. Me need time alone. That's all."

Sophia sat on Mishka's bed. "You want me to take you to doctor, darlin'? Talk to me. You know you can tell your mother anything. What's the problem?"

"Stop fret, Mommy. Me don't have nothing to tell."

"You sure?"

"Yeh."

"Well, there is always something to worry bout."

"Wha'?"

"Me boss tell me today that she have family emergency. Her mother sick bad so she mus' move back to England as soon as possible. Now me won't have work again. Don't hear nothing more from Calvin since Christmas."

Jamaica Tough

Saturday after noon, Tracy came to visit. Mishka sat at the doorway with a bowl on her lap, cutting up vegetables for Sophia's soup.

"Howdy," Tracy said.

"Evenin', Auntie."

"Sophie inside?"

"Mommy!" Mishka said. "Auntie here."

Sophia came out, flour on the front of her dress. "Tracy, long time no see. How you do?"

"Tired."

"How come?"

"Barely have time to sleep anymore. Whenever I'm not working I'm at church."

"Mishka," Sophia said. "Go get a chair bring come for your Auntie."

Mishka found the chair and brought it out. Tracy took it and sat.

"So where you work now, Tracy?" Sophia said.

"I work as a substitute teacher at Saint Andrew Preparatory."

"How you like to work with the children?"

"They're young so it requires more patience. Besides that they're sweet as pie."

"You have your career now, time to start have your own children before you get old like me."

Tracy laughed. "Not before marriage, Sophie, and I'm only twenty-nine."

"Hope you find a nice man there in the church. That's the only place you will find a man to put ring on your finger."

"You're right about that. Anyway, when was the last time you heard anything from my brother?"

"Calvin? Ha! Not since Christmas me sis. Last time im come here im tell me say im come back to bring the children to America to live."

"Oh, really?"

"So im say, me dear. You know im."

"It's about time. He's been there long enough and the kids are all grown up. Look at Mishka, she's as tall as you are now. If he can help them that would be nice. He called me and wanted to meet up while he was here, but I had a busy schedule at the time and he was only here for five days."

"That mean you never get to see the American wife."

"Please, Sophie."

"Calvin is really your brother. Same thing im say when me talk bout the wife. Me forgive im though, only because im still remember the children here an' want to help."

"I'm happy to hear that you forgave him for going off and getting married. I used to pray every day that your soul would heal."

"Tracy, you never been through them things, but me can tell you … when a man betray you, is one of the worse pain for any woman, no matter how strong she is. With all the things me an' Calvin been through here, im never married to me, me who turn im into a father and take care of the children. But im go all the way to America an' married to foreign woman."

Tracy raised her eyes to heaven as though she'd heard this story too many times.

"Alright, Sophie," she said sympathetically, with so slight a stress on the "*alright*". "I'm glad you can find it in your heart to forgive Calvin. So what were you saying about the children?"

Sophia sat beside Mishka on the step. "Oh, me glad im don't forget bout them too, cause im can help them better than me can."

"I shouldn't say this too soon, but I'm supposed to be going to America too."

"Oh yeh?"

"I'm going to the embassy soon."

"Who sen' for you?"

"No one's really sending for me. A friend of mine who goes to an Adventist church in Florida told me that there's a school on the church compound, and there's a kindergarten teaching position available. When she asked if I would be interested I had to laugh because I was sure there are many qualified teachers in America. But she said they weren't only looking for a teacher, they want someone who shares the Adventist faith. So I asked for more information and she hooked me up with to right person. I sent my resume and they offered me a contract. Can you believe that?"

"God is good, Tracy, you know that. You deserve a chance for workin' so hard at teacher's college all them years."

"So, Mishka," Tracy said, "How're you doing in school?"

"Fine."

"Just fine, that's it?"

"No Auntie, me like it."

"Haven't seen you at church in a long, long time. It's nice seeing Ricardo there more often lately. Hope to see you there again soon."

Tracy waved goodbye.

"Me hope you turn out like your auntie one day," Sophia told Mishka. "She have ambition."

On the way home from school on Monday, Mishka timidly went back to the clinic for her test results. This time, she didn't have to wait long. The nurse who tended to before came out and called her into a room.

"Doing alright today, Mishka?"

"Yes, mam."

She looked at her clipboard. "Your results are all negative. You're healthy."

"You sure?"

"Yes, I'm sure."

"Alright. Thank you, miss."

Mishka picked up her backpack to walk out the door.

"Wait a minute," the nurse said, pointing toward the chair.

Mishka sat. "What is it, miss?"

"You sure everything is okay with you at home?"

"Yeh. Why you ask?"

"Well, when you were here last week something just didn't seem right. After you left I kept thinking about you. You remind me of my daughter, she's the same age as you, born the same month too.You know, Mishka, I am as surprise as you are to see that your tests came back negative, because last week you presented yourself as if you knew something was definitely wrong."

"Nothing was wrong with me, miss."

The nurse rose and shut the door, then sat back in her seat.

"Look up at me," she said. "Why did you really come to do these tests?"

"Me tell you, miss, me only come to do a check-up is all."

She removed her glasses. "Look, child. Me do this job for ten years, see girls like you every day. Me can almost always guess why they're here, especially when them walk in here alone, and look the way you did last week. Girls your age who're sexually active will only ask for a pregnancy test, not tests for sexually transmitted infections, unless they're showing symptoms."

"What you try to say, miss?"

"Were you raped!"

Mishka's face froze, her empty eyes penetrated the floor.

"Were you?"

She choked back her tears and picked up her backpack before opening the door.

"You were, weren't you?"

A tear fell from her eye. She wiped it away. "Me have to go home now."

"If you change your mind and want help come back and see me. I can refer you to a professional counselor. Everything's confidential."

Mishka left without saying more.

She saw Roxanne calling and although reluctant, she answered.

"How you do, Mishka?"

"Alright."

"Me almost reach your street now, come outside."

"Come to me room."

"Miss Sophia inside?"

"She gone to look for work. Me an' Ricardo alone here."

A few minutes later Roxanne entered.

"Why your eyes look like you cry, Mishka?"

"Oh, nothing. Me scratch it is all. Anyway, how you do, you go through with the abortion?"

"Auntie give me four pill last night, the Quinine. Me swallow three, insert one up me vagina. Wicked pain cross me belly whole night! Me pass out big clot. Lord Jesus. Me nearly dead."

"Feel better now?"

"Me couldn't even stan' up last night. Worse pain me ever feel."

"Me glad nothing worse happen. Grieg still don't know?"

"No. Me done with im."

"Why?"

"Don't feel the same bout im since me get pregnant. It don't feel right to be with somebody who can't help if im breed me." She lay beside Mishka on the bed. "Me stay with Auntie now."

"You live there now?"

"Yeh. Her daughter, me cousin Tina, she tell me bout a work where she dance, in a club. Me go see the owner next week."

"You mean like ..."

"Go-go, but nice club Tina say."

"But wha' bout school?"

"Me don't go back since me find out me pregnant. If the principal know she kick me out anyway."

"You feel comfortable to dance in a go-go club, Roxanne?"

"Me don't think bout comfort. Me do it for money."

Mishka later made dinner because she knew that Sophia would be too tired to cook after a long day of job search. When Sophia came home, Mishka made a plate and brought it to the sofa where Sophia sat.

"Thank you, darlin'."

Ricardo glanced at Sophia's plate. "Wha' happen to mine, Mishka?"

"You foot broke?"

"Ricardo," Sophia said. "Please go outside an' pick two lime off the tree, mix some lemonade an' bring me some."

"Bring me some too," Mishka said, handing a plate to Ricardo.

Ricardo politely rose and did what the ladies asked of him.

They sat on the sofa and ate together.

"Mishka," Sophia said. "Ricardo."

The kids looked at her.

"If me don't get work soon, me don't know how me manage to keep on send you children to school. All me have left is a little change for food. Mishka, time to pay your school fee again, me don't have it. You pass exam for expensive school. Me proud of you, but me don't see the money to pay now. Lunch an' bus fare is another problem."

Chapter Nine

Three weeks later…

Because Sophia's hope for things to improve didn't happen soon enough, Mishka was forced to drop out of school. Days and weeks went by and she became lethargic, skipping household chores and barely speaking to her family. With nothing to do except hang around the house, she wrote in her journal and slept through most of the day. She felt hopeless, but there was a fire deep down inside telling her not to give up. Aware that Mishka was not in school, Roxanne stopped by one afternoon.

"Me get the work." she said. "Start tonight."

"You know if the boss look for more dancer?"

"Me can ask im. Who want work?"

"Me. Where's the club?"

"Near Port Henderson beach, Back-Road. Club name Paradise."

"Me come watch you tonight."

"Wha' bout Miss Sophia?"

"She have enough to worry bout."

“You can ride with me and Tina, eight o’clock. We have private taxi, a man name Winston. We mus’ leave early so Tina can show me roun.”

Mishka decided to go along right then. She went inside and changed into a pair of jeans and tee-shirt.

“Me don’t want to walk past Nathan yard,” she said as they exited. “Walk roun the other street.”

“Wha’ Nathan do to you, Mishka? Why you don’t want im to see you?”

“Me don’t want to talk to im right now.”

As they crossed the soccer field, she recalled the night she tried to run away from Paul but she held back the urge to tell Roxanne.

“So all you do is dance, right?”

“Wha’ else you think?”

“Me don’t have to sleep with the boss to get the job?”

“That’s what me think at first too, but Norman is a decent man, im married an’ have children. It’s jus’ business, Mishka. Im help all girls who work for im, that’s why it's hard to get the job—everybody want to work for im. Only reason why me get it so easy is because Tina is the supervisor an’ we cousins. She put in a good word for me. Norman like girls who pretty an' sexy. No reason why im shouldn't hire you. Tina say im have the best girls on the back-road an' them make good money. Man come from all over to watch girls dance there."

"You know a whole heap."

"You will see tonight."

They walked down a narrow dirt path to where Roxanne's aunt lived. A group of raggedly attired young men sat idly under a tree and watched as the girls approached.

"Psst," one of them said. "Who your frien', Roxanne?"

"You too fast," Roxanne said. "She don't want anybody."

"Me want her."

"Don't pay them no mind," Mishka said. "Them don't have anything better to do than give trouble."

The stopped at a blue wood shack, Roxanne cautiously pushed open a makeshift gate that was falling off its hinges. Mishka stepped in and closed it behind her. A heavy-set woman wearing a flowery tattered dress sat on the enclosed verandah. The girls greeted her and entered.

Inside, Tina and Roxanne tucked away clothing, lotions, and other feminine necessities in their bags before calling the taxi. On their way out, the woman called out to Tina.

"Lend me two-hundred dollah till tomorrow," she said.

Tina dipped into her handbag and tossed the women some bills. "Me want it back."

"Two-hundred dollah you treat your mother so for?"

"Me work hard for it."

The girls left.

Mishka sat next to Roxanne in the back seat of the car while Tina and the driver spoke casually. Although it was dark Mishka recalled riding along this road the day she went to the beach with Nathan. After crossing the causeway the driver veered left onto a road along the shore, secluded from the main road.

"The club jus' down the street," Roxanne told Mishka.

Mishka was captivated by the scene. The strip was lined with small convenient shops and scantily clad girls who admired each car that went by. Mishka gazed at them.

"Prostitution go on back here?" she said.

Everyone laughed.

"You mus' be new in town," the driver said.

"Is that such a bad thing?" Mishka said.

"Me don't say that, baby."

"Me have a name, it's Mishka."

"You have a feisty little frien' here, Tina."

"Me should introduced you two," Tina said. "Mishka this is Winston. Winston, meet Mishka."

He reached back and shook Mishka's hand, turned his head and smiled at her, his teeth stained brown.

"Blessings, Mishka," he said.

"Pleased to meet you."

"Tina tell bout the *Back-Road* yet?"

"Me lookin' at it."

"What you see now is not the problem, it's what you don't see."

"Go ahead an' tell it, Winston," Tina said. "You tell a better story than me anyway."

"This is the unofficial red light district," he said, with a British accent.

The girls laughed hilariously.

"This is the hub for sex trade. Mishka, see back here, you will find plenty go-go club, restaurant, hotel, pub. You will hear bout a place people call *massage parlor,* open twenty-four-seven. Them girls don't only give massage in there if you get me drift. All type of people come to the Back Road: teacher, lawyer, politician, policeman, an' thief. People come here to find all kind of things them can't get anywhere else in Kingston. All the hotels an' restaurants you see roun here, them mostly depend on dancers an' all them gal you see walk the streets. Them gal keep the place busy. Most people stay far from the Back Road at night, except for those who work here or people who like hedonistic entertainment, right, Tina?"

"After you finish tonight," Tina said, "There's nothing more to tell."

"You know the runnings roun here," Winston said. "Me tell your frien' so she won't get trick."

"Respect, mon," Tina said. "Ey, you hear bout the police who them find dead in the hotel room next to the club?"

"Me read it in the paper this mornin'."

Finally, they arrived at a white two-story building. Roxanne stepped out, Mishka followed. They waited for Tina to gather her bags and pay for the ride. Mishka looked up at the Paradise Nightclub. A faint sound of music came from the upper level. Next to the nightclub was a small motel, also painted white and separated from the nightclub by an alleyway leading to the beach. This must've been the motel Tina referred to in the car, where the police was found dead. It was difficult to tell that such a thing occurred a night ago. A blinking green sign in the window indicated that they were indeed open for business. People walked in and out in a businesslike manner, some of whom appeared to be ladies of the night. Shady-looking characters loitered in the dark of the alley, studying those who went about in the light. The scent of marijuana lingered in the air. As Mishka approached the entrance of the nightclub she heard the calming sound of waves crashing onto the shore. Tina waved goodbye at Winston's taxi and led the girls up a narrow winding staircase.

At the bar, an exceptionally tall gentleman and two uniformed police officers sat on silver stools drinking

Heinekens. Tina tapped the man on the shoulder and introduced Mishka.

"She want to work here," Tina said. He looked Mishka over. "Oh, yeh?"

"Yeh," Tina said. "She a good girl."

He looked at his watch. "Me soon talk to her. Show Roxanne aroun', explain the rules an' then get to work. Me have some friends stoppin' by little from now."

Although it wasn't a high-class gentlemen's club, it was clean and nicely arranged, the walls painted red. In the center of the room sat a pool table. To the left were three steps leading up to what looked like a mini boxing ring, a silver pole in the middle. Off to the right was a dim corner with two pink sofas, some tables and chairs. The girls walked down a hallway to the dressing room. Tina sat in front of a vanity and admired her face before concealing the dark circles around her eyes. She was high in color and had a bit of roughness to her skin. She put on a matching red thong and bra set and sequined leg garter. She handed Mishka and Roxanne each a pair of thigh-high boots before leading them back up the hallway. They stood by the platform and watched.

"Alright," Tina said, climbing up. "First thing, you have to get comfortable naked roun strangers and have them touch you when them give you money. Mishka, if you shy this is not for you. Second, you have to know how to dance in high heels without fall on your face. And last, every Jamaican gal can dance, but not all can climb a pole. Watch this."

She climbed all the way to the top and slid down slowly, coming to the floor in a perfect split. The police officers high-fived Norman and whistled at Tina.

"Do it again." Roxanne said.

After several trips by Tina up and down the pole, Mishka took off her sandals, put on the boots, and climbed up on stage.

"Better if you take off the pants," Tina said. "Will make it easier to climb."

"In front of everybody?" Mishka asked.

"Me tell you, this is not a place for shy people. If you can't dance in your panty in front of only six people, how you do it when we have a full house of horny man?"

Mishka froze in thought.

"Take it off!" the bartender said.

"You got the looks," Norman said. "Now, you got the courage?"

She took a deep breath like getting ready to start a race, and stepped out of her jeans. Tina moved aside. Mishka gripped the pole and shimmied up. Half way there, she slipped and landed on her bottom. Everyone laughed. Tina helped her up.

"Try again," she said.

After two more attempts, she finally had it. Like a child mastering his first bike-ride, she did it over and over until she was absolutely certain she wouldn't embarrass herself in front of an audience. The three men applauded. Sweating, Mishka slid back into her jeans and waited while the other two practiced.

Tina led them back to the dressing room to prepare Roxanne for her first night on the job. Mishka stood by and watched. Two other girls walked in with bags over their shoulders. Mishka looked away after noticing their green-eyed gaze at her.

"New girls?" one of them said, pointing at Mishka.

Tina introduced them. "Roxanne start tonight. Mishka might work here too."

Tina ushered Roxanne to one side of the vanity, giving the other girls room to dress. When everything met Tina's standards, she led Roxanne and Mishka back to the entertainment zone.

"Wait over there for Norman," Tina told Mishka. "Come with me, Roxanne."

Mishka sat alone, observing Tina and Roxanne as they danced to the music under a disco ball that enhanced the movement of their bodies. The two girls who had walked into the dressing room were now sitting topless at the end of the sofa where Mishka sat, talking, until two men walked up and handed them cash. In return, they moved to a corner and performed lap dances. Too embarrassed to watch the lap dances anymore, Mishka turned back to the girls on stage. Tina danced in front of a man who slid his hand up her thigh, leaving some bills in her garter. Mishka was surprised to see couples and single women there too. The police officers shook hands with Norman and left. Norman welcomed three nicely dressed gentlemen who had just walked through the door. The bartender served the men drinks. Norman glanced at Mishka, excused himself, and walked over to where she sat. He wore a crisp, button down shirt and jeans.

"Everything alright?" he said, sitting down next to her.

"Yeh, me cool."

"Gettin' used to this place?"

"Not so sure yet."

He handed her a bottle of water. "Changing your mind bout workin' here? Hope not, cause you have all-star looks."

"Thing is," she said, uncrossing her legs, "Me never do this type of work before but me really need one right now."

"Sure, that's how most girls start. Some don't last an' some grow into it, become pros, like Tina. The money good, real good, but it's not for everybody. Roxanne is a little wobbly yet, but she look good still. One of me girls leave cause she pregnant so me figure why not give Roxanne a try."

"Me an' her is bes' frien'. That's how me end up here."

"You learn the pole fast," he said, smirking.

Mishka didn't consider this a compliment.

"Tina's the best me ever hire. Look at her, she move like an acrobat."

"That me can see."

"Me see you move shy when Tina asked you to take off the pants. Think you can dance up there like that?"

"Long as it's only dancin'."

"It's more than jus' dancin'. Way more. You have to show your breast, even more. The fellows will try to put hands on you. This job is not for a preacher's daughter."

"Me mus' have sex with them too?"

"That's not a requirement. We don't do that on the premises. There is a rule here that most men understand, don't touch unless it's to give a tip. You do all the touchin'. If them violate this rule security here to deal with it." He patted her knee. "Look, how bout a trial? When you want to do it?"

"Soon, maybe."

"You have a cute face, fit for the stage. Why don't you go to the back an' me have Tina come in an' fix you up? You can give it a try tonight. Show me what you look like outside the blouse."

"Alright," she said. "Me do it."

He walked up to where the girls were, caught Tina's attention, and whispered in her ear. She immediately left the stage and accompanied Mishka to the dressing room where she handed her a long curly wig and black thong set. Mishka took the thong, held it up to the light and carefully examined it.

"It bran' new," Tina said. "Don't scorn it."

"Me have to make sure it clean."

Mishka undressed and put on the undies.

"Wait," Tina said. "

"What?"

"You can't go out there like that. Too bushy down there. Have to shave first."

"Me don't have anything to shave with."

"Don't worry we have everything here."

Mishka was embarrassed. She hadn't shaved anything except her under arms. It seemed as if not shaving "down there" was an abomination for girls who worked in this field. She quickly realized that moral implication shouldn't play a part in her thinking. If she wanted the job she'd have to fit in or walk away now. Tina opened a drawer, took out some items and handed them to Mishka.

"How me mus' use the cream?"

"Put some on an' shave it clean."

She sat on a chair with one leg up on the vanity. Tina stood by and watched.

When Mishka was finished Tina poured oil in the palm of her hands.

"Turn aroun'," she said, applying it to Mishka's back. "Your body mus' make customer want to take you home. Your dark skin will look better when it well shine."

She opened a bag filled with makeup. "You ever wear face powder an' them things?"

"No."

She enhanced Mishka's cheeks with a light shade of bronze blush. "You have a pretty mole above your lip, me brighten it with the liner for you."

She led Mishka to a full body mirror behind the door. Mishka looked in amazement at the transformation.

"Oh, no." she said.

"Wha'?"

"Me look like a different person."

"Wha' you mean?"

"The red lipstick, the hairstyle, the G-string. Me look too X-rated."

"You suppose to."

"But…"

"Make sure you keep a smile out there. Tell yourself that every man here is special. Look at them that way. You can dance?"

"Not like you but me can do what most girls do."

"When you go on out there make sure you move your bottom and legs to the music. Use the pole like how me show you. Take off your top after the first song, your breast them nice an' firm. Remember to use the looking glass on the stage, it will give you sureness."

Mishka climbed up and walked to the center of the platform. She saw Norman sitting at the bar with his nicely attired guests. She felt them watching her. Five-feet-seven, she looked down into the audience and saw everyone watching. The other dancers had walked off stage, leaving only her and Tina. Tina stepped away from under the light, waiting for Mishka to begin. A new song began to play. The men whistled. The stage was all hers.

She strutted around the pole flirtatiously and made eye contact with Norman. Facing the mirrors, she watched her body flow to the music. She suddenly felt alive, powerful. When she climbed to the top of the pole and slid down slowly to the floor, the crowd began to cheer. Tina walked up behind her and unhooked her bra, exposing her breasts and caressing them. Surprised, Mishka caught her breath. The men tossed bills onto the stage, their faces filled with desire. She had enough and wanted to run off the stage, but she kept smiling.

At the end of her performance there was an announcement for her to meet Norman in his office. She left the stage. In his office, Norman sat behind his desk waiting.

"Shut the door," he said.

She picked up a box of tissue from his desk and wiped her face.

"Impressive," he said. "Sure you never do this before?"

She smiled.

"You have the job."

"Thank you, sir."

"The customers like you, want to continue tonight?"

"Sure."

"Go back an' see Tina in the back room first before you get back on the stage. She will tell you how me run this place.

Tina patted Mishka's ass. "You do good."

"Thanks."

"Norman say you can work here?"

"Yeh. Thanks for all the help. Im say you mus' tell me how im run the place."

"Wait, let me ask you. You feel funny when me touch you on the dance floor?"

"You frighten me, but no, not really."

"Part of the job."

"Yeh, me figure so, like when you watch me shave."

They sat in front of the vanity.

"Alright," Tina said. "Let me to tell you the rules here in Paradise. You good at the dancin' so we won't talk bout that. We go on stage ten o'clock every night. You mus' buy drinks if you want, sometimes customer offer to buy. Oh, an' don't let anybody slip anything in your drink."

"Like wha'?"

"Me don't know the name of it, but Norman say it's something for date rape."

"People come here an' drop things in girl's drinks?"

"It can happen anywhere, but men might think we girls are easy target."

"Me don't drink anyway."

"Me have to drink something before goin' on the stage, it help me loosen up. Back to the rules. If we share a dance we share the tip. You can give lap dance if you want to. All girls here do it, that's how you make good tip. Don't let anybody feel you up, them not supposed to."

"Yeh Norman tell me that."

"If you have good client and want to work with them private, that's up to you."

"You work private?"

"Me do it if the money good and them pay for hotel."

They removed their tips from the garters and counted it.

"How much you make?" Tina said.

"One thousan' dollah, plus five-hundred from the dance we share.

"Good for the little time you here, right?"

"Better than nothing at all."

"Beware of some of the men you see here. Easy to pick them out. Them the ones who sweet talk you the most. At the end of the day all them want is to fuck you. You won't find a husban' here. This is a job not a place to find a date."

"Let me ask you, police come here for watch girls dance too?"

"Sometimes, but in plain clothes. The ones you see here earlier, them friends with Norman."

"One more thing, we mus' work all night?"

"The club close at four but you can stop work three o'clock if you want. Mishka, most important rule, don't invite your boyfriend here. Norman don't like that. It can cause big problem for your job. Bout a year ago, one girl, her boyfrien' come here jealous and stab a customer. Norman fire her same time."

They later resumed their duties on the dance floor.

On their way home, it suddenly occurred to Mishka that Sophia knew nothing about what she'd done. The streets were empty, everyone in bed. The taxi dropped them off at Tina's house.

"You think me can stay here till daylight?" Mishka asked Roxanne.

"Auntie cool, she won't mind."

They went in and lay in bed together.

"Mishka," Roxanne said, "Don't tell Miss Sophia you go with me. She might vex and complain to me mother, say me influence you."

"Me know," Mishka said.

"Me don't care who know," Tina said. "Nobody give me anything for good name."

Mishka was awakened by her cell phone. She rolled over and looked at it—Sophia. Mishka didn't answer. She rushed into the bathroom, washed off her makeup and slid back into her jeans. She was as pure as she did before going to the nightclub. Roxanne's aunt made breakfast but Mishka didn't stay to eat. Roxanne with walked her up the street.

"Me glad you get the work," Roxanne said.

"Me too, but me can't tell Mommy nothing at all bout it, she will kill me."

"You come back tonight?"

"Me find a way."

They were halfway to Mishka's home.

"Me turn back now," Roxanne said. "You alright from here?"

"Yeh. Call me later. Me don't have no more minutes."

Walking up the street, Mishka saw a police car parked in front of her house. She panicked, turned, and walked in the opposite direction. She hid around the corner and waited until the car drove away from her house.

She pushed the gate open and entered. Sophia sat on the step with a concerned look on her face. She rose and walked toward Mishka.

"Where you was?" she said, holding Mishka by the collar.

"Me find work, bartender, sell drinks."

"Where? An' why you take up yourself an' leave here like that? Me call and you don't pick up your phone. Police jus' file missing report for you. What's really goin' on, Mishka?"

"Mommy, me tell you me work at a bar Cross the Waters. Me frien' tell me bout it. Me work late that's why me stop at her house till day light."

"Me hope that drinks is all you sell, Mishka. You know me don't want you to do nothing out of order for money, you know that! So me hope you tell me the truth. Me don't understan' why you couldn't wait for me to come home before you leave here. Whole night me don't sleep."

Mishka reached into her pocket. "Here, you can use this to buy food. Me work for all of we, not only me."

Sophia took it. "One thousan' … Mishka, you sure all you do is honest work?"

"Yeh, honest work is all me do. Me can go back and finish school now so me can graduate."

Sophia was teary eyed. Mishka held her. "Why you cry, Mommy?"

"Me don't want you to feel obligated to work for we. That's for me to worry bout. You still me baby."

"Don't cry, Mommy. Me do anything for me family. You work hard to send me to good school. Now that you can't find work me help. We help each other."

Relieved that Sophia didn't pursue finding out more about her job, Mishka went to her bedroom, changed her clothes and showered. It broke her heart to see her mother cry for the first time. She felt guilty about lying, but she didn't want to add disappointment to Sophia's stress.

Sophia walked into the room before Mishka was dressed. She hastily wrapped a towel around her waist to conceal her new haircut.

"How much days you work?" Sophia said.

"Friday, Saturday, Sunday. Most busy time."

"Oh. You look tired. Go get some sleep now, me go shop for dinner, cook something for you to eat before you leave again later."

She went to bed thinking about her new job and how easy it seemed for the other girls to do. The dance with Tina—not even in her wildest imagination had she see it happening. She was raised in an environment where people didn't tolerate gay behavior. Tina said that touching her was the nature of the business and complimented her breasts, smacked her butt. She lay there bewildered at the thought that Tina might be a lesbian.

Late afternoon, Mishka felt a hand on her shoulder. She opened her eyes and saw Sophia. "Dinner ready."

Mishka rose and walked to the kitchen.

"Boy name Nathan come look for you. Me tell im you sleepin'."

"What im say?"

"To tell you im come look for you. Who im?"

"Same boy me an' Roxanne go beach with, im live where the supermarket is."

"But why im come here to look for you?"

"Cause me don't see im long time now."

After eating, she saw Roxanne calling and stepped outside to answer. She later dressed, kissed Sophia and left with her bag.

She met Roxanne near the ball field.

"Wha' you tell Miss Sophia?" Roxanne said.

"Say me work a bar, sell drinks."

"Wha' she say?"

"She nearly box me down, vex cause me take up an' leave yesterday, even call police an' report me missin'. She say she hope all me do is honest work for money. Me feel it's honest work."

"Jus' be careful. Don't let anybody at all know what you do. If anybody find out, the whole Jones Town will hear bout it. Them will call you dirty gal, whore. Tina say we mus' always use the same taxi man, only im know where we work."

"You right."

"You make good money last night?"

"Three thousan' dollah. Me only give Mommy one-thousan' so she won't get suspicious. Me really want to go back and finish school."

"Me want to go back too, for cosmetology. Me want to open a parlor one day. Maybe we can do it together.

The men at the nightclub were requesting lap dances from Mishka. She felt awkward at first, but told herself that it was only work and she wasn't being forced to do it. When she walked over to the guy who'd been asking her for a dance since she arrived, he had a smile on his face. After minutes of rubbing her body on his lap, she held out her hand.

"Three-hundred dollah."

"Me don't have so much." He handed her two-hundred.

"Me say three hundred."

He smiled. "Go easy, baby, me pay you next time."

"Me want it now. Nothing in here free. Give me one-hundred more."

He insisted on not having any more so she walked over to Norman at the bar.

"One dirty man over there don't want to pay me."

They walked over to where he sat.

"You got a dance from me girl?" Norman said.

"Brethren, me tell her me pay next time. Me come here every weeken', spend money at the bar, still support the thing."

By the scuff of the neck, Norman lifted him from the chair and pushed his back against the wall. From behind his waistband, Norman drew a handgun and pointed it at the man's temple. Mishka held onto Norman's elbow, pulling him away from the man.

"It's alright, Mister Norman," she said. "One-hundred dollah don't worth this kind of trouble."

He lowered his firearm and stood directly in front of the man. "You take me business for fuckin' joke?"

"Me leave your place now," the man said, fixing the front of his shirt.

Norman turned to Mishka. "Next time make people pay before you do anything, one of the rules Tina forgot to tell you bout."

She continued her duty, collecting every penny due to her.

Chapter Ten

Two weeks later ...

Back in school she felt like an outcast. She looked around at her peers, wondering if any of them were faced with similar circumstances at home. It was difficult to tell. They all seemed happy. There were no signs of hardship. Many of them lived within the vicinity of the school where there was no crime or poverty. If she kept quiet about where she lived and how she was able to attend Alpha, she would look like one of them—from a perfect home. She sat in the corner of the room and away from the cliques. She felt them cold-shouldering her. A group of girls who sat behind her whispered among themselves and rolled their eyes whenever she turned around. She tried to ignore them, it was too late to make friends and they had nothing in common. She fell back into her mental bubble where no one posed a threat.

At recess, her homeroom teacher handed her a note. She read it. "*Please see me, Sister Katherine.*" She thought that she was in some kind of trouble and immediately went down the hall to her guidance counselor's office. The traditional wimple and veil covering her head, Sister Katherine sat behind her desk working on the computer. She looked up and beckoned Mishka to step in. She entered and held up the note.

"You want to see me, mam?"

"Yes, Campbell, please have a seat."

Mishka settled in the chair and waited.

"It has been brought to my attention that you've been absent for quite some time, almost a month."

"Yes, mam. Me mother, she lose her job an' that make things hard for the time I was gone."

"Ah, I see."

"You expel me because of the absence, mam?"

"Oh no. Not at all. I asked to see you because the law requires that I recognize lengthy absences. Now that you're here, I also have to document the reason you haven't been here. It's all confidential."

"Alright, mam."

"How're things at home now?"

"Better."

"Happy to hear. Have you spoken to your teacher to see about make-ups?"

"After class this evening, we meet to talk about it."

Katherine put on her glasses and examined some papers on her desk.

"As far as I know," she said, "You've been a wonderful student. Your grades were above average before the absences."

"Yes, mam. Me willing to do everything to make it up so me can graduate."

"I was really happy this morning when I heard that you were back."

"Thank you, mam."

Katherine gave her a smile of endorsement. "If you work a little harder to get back on course you'll be sure to graduate."

Mishka became disheartened each time she recall her brief relationship with Nathan before Paul attacked her. Everything seemed to have changed so quickly. She missed him, but was too ashamed to face him. She sat by the doorway hand-washing her uniform when Sophia hurried in from the street.

"Come inside," she said, urgently. "We have to talk now. Where is Ricardo?"

"Im help' me cook dinner."

"Go get im an' come now."

Mishka dried her hands on her blouse and went into the kitchen where Ricardo stood over the stove.

"Mommy want you."

They gathered on the sofa.

"Wha' so serious, Mommy?" Mishka said.

"Calvin call when me fill out application at the airport, say im come for you to take you to America!"

"You did sen' the birth paper?" Mishka said.

Sophia said nothing for a moment. She eased back on the sofa and folded her arms.

"Yes, me sen it to im other day."

"Me don't want to go," Mishka said.

"Me make it without im," Ricardo said.

"Don't act too jumpy now," Sophia said. "Im don't come tomorrow."

"Why you never tell me when you sen' the birth paper?" Mishka asked.

"It wasn't an easy decision. Me don't want to let you go, but it's for your own good, not mine."

"Me don't want to go," Mishka said.

"Both of you mus' go, especially you, Mishka."

"Me don't know im, Mommy," Mishka said. "How me mus' live with a man me don't know? What if me go to America an' don't like it?"

"Look aroun you!" Sophia said, intensely, sweeping her arms out to indicate the neighborhood. "Look where we live an' all the things that go on here. You want to live this way all your life? If you don't go you know what will happen to you here?"

Mishka didn't respond.

"You will finish high school and can't go any further, get pregnant then your life over. That's what you want, Mishka?"

Mishka looked down at her lap.

"Life too rough here for women," Sophia said. "Worse when you poor. That is why you see most women sit home with them children, can't pay for education, can't find work an' can't feed them children, no father to help. Same like me."

"Me stay here with you, Mommy," Ricardo said. "Make sure you alright."

"Don't fret bout me, you have your whole life ahead of you. Don't stay here an' waste it. You a good boy. Me proud of how you not like them other boy roun' here who take to gun. Me know that the good Lord sen' Calvin back here to take you to America so you can become something."

"Me already know what me want to do with me life," Ricardo said. "The pastor at church say if me join the cadet at school now it will give me a jump start to the police force. Pastor say that im will give me good recommendation."

"Me don't want to go," Mishka said.

Sophia raised her hands above her head. "Mishka you mus' go! Please, me beg you. Me don't want to see you end up like me. At your age me already a mother. You can do better, educate yourself, get decent work. You have good potential but me can't pay for university for you here. This is the only chance you will ever get an' you shouldn't waste it."

"But, Mommy…"

"Me say you mus' go!"

Back to washing her clothes, Mishka felt betrayed by Sophia's secret agenda to send her away to America. Calvin had told Mishka that America was a wonderful place filled with opportunities, but she couldn't put together a mental image of having a future there. Sophia made a strong case that Mishka should leave Jamaica, but despite the growing darkness that Sophia emphasized, Jamaica was Mishka's home. It was all she knew.

In the face of Sophia's persuasiveness, Ricardo was rebellious toward his father for obvious reasons. Mishka had never seen him talk back to Sophia. Growing up, he was reserved and showed very little humor. Now, it seemed as though he was determined to show what a man can do for good. She realized she didn't know much about her brother as he was coming into manhood. Under the tutelage of his pastor, perhaps Ricardo found the role model he longed for from his own father, someone to look up to and keep him on the right path.

As she hung her wash on the line, she recalled Sophia's pleading eyes and how desperate she appeared for Mishka to leave Jamaica. She knew that Sophia was right about the challenges ahead, but Mishka wasn't fazed by it. She lived in a society where social constraints were part of being a woman. She saw it in her mother each day. It's who she herself would have to become had there been no Calvin.

She noticed Sophia's smile of victory as she walked through the front door.

"Me get security work at the airport!" she said.

"True?"

"The good Lord answer me prayer. The boss want me to start train tonight."

Mishka held Sophia. "Glad you never give up, Mommy."

"Me weather worst storm than this. God only give what me can bear. You don't have to work no more. Me take care of things now. Me go get ready to start later."

Mishka picked up her phone and called Roxanne.

"Come here now," she said. "Me have to talk to you."

Sophia waved goodbye on her way out the door. "Make sure you lock up the place before you fall asleep, hear me?"

"Yes, Mommy."

Roxanne later walked in and went straight to Mishka's bedroom.

"Everything alright?"

Mishka hissed. "Don't know at all."

"Wha' trouble you?"

"First, Mommy find work. Then me father supposed to take me an' Ricardo to America next month."

"You go?"

"Don't want to but Mommy force me, for better life she say. Ricardo say im stay here."

"Why Miss Sophia have to force you? Wha' you think you miss here?"

"Wha' me miss in America?"

"Miss Sophia already tell you, better life."

"Me don't know Calvin good, Roxanne. Im left here when me a baby an' only come back one time to look for me."

"You fret bout the least. Look how hard it is to make it here."

"Same thing Mommy say."

"If somebody bring me go abroad, anybody, me leave here in no time. You better go to America, better yourself and help Miss Sophia."

"Me plan to better meself here. Another thing, how me tell Norman that me don't work for im no more?"

"Wha' so hard bout that? Say you have to leave."

"But Norman a nice man. Im hire me when me need work bad. Im will think me ungrateful to leave there now."

"You won't be the first or last to leave. Girls like we look for work all the time … when you leave someone else take your place."

"Me don't want to leave Jamaica."

"You will get to love American. When you make it there don't forget bout me."

As Mishka went over some homework in her bedroom she heard several taps on her window. Ricardo had gone to bed and Sophia had a key. Mishka suddenly thought of Paul and turned off the lamp.

"Mishka," a voice said, softly.

"Who is it?"

"Nathan."

She kept quiet for a moment. She thought that he had forgotten about her and didn't expect he'd come back. She turned on the light, opened the front door and saw Nathan standing there. They looked at each other.

"Miss Sophia inside?" he said.

"She gone to work."

He followed her to her bedroom and sat next to her on her bed.

"Wha' me do to you?" he said, his eyes pleading. "Why you avoid me so? Last time we talk you promise to come check me. Me wait outside for you till one o'clock. Why you do me that, Mishka?"

She thought of an excuse.

"Me did feel sick."

"But why you don't answer when me ring your phone? Me come here an' ask Miss Sophia for you, me ask Roxanne for you, me know them tell you."

"But…"

"Me still love you, want you back."

She didn't believe he'd still love her if he knew what Paul had done, and her dancing at Paradise. It was too late for them.

She hung her head. "Me goin' to America to live with me father."

"When?"

"Soon."

He sighed deeply. "Can't believe you leave me so."

They both sat quietly, Mishka, aware they had no control over their destiny together. She had loved him at one point too but the night she was raped changed everything.

Chapter Eleven

Three weeks later ...

Parting with Nathan was excruciating. Sitting next to him felt so different from before when Mishka saw their wonderful future ahead. Now it seemed a morass. He had a pained look in his eyes and was unable to look at her and say goodbye. She couldn't keep away the guilt for everything that had occurred. She too had to accept that things would never be the same between them. Graduation was only a week away and she was determined to be a part of it. Her grades were intact again and she finally felt a sense of optimism. Sophia seemed to have regained her confidence as a parent and Mishka was proud of her mother's vigor to rise again. For all the setbacks that her family had undergone, she was eager to complete high school successfully and prove to herself that her circumstances wouldn't define her. She was as good as the elites whom she walked the corridors with each day.

She turned on the outside light and went to shower before bed. Under the faint spray of water she heard someone fumbling with the door. She wiped water from her eyes, looked up, and saw a hand reaching above the door, unlocking it. Paul opened it and stepped in. She screamed. He put a finger on his lip, gesturing her not to make a sound. She immediately began to fight her way past him. He caught her arm in a vicious grip, pulling her back inside. She wrestled with him, still trying to break free.

"Help!" she said.

He covered her mouth. She yelled harder under the palm of his hand. He grabbed her by her wrists, twisted them behind her back, and shoved her inside of the bathroom. She slipped and fell. He brought her back to her feet and shut the door.

"You still don't learn, eh?" he said, turning off the shower. "Why you run from me?"

"Me don't tell nothing," she said, shaking with fear.

"Me know you wouldn't do that."

"So what you want from me then? Me mother soon come out here to see why me bathe so long."

He held her by her throat and pushed her against the wall.

"Me tell you before, don't lie to me! Me know Sophia gone to work tonight.

She stood there quietly, hoping for him to release her.

"You turn whore now?" he said. "Me know wha' you an' Roxanne do over Back Road. Sophia know?"

He let her go. She used her hands to cover herself.

"Me no whore, only dance, an' how you know what me do."

"Me know everything. Me the one who govern roun' here, lock the street every night. Make sure when me ready for you again you ready too. An' don't worry, me keep your secret. Marlene don't know Roxanne a whore either. Tell her me keep her secret too."

On his way out, he touched her breast as if he owned her. Sure that he was gone, she wrapped a towel around her body and ran inside to her bedroom. She realized she was being blackmailed by a powerful force from whom she had no escape. If confessing to Sophia would guarantee he'd leave her alone, she would have done it in a heartbeat. She would have no peace unless she did whatever he wanted, whenever he wanted. She became furious that he came back to intimidate her, making it obvious that he still had control over her. Will she do something to protect herself? Or will she submit again?

Chapter Twelve

One week later ...

It was the day of graduation. Sophia and Tracy had taken the day off to support Mishka. They watched as she stood before her dresser putting the finishing touches on her makeup. She put the cap back on the black eye liner and picked up her straightener. After a few minutes she was satisfied with the way her hair looked and unplugged the straightener. Sophia walked over and carefully set the graduation cap on Mishka's head. She moved around Mishka, walking a circle, admiring Mishka from head to toe. She stepped closer and held Mishka's hands. Her eyes began to well up.

"Me don't know what it feel like to graduate from anything," she said. "Feel good to watch you."

"Don't cry, Mommy," Mishka said, holding Sophia.

Tracy leaned in, her arm wrapped around Sophia. "It's alright Sophie, nothing wrong with a tear of joy."

Mishka wiped the tears from Sophia's eyes.

"Me always want to make you proud, Mommy. Thank you for all you do to get me this far."

"You make your auntie proud too," Tracy said hugging Mishka.

Outside, Marlene sat in a chair in front of her home, Paul next to her, smoking.

"You look good, Mishka!" Marlene said, smiling. "Sophie mus' feel like a million dollah now."

"Try a billion!" Sophia said, smiling back.

Mishka didn't respond. She saw Paul looking at her. She glared back at him.

Marlene joined Mishka's family.

"Me walk with Sophie to bus stop," she told Paul.

He nodded, blowing smoke into the air.

Mishka felt no animosity toward Marlene, but she was uncomfortable in Marlene's presence. Mishka walked next to Tracy while Sophia and Marlene walked next to each other, talking. At the bus stop, Mishka was relieved when Marlene said goodbye and went back home. Sophia chartered a taxi to Mishka's school.

Sophia and Tracy joined the parents and guests in the auditorium. The students were later awarded diplomas. When it was Mishka's turn, she looked down in the crowd and saw Sophia glowing with satisfaction. Exiting the ceremony, Mishka's little group was approached by Sister Katherine.

"Congratulation, Mishka," she said.

"Thank you, mam."

Katherine turned to Sophia. "She's a bright young lady. Hope she can continue on to university."

"Yes, mam," Sophia said. "Me do everything to see to it."

Mishka and her family later celebrated over lunch.

Sophia went to work that night. Mishka dressed and reached under her mattress for all the cashed she'd saved from working. She counted it, placed it in her handbag, and called Winston. On the way out the door, she saw Ricardo fixing his tie around his neck.

"You go to prayer meetin'?" she said.

"We have Crusade. Auntie say me must invite you."

"Next time. Me have something important to do."

"Wha' so important?"

"Wait up for me when you come back home. Me see you roun ten o'clock."

He picked up his bible from the coffee table and tucked it under his arm. They walked outside together. He proceeded up the street. Mishka waited for Winston. Not long after he showed up.

"Take me to Paradise," she said, getting in.

They took off.

"Me think them girls say you don't work there no more."

"Yeh, good while now."

"If you don't work there why me take you then?"

"To see Norman bout something."

Entering the nightclub casually attired and her hair in a ponytail, she was barely recognized by regular patrons. Roxanne and the girls were on stage entertaining. Mishka didn't want them to see her. She went straight to the bar where Norman sat on his stool watching the girls and sipping his Heineken. She tapped him on the back.

"Mishka!" he said, over the music. "Long time no see!"

She wrapped her arm around his shoulder. “Me need to see you!”

He walked with her to his office. She closed the door behind them.

“What’s up?” he said, sitting behind his desk. “You come back to work?”

“No, but me thank you for the time you hire me to work here, get me family out of a bad jam.”

“Hope you come back one of these nights. You’re a good draw, always keep this place lively.”

“No, not comin’ back. Me work here cause me was really in need of money. Thanks to you things better now.”

He nodded. “Me understan’. Not everyone take this job for a profession. Me respect you a whole heap and if you ever want to come back you welcome anytime.”

“Mister Norman,” she said, hesitantly. “Me want to ask you something.”

“What’s that?”

“Me can trust that you won’t tell anybody what we talk bout?”

“Me ever give a reason not to trust me?”

"Not even Roxanne. Me don't want anybody at all to know."

"Alright."

"You know where me can get a small gun to buy?"

He leaned forward. "Wha' you need it for?"

"Somebody want to hurt me."

"Who would want to hurt a girl like you?"

"This man me know, im won't stop fuck with me. Im frighten me when me bathe, push the bathroom door an' come in, wring me hand when me try to run from im. Im know me used to work here an' threaten me, say im tell me mother if me don't let im fuck me."

"How im know you used to work here?"

"Don't know. The only people who know me used to work here is Roxanne, Tina, an' we taxi man name Winston."

"But me don't understand … im come as far as in your bathroom to fight with you? How you an' im know one another? You and im used to …"

"No, no. Nothing like that. Im live near me. Im want to make me sleep with im, force imself on me. Me don't want nothing to do with im. Im know that."

Jamaica Tough

He leaned back in his chair and took a long sip of his Heineken.

"Any man live roun your house?"

"Me brother. Im only sixteen-years-old, good boy, im can't help me."

"Ever fire a gun before?"

"No, but me can learn."

He took a set of keys from his pocket and opened a safe above his head. He took a box from the safe, placed it on the desk and reached in.

"This is of no use to me," he said. "Too small." He handed it toward her. "Smith and Wesson, twenty-two."

She took it. He sat back in his seat.

"Why it so small, but so heavy?"

"Cause it's not a toy."

She sat there quietly, admiring it, thinking it through.

"How much you want for this?"

"How much you have?"

She placed it on the table and opened her bag, emptied it on the desk.

"Four-thousan'."

"Me give it to you for five."

"Me have to think of a way to get the rest an' come back."

He stopped her as she gathered the bills and took a brief pause.

"Me like you, Mishka," he said. "Take it. Four-thousan'."

"Me don't want to owe you anything."

A few seconds passed as he estimated her honesty.

"Tell you wha'," she finally said. "If you let me work here for one more night, tonight, me make the money an' pay you. Me even pay you extra, five-hundred more than what you ask. You know me good for it. Jus' give me one night an' me sort it out for you."

He slid the twenty-two across the table. "Don't fret bout it. You don't have to do all that. Take it. Protect yourself."

"No. Me want to pay you. Don't like to owe people money. Me left some things here in the locker. If you let me, me go out there now, make the money, an' pay you for it tonight."

"Me say don't fret bout it," he said, irritably. "Give me the four-gran'. You don't owe me nothing else after that.

One-thousan' dollah can't break me bank. Take the thing an' protect yourself."

She recounted the bills and handed them to him. "Here, four-thousan'."

He reached for the firearm on the table. Mishka's eyes widened. She watched as he released the magazine.

"It hold ten," he said. "If you ever have to use it, make sure you have good aim cause a man is stronger than you. If you miss im will use it against you. It's not a play thing."

"Me don't intend to play with it."

He held it assuredly. "Watch this. It clean, untraceable, serial number file off. Walk with me outside."

He lifted his shirt and tucked it in the front of his waist. Mishka followed him through the club where the music was pumping. Alone, they stood on a balcony overlooking the beach.

"Look here," he said. "Very important, the safety. Make sure it on when the gun not in use." He handed it to her. "Let me see if you can manage it. Can't have a gun an' don't know how to use it."

She took and admired it once again, stroke it with her fingers. He positioned her directly in front of him. She located the trigger. She gripped it tightly. Her finger awaited his permission.

He raised her hands above her head.

"Point straight up," he said. "Now, fire two."

She aimed at the moon, closed her eyes, and squeezed.

She lowered her arm slowly and handed the pistol to him.

"Good," he said. "It work."

"Me ears," she said, holding it.

"It soon stop ring. Listen, don't show this to no one unless you plan to use it. Nobody mus' know you have it. Only use it for life and death."

He wiped the pistol on his handkerchief thoroughly.

"All yours," he said, handing it to her. "No one have evidence me touch it. Remember, Mishka, if you use it you will open a whole new can of worm. Me give it to you cause me know you a smart girl. Don't be a fool. Life or death only!"

As she began to put it into her handbag, he stopped her arm. "See, you forget something already."

She paused. "Oh, the safety."

He smiled at her, opened the door, and walked inside.

"Life or death only," she said to the pistol.

She enabled the safety and cautiously put it in her handbag. She left the nightclub and found the waiting driver.

She was back in Jones Town. The streets were scanty, one convenient shop still open. In the back seat of the car, she reached into her handbag for cash to pay for the ride, touching the smooth surface of her pistol. She handed the money to the driver.

"Thank you, Winston."

"No problem."

Getting out, she panicked. Paul might be watching her every move. She noticed that the outdoor lights were off. Ricardo must've gone to bed. She opened the gate and entered. The taxi drove away. Relieved to make it almost to her doorstep, she saw what appeared to be a bicycle parked under the tree and against the fence. She ran back toward the gate. Paul stepped out of the shadows, blocking her path.

"Where you go?"

She clutched her handbag and thought quickly.

"Me forgot to buy something at shop, Excedrin, for headache."

"You go whore tonight?"

"Wha' you talk bout? Me tell you, me no whore, only dance."

"Me want you to dance for me tonight. Me bring you back where we was last time, my place."

"Me don't do private dance."

"Me pay you jus' the same, make one of me soldier drive you back home after. Me hear that all the man on the Back Road go crazy for you. Me want to see wha' them go crazy for."

"Don't feel up to it. Me have a bad headache."

"Me make it go away. Go buy the tablet and come back. Me wait for you here."

She opened the gate and walked up the street. Without looking back she held on to her bag and ran past the shop. Approaching Tracy's house, the gate was shut but she kicked it open. She pounded on the door, hoping Tracy would come out before Paul caught her. Tracy's sleepy voice came from inside.

"Let me in!"

Tracy opened the door. Mishka stepped in and locked it.

"What happen?" Tracy said.

"A man run me down."

"Which man?"

"Me don't know im, first time me see im."

"Where you coming from so late and where's Sophie?"

"She gone to work. Me go shop to buy pill. The man come out from the bush and frighten me, grab me blouse. Me run."She went home when the sun came up. Paul was gone for the moment. She knew he would make it a point to come back and confront her for running away from him again, deceiving him. Keeping her handbag close at all times would be her last resort. The postman rang his bell out front. She looked around to make sure Paul wasn't around before going for the mail. The postman smiled at her. She knew him. He lived up the street. He reached into his delivery bag and took out a large envelope. She took it and went back inside. She knew that the envelope meant something important because they never received mail at home. She hurried inside and shook Sophia awake.

"Mommy," she said. "Look!"

Sophia's head was slightly tucked under a pillow.

"Me tired," she said. "Me look at it before me go to work later."

"No, Mommy, a big letter. Look now!"

Sophia rolled over and rubbed her eyes with the back of her hands. Mishka handed over the envelope. Sophia opened it and looked at the documents enclosed.

"Oh," she said. "Immigration letter for you and Ricardo. You consider wha' me say bout goin'?"

"Yeh. Me go."

Sophia sat up and scanned the papers.

"It have appointment date for interview. Tell Ricardo come here to me."

Mishka went and came back with her brother.

"You decide if you want to go to America with your father?" Sophia said. "See letter here, from embassy."

"Me done tell you wha' me stay here an' do," Ricardo said.

Sophia pointed her finger at him. "You better do something. Me don't want you to stay roun' here an' get with bad company, turn gunman, an' make police kill you. Me don't have no money to bury you."

Next day, Sophia woke Mishka to accompany her to the market. Mishka hid her handbag under her bed before leaving. On the way to the bus stop, she became increasingly paranoid. She felt as though she was being watched. She knew how desperate Paul would be to get her back. Perhaps he or one of his men was on to her. She remained alert and walked close to Sophia, hoping they'd get to their destination fast. Her heart leapt each time a man rode past her on a bicycle. Finally at the bus stop, they flagged down a taxi and squeezed in.

The Coronation Market was teeming and filled with energy. Folks came from all over the island to sell things in the nation's capital—large variety of fresh, exotic harvests, dry goods, apparel, and various healing herbs. People worked tirelessly in the heat of the sun to make a living. Boys and men of all ages skillfully pushed handcrafted pushcarts, transporting goods from one end of the market to the other. Mishka and Sophia pushed their way through the frenetic hustle and bustle, careful not to get a foot run over by the wheel of a vehicle. Vendors arranged their items on wooden stalls sheltered by blue tarp. A boy wearing only shorts and slippers walked up to Mishka with a box on top of his head.

"Miss," he said. "Buy some scallion from me please. Only twenty-dollah."

Mishka politely declined and kept on. Cops walked around and examined the atmosphere, making sure that each person was lawfully permitted to sell in the market.

"Let we go an' buy fish first," Sophia said. "We can come back out here after."

Not far away, they stopped at an enclosed area where women sat over buckets scaling and gutting freshly caught fish. The smell was potent. Mishka couldn't wait to leave. Sophia stopped at a stall, picked out some red snapper, and handed it to the vendor.

"Leave the fish head for me please," she said. "Me soon come back."

"Take your time mum," the woman said. "Me clean them up nice for you."

Later that evening Ricardo came home with Tracy after church.

"Me smell food," he said, walking into the kitchen. "

Hope there's enough for me," Tracy said.

"Sit down," Sophia said. "Me an' Mishka jus' finish steam some fish we get from town today."

"I'm starving," Tracy said. "I've been fasting since sundown yesterday."

"The rice nearly done," Sophia said.

Tracy kicked her feet up on the sofa. "Am leaving for America next week, Sophie."

"Congratulations, darlin'!" Sophia said from the kitchen. "Me wish you a safe journey. Mishka soon gone to New York too. Me take her to embassy Monday mornin' bright an' early. Calvin come for her after she get the visa. You an' her should keep in touch there."

"I will but I'm not sure we'll see each other. I'm going to Florida. I think New York is far away. I'll find out from Calvin."

Sophia walked in from the kitchen "Yeh, do that."

Mishka came out and sat on the floor next to Tracy.

"Ricardo told me he's not going," Tracy said to Sophia.

"Me wish im would go, but im old enough now. Me can't force im too much."

"I know how boys are with their moms," Tracy said.

"Mishka didn't want to go either. Me talk sense into her. Ricardo say im stay here an' turn head of police one day."

They cackled.

Ricardo changed out of his suit and came out. "Who laugh last laugh the bes'. Me make everybody see."

"Son," Tracy said. "I hope you'll stay here and do something productive, even if your dream doesn't come true."

They sat and had a wonderful fish dinner together, Mishka relieved that Tracy didn't mention anything about the night she ran to her house and away from Paul.

Chapter Thirteen

One week later ...

The lights came on in Mishka's house at five o'clock and the dawn was beginning to announce itself. The strong smell of brewed mint told Mishka that Sophia was active around the house. Mishka was mentally exhausted and hoped that Sophia would sit and have her tea before coming in to wake her. She fell into a brief snooze, until she heard her bedroom door creak open. Her eyes felt heavy but she opened them and saw Sophia walking in.

"You don't plan to get up this mornin?"

Mishka yawned. "Me up now."

"Put on something decent today, the blue frock Tracy give you for your birthday."

"Why me mus' wear tha' church frock? We only go to the embassy."

"Me say you mus' wear it. The people at the embassy want to know that decent Jamaican go into them country.

You can't go there dress any ol' way. Put yourself together properly."

"Alright, Mommy. Me wear it."

When the taxi dropped them off at the embassy, already a long line stretched along the sidewalk. Two hours later they finally reached inside. In the waiting area, Mishka looked over at Sophia who seemed preoccupied in thoughts. She sat quietly, her arms folded across her chest.

"You alright, Mommy?"

"Can't believe me will have to say goodbye to me only daughter."

Mishka hugged her mother.

A voice called out for Mishka to come to a window. Sophia and Mishka rose. The blonde-haired gentleman behind the glass had a friendly smile. The sleeves of his button-down shirt were rolled up. Sophia reached into her bag and slid some papers through the opening under the window.

"You are the biological parent or legal guardian of Mishka, yes?" he said.

"Yes, sir."

He examined the documents sheet by sheet.

"Everything looks great," he said. "Good luck in the U.S., Miss Campbell."

Mishka was relieved to know that soon she no longer had to live in fear of Paul. The thought of leaving without saying goodbye to Roxanne saddened her. Keeping her departure a secret might be the only way she'd leave Jamaica safely. She needed to leave quickly before Paul finds out. He said that he knew everything. Will he come back before she left the island?

She cuddled with Sophia that night, the only place she felt secure for the moment.

"Me goin' to miss you, Mommy," she said.

"Me miss you already, but we mus' do what's best sometimes. It hard but we have to do it."

"You want me to go for better life, so let's look at the good side."

"It not so simple. Someday you will know this pain, but it's the right pain, to help your children."

"Soon as me make it in there me come back to help you out of Jones Town."

"Don't fret bout me. Go there an' get yourself together, get good education an' work hard."

"You take the day off tomorrow? The last time we will spend together."

"Me already have the day off."

Sophia held her tight, not only to let her know that she was loved, but also to give her the strength to go.

"Me hope you take this opportunity an' put it to good use. Don't go there an' get mix up with bad company because you will get deport back here. Me don't have nothing here for you to come back to. Stay there an' do your bes', hear me?"

"Yes, Mommy."

Sophia drew the sheet over Mishka's shoulders.

Finally, it was Mishka's last night in Jamaica. Not having the courage to say goodbye to Nathan ripped her heart apart. Sophia had gathered some sentimental items she kept over the years and wanted Mishka to take along—her beauty pageant certificate and the page from the newspaper with her name for having passed the high school entrance exam. They later sat together and ate dinner.

"Don't know how me manage now without you, Mishka. It will take a long time to get used to."

"Ricardo will be here." She looked at her brother. "Take good care of Mommy."

"Me always do that," he said. "She good here with me."

"Mishka," Sophia said. "When you get there, whatever you do, always remember that education is the key anywhere you go. It's the only way you won't end up like your mother. Me tell you that from you a little girl. Don't let anybody fool you bout love an' get you pregnant before time. Always remember Tracy, see, she want to get marry first before she think bout baby. Don't disobey your father and Jackie. Don't do or say anything to upset them. When you reach, ask your father for a phone card and call me."

Mishka nodded and gave Sophia a long, emotional hug.

Mishka looked at her suitcase in the corner, packed with everything she owned. She remembered her diary and reached under her mattress for it. After a deep breath, she sat on her bed and opened it to where she left her pen. She read the last sentence: "*Why did this happen to me?*" She closed and placed it in the pocket of her luggage. As she climbed into bed, the pistol crossed her mind. She needed to get rid of it. What to do with it? She came up with an idea—bury it in the yard. She looked in at Sophia and saw she was fast asleep. Ricardo was too. She quietly slipped into the kitchen for a black plastic bag which she brought back to her bedroom. She removed the pistol from her handbag and wrapped it tightly in the plastic bag. She opened the front door, turned on the outside lights, and looked around to make sure Paul wasn't there. She walked over to the root of the mint tree and looked for a spot. Between the tree and fence would work. She reached for an old rusted shovel leaning against the fence. From where she stood, the gate looked shut, but she went and locked it. At the tree, she dug a shallow hole. She placed the pistol there and covered the hole with dirt. Behind the gate was a large rock. She rolled it from the gate all the way to the hole, sweating and breathing hard. She shoved it on top of the buried pistol. No one would know what was under the stone. Back inside, she checked the windows to make sure they were locked before going to sleep.

Sophia jostled up and made breakfast. Mishka prepared for her departure. Later, there was a knock at the front door. Mishka opened it and saw Calvin.

He smiled and hugged her. "Mornin."

"You come early," Mishka said.

"We have to be at the airport by ten. Where's Sophie?"

"She cook breakfast."

He went in and greeted Sophia.

"You want a cup of tea?" she said.

"That's all you have?"

"What me have you won't want, it's not American food."

He looked over her shoulder and into the pan on the stove. "Callaloo an' fry dumplin'."

"Sit down," she said. "Me dish some for you."

Ricardo came out neatly dressed for school, barely acknowledging his father's presence. He pulled out a chair and sat at the table where Calvin and Mishka waited for their meal. Calvin peered at Ricardo who had his face planted in the sport section of a newspaper.

"Mornin," Calvin said.

"Mornin," Ricardo said, still reading.

After Sophia set breakfast on the table, everyone dug in, barely a word spoken, only the sound of utensils and chewing.

"So you want to stay here?" Calvin asked Ricardo, breaking the silence.

"Yeh," Ricardo said. "Me stay an' take care of Mommy."

"Well, you can't say me didn't try."

"Everything alright, mon. Me good."

"What you plan to do with yourself here?"

"Police force."

Calvin laughed. "What chance that will happen?"

"Me will make it happen."

Mishka didn't have an appetite. She drank her tea and excused herself from the table. Calvin finished his meal and thanked Sophia.

"You ready, Mishka?" he said.

"Me go get me things."

"Don't forget your passport, Mishka," Sophia said.

"Let me give you a ride to school, Ricardo," Calvin said.

Ricardo tossed his backpack across his back. "No problem."

Calvin took the suitcase from Mishka and carried it outside. Sophia walked with them to the car and kissed Mishka goodbye.

"Take care of yourself," she said.

Mishka saw Paul pushing his bicycle leaving Marlene's house. He looked inside of the car and saw Mishka. He gave her an angry glare as he rode past the car.

Calvin took off.

"Who was the man on the bicycle?" Calvin said.

"Im run the place," Ricardo said.

"That's why im look at me so?"

"Them don't like to see strange face roun here."

At Ricardo's school, Calvin reached into his pocket and handed him some cash.

"If you change your mind bout comin' me only a phone call away, alright?"

"Thanks. Take care, Mishka."

"You too," she said.

Ricardo jogged across the street toward the entrance of his school.

Calvin took off.

"How come you decide to leave and not stay here with Sophia?"

"For a better life, rough here."

"Your brother don't think so though, eh?"

"Don't know. You would have to ask im."

Chapter Fourteen

Four hours later ...

After landing in New York, the plane sat on the runway for nearly twenty minutes, and already, Mishka missed the ones she'd left behind in Jamaica— Sophia, Ricardo, Roxanne.

"Why we wait here?" she said.

"JFK is a busy airport, almost like getting stuck in traffic."

When they finally got off the airplane, Mishka looked all around, so much to see. They waited in another long line with fellow passengers.

"Why we wait here now?" she said.

"Anyone coming into the country must go through customs and immigration to prove legal entry, same like I have to do when me enter Jamaica, understan'?."

She nodded, feeling lost.

Jamaica Tough

"Two most important things you must start doin', Mishka, speak proper English so people will understan' you better, and learn to count coins, alright?"

At the baggage area, people were everywhere, some held up signs with names on them. Mishka assumed they were meeting strangers. Waiting for her bag, she gazed at the diversity surrounding her—blacks, whites, Asians, people of all kinds. After picking up their luggage she saw Jackie, smiling, coming to help, and a young lady with her.

"Welcome," she said hugging Mishka. She reached into a shopping bag she was carrying. "Here's a jacket. I didn't think you owned one coming from Jamaica."

Mishka took the coat and immediately put it on, zipping it up to her neck.

"Thank you very much, mam," she said, shivering.

Calvin introduced Mishka to the young lady who was with Jackie.

"This is Jackie's daughter, Nicki."

Mishka smiled at Nicki. "Pleased to meet you."

Calvin and Jackie loaded the luggage into the trunk of their SUV, and off they went, Mishka and Nicki in the back seat.

"How was the plane ride, Mishka?" Jackie said.

"Just fine, mam."

Jackie laughed. "You don't have to call me *mam,* Jackie is fine."

She remained quiet almost all the way, observing the traffic signs, bright lights, bridges, wide roadways, and towering buildings.

"What JFK stand for?" she said.

"John Fitzgerald Kennedy. He was the president of the United States, but was assassinated." "Assassinated?"

"Shot and killed."

"When was he assassinated?"

"In the sixties. We learn about him in school, part of our history."

"How're you managing the weather, Mishka?" Jackie said.

"Not good at all."

"You don't see anything yet," Calvin said. "Wait until November to March when it snow. Me have to take you to get warm clothes."

"Nothing inside me suitcase will be of any use."

"Get used to saying *my* and *I*, Mishka," Calvin said.

"Sorry," she said. "*I* forgot."

They all laughed.

When they exited the highway into Brooklyn, Mishka noticed that fewer people were on the streets. She supposed it was too cold to be anywhere except in bed. At the airport, most of the people were white, but now most were black. There were stores on every corner.

"Those tall brick structures," she said to Nicki, pointing, "business places?"

"No, they're where people live."

"Oh." She tapped Calvin on his shoulder. "*I* need a phone card to call Mommy, please."

Calvin turned onto a street and parked in front of a two story building.

"This is where you live, Nicki?"

"Yup," Nicki said, climbing out of the van.

"Look like the general penitentiary in Jamaica."

"Most of the buildings you'll see in New York will look like Jamaican prisons."

She felt far away from home, and nothing she'd seen was what she imagined. Calvin unloaded the bags, after which he walked up a flight of stairs and opened the door to their unit—three bedrooms, a living room, two baths, a kitchen, a long hallway, and some closets. In the living area, Mishka put her things in a corner and walked over to a window facing the street. She looked down at the cars going by.

Calvin handed her a phone and a phone card. “Call your mother.”

Mishka looked at all the numbers on the card. “How do I use it?”

“Let me show you.” He sat next to her and taught her each step.

Finally, she waited for Sophia to answer.

“Mishka!” Sophia said. “You reach alright?”

Sadness suddenly overtook Mishka.“Yes, me alright.”

“Why you soun’ so?”

“Tired.”

“Lord, baby, me miss you so much already. Can’t stop cry.”

They both went silent.

“Miss you too, Mommy.”

“Anyhow, me glad you reach alright. Always remember what me say before you leave. You know me address, write when you can, an' call me anytime, you hear?"

"Yeh."

She handed the phone back to Calvin, not wanting him to see her emotion. She needed to be alone, but didn't want to make anyone feel uncomfortable. Taking a shower would be her only escape. She went into the bathroom, shut the door, and sat on the floor, her forehead pressed against her knees. She felt disconnected from everyone and everything around her.

Next day, she woke up and looked around at what appeared to be unfamiliar surroundings, soon remembering she was in America. Still in culture shock, she recalled her conversation with Sophia. Mishka should've been happy to know that she no longer had to live in fear and carry a gun, but for some reason, still, joy remained absent from her life. Not too long ago when she'd fallen in love with Nathan, though it seemed a century ago, joy was all she felt. Then somehow she crashed into a wall. Now that she was here, there was no time to grieve, no time to ponder, no time for self-pity. There was too much to take in, to learn. There was her future to think about. Joy must come later, if it were to come at all. She wanted to make amends for her brief descent into the skin trade, and to live up to the principles Sophia instilled in her. In addition, she had a promise to fulfill—return home and move Sophia to a better neighborhood and away from Paul.

The strong smell of breakfast led her into the kitchen.

"Good morning," Jackie said. "Hungry?"

Mishka looked into the frying pan. "Is that pork?"

"Bacon. I know it isn't ackee and salfish but you should try a good American breakfast sometime."

"Are there Jamaican markets here?"

"Yes. I'll take you to one over the weekend. They have the best Jamaican food in Brooklyn."

Calvin walked in and sat at the kitchen table. "Me take you shopping today, Mishka. Eat something and get ready."

Mishka didn't know what to think about New York, it looked a lot different during the day—more people, buses, cars everywhere. There wasn't any trash on the street, but something about it seemed untidy.

"We're goin' to Manhattan," Calvin said. "Keep your eyes open. Look around. You will have to move around by yourself."

Finding a parking spot seemed impossible. Manhattan was more active than Brooklyn—bumper-to-bumper traffic, sirens going off, billboards all over, street vendors, yellow cabs, and numerous stores. It was difficult for her to focus on anything because of the constant movement. They finally parked in a lot and walked three blocks to a department store. In Jamaica, Mishka was used to seeing people shop for everything in downtown Kingston. She hadn't been inside of a store.

"Look for warm clothes," Calvin said. "Sweater, pants, gloves, hat, and jackets."

Overwhelmed by the variety of items surrounding her, she agreed to everything Calvin suggested. He picked them out and she tried them on. Next, they went to the shoe department. When she headed for the sneakers, Calvin stopped her.

"Get a pair of boots. You will appreciate them when it snow."

He strutted around like a rooster, proud to show off his new world to his daughter. When they were finished, she walked out with large bags filled with new apparel.

On the way home, they rode in silence, only the sound of the radio playing. Calvin was occupied behind the wheel, muttering to himself how slowly they were moving in the thick of traffic. Mishka looked over and saw how much she resembled him, his determined nose, almond eyes.

"Does it feel odd when I call you, *Daddy*?"

"Odd cause you're all grown up now. When me left Jamaica you were only a baby. Now me look at you and see how much me miss out, how much time fly. You're almost as tall as me now."

"You know, when I was younger I didn't think I'd ever see you again. I thought you forgot about me and Ricardo."

"Sophia ever tell you how me end up here?"

"No."

"When you were about three-years-old, somebody tell me bout a farm-work-program at a place name Belle Glade. That's down in Florida. Back then, me used to drive taxi for an elder name Boy Blue. Im had some cars that people run as taxi for im. The deal was, we work the road six days a week, an' pay Boy Blue half of what we make. By the time me done pay im every weeken' me don't have nothing

Left. Sometimes me couldn't even buy food, clothes for you an' Ricardo, but Sophia never complain. Deep down, it made me feel like less of a man knowin' that me work so hard, yet couldn't do more for me family. Anyhow, long story short, me apply for the farm-work an' get through, left Jamaica. Six months later when it was time to go back, couple guys who left Jamaica with me on the program say them not goin' back. Me didn't plan to stay, but at that time me know what me go back to in Jamaica—nothing, wasn't even sure if Boy Blue would give me back the taxi to run cause me owe im some money. One of me cousin, Lillian, she live here in New York, me call her from Belle Glade to tell her what was goin' on. She say me mus' come to New York an' stay with her till me get meself together, so that me can better help me children. That sound like the only chance me had to get something under me feet to help me family. Lillian migrate here before me, on the same farm-work-program. She never go back home. The day before me supposed to take the plane back to Jamaica, me leave Belle Glade an' take the greyhound bus all the way here." He pointed behind him. "Bus let me off in Manhattan. Lillian an' her husban' come meet me. She hook me up with a little work under the table, pay well below the minimum wage, but me take it cause me didn't have work permit an' me had to make a livin'. Me save some money an' rent a room from a man, in the basement, live there an' work for three years, until me meet Jackie. Jackie was about to graduate college, an' goin' through a divorce. Both she an' Nicki live with Jackie's mother. As time pass by me an' Jackie get to know each other, till we get married. That's how me get papers to stay here legally. Jackie a good woman. She love me an' always want me to bring you an' Ricardo here. Me never forgot about you. But me needed to make sure of a solid foundation before you come here. It never happen as soon as me want it to. Everything takes time. Me figure it would be bes' if you come here when you're old enough to take care of yourself. Me didn't want to burden Jackie with two more young children."

"When did Mommy come out of the picture?"

"Well, to tell you the truth, me an' Sophie drift apart when me meet Jackie. Me know she still hate me for it."

"She doesn't hate you. She was hurt."

"Me can't make an excuse for it now. The best me can do is be a father to the children me an' her have together."

"I guess after hearing about your life after you came here I can forgive you for the time you missed out on."

"When people come to America things don't happen right away. Good things can happen for you here if you have patience and ambition. You will soon learn bout the American Dream. Everyone come here to live it, but you have to work hard to earn it."

"You know, maybe one day you should tell Ricardo all you've told me about why it took you so long to go back to Jamaica, not so he'll change his mind about coming here, but so that he won't keep carrying around that bad feeling for you. Maybe he will understand how and why you did what you did."

"If im willing to give me the chance, sure. Doubt that will happen now. Me have a feeling Ricardo done write me off."

"You should still try."

"Maybe one day."

"As far as you and I go, hopefully with time we'll get to know each other, like father and daughter should."

They were back in Brooklyn, blocks away from home.

"So, what sort of work you do here?" she asked.

"Fireman. Jackie is a school teacher. Nicki is a waitress at one of them expensive restaurant, lower Manhattan."

"You're a fireman?" she said, laughing.

"Yes. Here, people say *fire fighter*."

"You like doing that, fighting fire?"

Calvin laughed. "Like anything else, you have to have a passion for it. Mine is to help prevent destruction, maybe save a life. Imagine what it would feel like if you find yourself trap in a burning house."

"It looks like we have something in common, not to fight fire, but I want to do something that will help other people, especially children. So much bad things can happen to children when they're young and vulnerable."

She enjoyed her time with Calvin and admired him. Rather than the father who abandoned his children and their mother, Mishka now saw Calvin as a man who kept it together long enough to ensure a life of opportunity for his children. She hoped that Ricardo would someday open his heart to his father.

Over dinner, Jackie probed Mishka about leaving home.

"Miss my mother more than anything," she said.

"I'm sure your father wouldn't mind sending you back to visit, right sweetie?"

"No rush," Mishka said, after she remembered Paul. "I'll go back whenever I have myself together here. That's what my mother wants me to do anyway."

"Any career choice yet?"

"Haven't really decided yet, but I'd like to go to university."

"Did you finish high school?"

"Graduated last month."

"Good. You need to be a high school graduate before you can attend college. I keep telling Nicki to go and get her GED. She likes making money better."

"Mom, I'll do it before the end of the year," Nicki said.

"What's a GED?" Mishka asked.

"It's equivalent to a high school diploma," Jackie said. "For drop outs."

"How are the colleges here, pricewise?"

"Expensive," Jackie said. "If you get in there and study hard you can get a scholarship. There're many resources available for those who can't pay—grants, loans."

"In Jamaica," Mishka said, "If you can't afford it you simply can't afford it. I'd like to find a job as soon as possible to put myself through school here."

She woke up to the lonely apartment. Everyone else went off to work. She showered and made herself a cup of tea, and noticed some cash and a note sitting on the counter. She read it and called Calvin.

"I'm going to look for work today," she said. "If you call and I'm not here that's what I'm doing."

"Remember, when you take the bus, ask the driver for a map and study it so you will know where you are. Me get a cellphone for you next time me off from work. It's chilly out here, dress warm."

Dressed as if she was going into a blizzard, she took a series of buses until she saw a *Now Hiring* sign in the window of a bookstore. She got off the bus at the next stop and walked back to the bookstore. A nicely dressed young man who looked to be in his late twenties walked up to her.

Instinctively, she clutched her handbag. She caught herself and hurled her bag over her shoulder.

"Can I help you find something?" he said.

She recognized his accent and smiled. "You from Jamaica?"

"Yeh, mon."

"So funny. The first stranger I meet is from home."

"Where you from there?"

"Kingston, Jones Town."

"Oh, straight from out of the jungle," he grinned. "Me family still live there, Red Hills. What book you looking for?"

"Oh, no." She pointed at the sign in the window. "Me come to see if you need workers—this is a big store just for books, no wonder."

He laughed. "You jus' left Jamaica?" "Two days ago."

"Me can tell."

"Are you the one I should talk to about the job?"

"Me? No. See the lady over there at the register?" he pointed. "The one with the glasses, talk to her."

"She's the owner?"

"Manager. Talk to her and see what she say. She name Miss. Parker. Tell her you want to know if she's accepting applications. Say you know me, we friends. She like me."

Mishka switched to her best English and was glad Ms. Parker, after studying her application form, asked her to return the next day for an interview.

She went back to the bookstore to see Ms. Parker, a white, older dark-haired woman.

"Good to see you again, Mishka," she said.

Mishka smiled. "Good to see you too, mam."

They sat at a table. "So, on your application, I see you have no experience in sales?"

"Yes, but I'm willing to learn. I catch on to things very easy and good at following instructions."

"Well, most people who start here have done it before. In your case, well, I was especially moved by Gordon's glowing recommendation. Are you two …?"

It took Mishka a moment to pick up on Ms. Parker's insinuation.

"Oh, no," she said. "We're just very good friends."

"Well then, let's give it a try, shall we? If you're half as good as Gordon we'll have an excellent employee."

"Thank you so very much, mam," Mishka said, shaking Ms. Parker's hand.

Now working at Barnes and Noble, Mishka kept busy. Gordon trained her and she got the routine down very quickly. Selling books was much easier than her duties at the nightclub. She was captivated by the different categories of publications, and already, she'd seen some books she wanted to read. Calvin and his wife seemed pleased with Mishka's responsible approach, commending her for independently gaining employment in such short period of time. She felt great, and mentioned nothing about her previous job in Jamaica.

One day after work, Gordon saw her standing at the bus stop and pulled over in his Mustang.

"Let me give you a ride," he said.

She felt vigilant being one-on-one with a man, but tried to relax after telling him her exact address.

"How you like the job?"

"It's alright," she said, feeling easier as they drove block by block. "How long ago you left Jamaica?"

"Since me thirteen years old. Me twenty-five now."

"You could've said twelve years ago."

He laughed. “Me jus’ test you, mon.”

“Math was one of my favorite subjects at school.”

“You know, if you didn’t say anything the first time you come to the store, me would think you been longer.”

“People who been here longer supposed to look a certain way?”

“Most times, yeh. You look Americanize already. Who you here with?”

“My father.”

“Daddy’s girl?”

“Wouldn’t put it that way. I’m still getting to know him, long story I’d rather not talk about right now.”

“Sorry me ask.”

“It’s okay.”

“Me can have your phone number? Maybe we can be friends, hang out sometime?”

“I guess having a friend here wouldn’t hurt.”

He handed her his cellphone. “Ring your phone and save my number.”

Men seemed to notice her and show respect here more than the men in Jamaica. Gordon asked her to a movie, and though she wanted to go, she told him she wasn’t sure.

"You don't have to be afraid of me," he said. "Me don't bite."

"I'll let you know later, after work."

Chapter Fifteen

One week later…

Mishka couldn't shake her anxiety about her first date in America. She and Nathan didn't exactly go on dates so she didn't know what to expect. Gordon appeared to be a nice guy, but her guard was up. She didn't trust men. On the night of their date, she saw Gordon calling and picked up.

"Me pick you up at seven," he said.

She showered and slid into a pair of slim pants and a black blazer. From working at the nightclub, she remembered how to apply makeup. She looked stunning as she walked to Calvin's bedroom to say goodbye.

"Who you goin' with?" he said.

"A friend from work, Gordon."

"Where is he?"

"Outside. He drives."

"Tell im to come in so me know who you goin' with."

"Are you kiddin'?"

"No."

She called Gordon and asked him to come upstairs. Calvin stood in the living room and waited with Mishka. Gordon rang the doorbell. Calvin answered. Mishka introduced them. Gordon reached out and shook Calvin's hand.

"So you want to take out me daughter?"

"She in good hands. Me bring her back safe."

"You're how old?" Calvin said.

"C'mon, Dad!"

"Calvin looked at her. "Wha'? me can't ask?"

"Twenty-five," Gordon said.

"Where you live?"

"Canarsie, not far from here."

"Me know where Canarsie is. You understan' she jus' come from Jamaica an' don't know her way here well?"

"Yeh, mon. Me the one she first talk to when she come to look for work at the store. Me put in a good word for her."

"Me want to make sure she's not in any danger. She's me only daughter."

"No problem boss."

"Alright," Calvin said, sitting down. "Be careful out there." He looked up at Mishka. "Call me if you need anything."

"We're only going to the movies, Dad," she said, opening the front door. "I should be fine."

They were on their way to Manhattan. She didn't see it necessary for Calvin to interrogate her date. She would understand if Gordon had changed his mind about taking her out.

"Why so quiet?" Gordon said.

"My father."

"Wha', you feel shame?"

"Who wouldn't?"

"Relax mon, people crazy nowadays, daddy only do im job."

"I'm an adult."

"Didn't he act the same with other boys?"

"He didn't raise me."

He looked at her. "Don't say me get into your business, but who raise you?"

"My mother. My dad left and came here when I was a baby."

"Oh, okay. What movies you like to watch?"

"I thought you had something picked out."

"Action or comedy?"

"You decide. Besides, I don't know anything about American shows."

"We'll see when we get there." They were at a red light. Gordon looked at her, a silly grin on his face. "Look like you the one starring the movie tonight."

"You don't have to be so kind, but thanks."

"Me don't try to be kind. You look good, like a modeler."

"Can I ask you a question?"

"Yeh."

"Do you have a girlfriend?"

"If I did, wouldn't that be cheating?"

"Wouldn't be the first time a guy would do such a thing."

"So you think we're all dogs?"

"Just guys."

"I had a girl but we mash-up some months ago."

"Why?"

"Been wondering that myself. We got tired of each other I guess."

She didn't want to stir up anyone's past, including her own. "If you say so."

"Not worth talkin' about. Me like you now."

Finally in Times Square, Gordon parked a block away and they walked to the theater. The atmosphere reminded her of a carnival by night. There were electronic posters everywhere, colorful blinking lights, vendors, and people walking the street. It was an amazing sight to see. Inside, she removed her coat as they stood in the theater line waiting for tickets. Gordon later bought popcorn and smoothies.

"We goin' to see Training Day," he said.

"Is it good?"

"Most likely, yes. An actor name Denzel Washington star it. He's one of the best on American big screen."

They sat close, enjoying their treats and watching the film. He wrapped an arm around her and pulled her close. She stiffened at his touch. The memory of that horrible night resurfaced. She recalled Paul's filthy hands touching her and gently removed Gordon's arm from around her shoulder.

"I have to use the restroom," she said.

She went into the bathroom, shut the door, and stood against it. Her eyes were closed. She tried to erase Paul from her memory. She tried to convince herself that he was history, miles across the ocean. She walked over to the sink and splashed water on her face before going back into the theater to sit next to her date. She was physically attracted to Gordon. His trendy good looks, courtesy, and flirty comments made her smile inside. She didn't want him to feel as if he'd done something wrong.

"Wha' you think bout the movie?" he said.

"Little bloody, but like you say before, Denzel is a good actor."

She rested her head on his shoulder.

She and Gordon became an item at work. They often lunched together at a pizza shop located next to the bookstore. He gave her a lift home whenever they worked the same hours. She was still puzzled by her sudden aloofness at the theater. She wanted to be normal again and have a relationship. One evening after work Gordon asked her out to dinner in the city, of course, she agreed.

When they arrived at the restaurant, she examined the menu carefully before ordering.

"What's that you're drinking?" she said.

"A mix Daiquiri. Wha', you want one?"

"I'll try yours first."

She took a sip and ordered her own.

"Hope me don't get wasted."

Gordon laughed. "Drink it slow."

She finished her lobster Alfredo and ordered another cocktail.

Driving back home, Gordon's hand was on her thigh the entire time. She wasn't as tense as at the movie theater. She rubbed his head from time to time. They gazed at each other at every stoplight. This was more than their previous date. She became curious about him as he seemed receptive to the touch of her hand stroking his braids.

"Me swing by my house real quick," he said, "So you know where me live."

She recognized his neighborhood from riding past on the bus. His apartment was clean, reminded her of Nathan.

Jamaica Tough

He showed her around, told her all about his family back in Jamaica.

"Have you ever thought about going back home?" she said.

He shook his head no. "Can't see myself back in Jamaica to live. Only visit."

"Why?"

"Cause you get used to certain things here that don't exist in Jamaica."

"Like what?"

"Less crime, more justice, access to the simple things. After a year here you will see what me mean."

They took off their coats and relaxed a bit.

"Jeez," she said. "It's colder in here than it is outside."

"Me light up the fireplace, warm you up."

She settled herself on the sofa and rubbed her hands together, waiting to get warm.

"I could hang out here more often, Gordon. Nice place."

"Don't want your ol' man to chop me up."

They laughed.

"Knew I'd hear that from you someday." She looked at her watch. "Let's watch a movie, it's
still early."

"What you want to watch?"

"More Denzel?"

He smiled. "Me don't have any Denzel right now. How bout a movie name Saw?"

"Someone at work was talking about that. Is it the one where all the people get their heads cut off?"

"Wha', you don't like that?"

"No, can't watch it … sound too brutal."

"How bout some stand-up comedy?"

"Laughter is good."

"Use the bathroom cause this brother name Chris Rock might make you wet your pants."

Gordon microwaved popcorn. They sat close and laughed aloud. After a while, Gordon lifted her leg and removed her stiletto, then the other. She was just buzzed enough from her Daiquiri to consider it was sweet of him.

"Sorry if my feet smell," she said.

"If they did, I'd put them back on right away."

"Well since they don't let me put them on your lap."

So far, she felt relaxed. She saw Gordon's glimpses at her thighs.

"You want to say something?" she said.

"Mind if me massage your feet?"

"What a treat."

His hands were amazing. She could've fallen asleep right where she was. Her gratitude later moved her to reward him with a deep kiss to which he thoroughly responded. She hadn't kissed anyone since Nathan and almost forgot what it felt like. In their anxiety, they tugged at each other's clothing, knocking over a lamp, until they were both bare.

Nudging her legs apart with his knee, he poised himself above her. The moment she felt his skin against hers, something suddenly closed down on her feelings. Even the alcohol didn't stop it. She went along, fought as best as she could, to see if she would feel any further excitement, as she had with Nathan. There was nothing. She seemed stripped of sensation, desensitized, the strangest thing. Then a flashback of Paul's face overwhelmed her, as if Gordon suddenly became that hideous guy. *Feel something*, she commanded herself, but it was all ice, like a dentist's Novocain. She wanted to cry out, but remembered Paul's machete, his gun pointing at her. She pushed Gordon away and sat up.

"Wha'?" he said.

"I can't do it."

"But me think you want to."

She picked up the lamp and set it back in its place before turning it on. She rummaged through their clothes and found her pants.

"Please take me home."

"Now?"

"Yes."

"Me do something wrong?"

"No. Please take me home."

She was dressed. He picked up his sweater and pulled it over his head.

"No problem. Me take you home."

She walked down the hall to the bathroom and fix her hair. She came back and picked up her handbag. Gordon was at the door, holding it open.

"Sorry," she said, walking past him. "Didn't mean to lead you on."

Jamaica Tough

She couldn't tell him the real reason why she stopped. She didn't want to play the role of a victim and thought he might've been turned off by it. Will she ever recover?

Chapter Sixteen

One week later...

Things grew awkward between them. She was perplexed and almost ashamed about having been aroused then unexpectedly felt terror. She was losing hope of ever having a normal relationship, and if she ever planned on having one that involved intimacy, she'd have to find a way to overcome her fear. Working with Gordon became uncomfortable. Each time he was around she remained polite. He didn't mention anything about her suddenly turning into a zombie in the heat of the moment. He continued offering her rides home after their shifts. She often took out her book and read on the way. At home, she thought about having managed to escape from Paul, but wondered why the memory still lingered. She picked up her cell and dialed Sophia. She heard her mother's familiar voice.

"How's everything darlin'?" Sophia said.

"Not bad. How're you?"

"Alright. Me an' Ricardo here. Still can't get used to not havin' you aroun', but me glad you call."

"Miss you too."

"So tell me bout America, how you like it?"

"Some very nice people live here. I found a job at a bookstore, the first place I asked, I ran into a guy from Jamaica."

"Me glad you find work. You like it?"

"Yes, It's nice to see how much Americans like to read."

"Me proud of how you blend in. You even talk like American and you not there two full months yet."

"How's Ricardo?"

"Im alright. You know wha', Mishka, I never know Ricardo was so bright. Im pass all im subjects, soon leave school. Now all im ever talk bout is police training."

"Didn't take him seriously at all. Tell him hello for me. Have you seen Roxanne?"

"Yeh, she was here last Sunday, ask me if you gone to America yet. You didn't tell her when you leavin'?"

"Didn't get a chance to tell her. Anyway, how's Miss Marlene?"

"She jus' left here before you call, say Paul fight with her."

"For what?"

"You know me, don't ask her why, but she almost look Chinese, have two big black eye. She can hardly see."

Hearing Paul's name made Mishka cringe. "I'm going off to bed now, need some sleep. I miss you and wish I could see you."

It was her day off. Gordon called and convinced her she should get the grand tour of Manhattan.

"I won't do anything but sit here all say," she said over the telephone.

"Them have an observation deck opened to the public, top of the Twin Towers, nice view of the city."

Besides going to Times Square, Mishka hadn't explored the wonders of the Big Apple.

"What made you think about taking me to see the city?"

"Something to do, that I know you will like."

"Hey, I want to apologize for the other night."

"Don't fret bout it. It didn't work out, we can still be friends."

"So what time are you coming to pick me up?"

"Better if we take the train there, traffic too heavy in Manhattan."

"You come here to meet me?"

"Meet me at the train station near your house. Me go get ready now."

When she arrived at the station, Gordon gave her a hug and led her to the platform. This was her first time walking underground and even to ride a train. People looked at their watch and anxiously waited for the next train to pull into the station. Next to where she and Gordon stood, a man slept on a bench under a blanket.

"I didn't know that poor people live here," she said.

"We call them *bums*."

"That's not nice!"

"The only ones me feel sorry for are the war vets. The alcoholic and drug addicts cause it on themselves, and they can go to rehab."

She rolled her eyes at Gordon and looked down at the train track.

"Oh my gosh!" she said. "What a big rat!"

The people close by looked at her and laughed.

"Lower your voice," Gordon said. "Everyone doesn't need to know you're new here."

"Sorry, he scared me. At first I thought it was a cat. What if he get run over by a train?"

"They know their way aroun'."

Soon a loud horn sounded and the train came into sight. She shivered from the wind of the cars zipping by. The train came to a stop. People rushed off and on. A group of school teens giggled at a man who had his jacket caught in the doors.

Gordon held Mishka's hand and led onto the train. All seats were occupied so she held on to a pole, Gordon just behind. Across from her two men shared an intimate kiss.

"What the hell?" she said.

"Welcome to the land of the free."

"Me can see that."

Yes, she had danced with Tina at the nightclub, but she would never tell. The train ride was fast and bumpy. Her heart was thumping and she couldn't wait to get to Manhattan safely.

Jamaica Tough

Among the throng of the morning commute, she and Gordon exited the train at an underground concourse and shopping mall.

"Everyone's in such a rush!" she said.

"That's why they call it rush hour."

"But why're they walking full speed?"

"That's how it is in the financial district. They might be running late for work or tryin' to catch the next train. Time is money, you know?"

They exited the concourse and walked onto the street. "See the traffic me talk bout?" Gordon said. "We wouldn't reach this far yet if me drive."

Mishka was overawed by how tall the skyscrapers were. She stopped and stared at them.

"See those two tall buildings next to each other? That's where we will go. We call it the twin tower."

"We'll go all the way to the top?"

"Hope you're not afraid of height."

A man hurrying by hit her on her leg with his briefcase. He apologized and carried on.

"I wish these people would slow down."

"Pay attention and step out of the way when you see them comin'."

"I'm not used to this rushing."

Gordon held her hand as they waded through the flow of people. They waited to cross the street. Mishka walk carefully between stopped vehicles.

"I'm hungry," she said.

"Let's go to that coffee shop. They have a breakfast in there. We can get something to eat real quick."

"What kind of breakfast do they have?"

"All American—bagel and cream cheese, egg and cheese sandwiches, coffee, tea, juice."

They sat by the window of the mini restaurant, eating and talking, Mishka curious about the panoramic view that Gordon would take her to see. A few minutes later, from where she sat, she looked to her right and saw people outside pointing toward the sky, panicking and reaching for their cell phones.

"What's going on?" she said, pointing outside.

"Maybe them see God."

She rose. "Stop joking. Something's happening!"

Customers began rushing out the door. They stood outside and looked across the way, up at the towers. Mishka and Gordon abandoned their meals and headed for the door, Mishka leading the way. The moment they stepped outside, an enormous explosion shook the ground, causing Mishka to duck to the pavement, grabbing a hold of Gordon's elbow. Everyone suddenly stood still, gawking up at the north tower where a terrifying cloud of smoke poured out of a hole high up in the building. Thousands of papers floated in the air. It seemed like a catastrophic accident. Someone close by said that a plane had crashed into the building. Alarms sounded everywhere. It wasn't long until firefighters and police officers began to swarm the street. It all seemed unreal to Mishka. People were streaming out of the buildings and onto the plaza. Some had dust on their clothing.

"Look!" Mishka said, pointing up at the tower that stood next to the one burning. "Another plane! It's going to crash!"

The chaos heightened, the crowd thickened, people ran along the sidewalks and into the street. Traffic was snarled, horns sounding. Mishka found herself being shoved along.

She looked back for Gordon who waved frantically. To escape the pressing crowd, she stepped into the gutter but was knocked over by a swerving taxi. People pushed by, some stepping on her, no one paying attention, but rushing. She struggled to her feet and was knocked back against a parked car, hit her head. In tremor, she began to hyperventilate and felt liquid running down the front of her face. She touched it—blood. She struggled to her feet again, barely able to see, impossible to locate Gordon. She ran with the flow up the street, being bumped and shoved by others. A police officer came running toward her. He tugged her arm, ran up the street. She followed, almost blinded from blood. He handed her over to paramedics who lifted her into an ambulance packed with others. He guided her to sit on a hard surface. People shouted, moaned. The ambulance took off, sirens screaming.

She felt a hand on her shoulder.

"My name is Brad Calahan," a voice said, "I am a Medic."

"I can't see anything!"

"Don't rub your eyes. Try and relax. I'll help you."

"Okay."

"I'm going to put on a nasal cannula to stabilize your breathing, and then I'll clean your eyes with saline. Tilt your head back."

"It burns so bad."

He began to clean around her eyes. "What's your name?"

"Mishka. Mishka Campbell."

"Do you have a history of any respiratory illnesses such as asthma, tuberculosis?"

"No."

"Are you on any medications, or have allergies?"

"No, nothing. I'm healthy."

"Take some deep breaths. You have a gash on the forehead, along your eyebrow. You'll need stitches. Try to open your eyes now."

She began to feel some relief and opened them to see the dark haired medic standing over her, bits of gray hair at his temple.

"Any better?" he said.

"My head's killing me."

"It's bleeding quite a bit."

He took her hand. “Hold this compress against it. Don’t let up.”

“Is it cut deep?”

“You’ll be fine, I promise. We should be at the hospital shortly. They’ll stitch you up and you’ll be good as new. I have to go and help others now. Hold that compress down until we get there.”

He was gone.

There was so much going through her mind—what the hell’s happening? Did Gordon make it out alive?

Still pressing against her forehead, she sat up and saw a woman in front of her, a large white bandage around her head, blood on the front of her blouse. The ambulance finally pulled into the bay of an emergency room. Everyone stepped out.

The ER was in frenzy. Medical staff tended to the critically ill first. Finally it was Mishka’s turn. The doctor looked her over as she told him what had happened.

“Do you have anything for my headache?”

“I’ll have the nurse come in with Tylenol before I numb your forehead and suture the wound.”

“Suture?”

"Sow it up. Your brow will cover the scar."

Buses and trains were suspended. She began her journey back to Brooklyn. She knew it would take hours to walk all the way home. She reached into her pocket for her cell phone, but only found some coins. She checked her other pockets, nothing. Still disoriented, she suddenly realized that her handbag was gone. She recalled seeing Gordon pick it up off the seat inside the restaurant before they walked out. Crossing the Brooklyn Bridge, she looked back and saw boundless trail of smoke drifting into the sky. She kept her eyes and ears open for Gordon among the throng of people. Beyond the bridge, she didn't know which way to turn toward home, but along the way, she asked for direction. Someone with a portable radio mentioned strange names—Saddam, bin Laden. She felt bewildered.

Finally, she reached her brownstone and saw Jackie's car parked out front. She ran up the stairs and rang the doorbell. Jackie opened it.

"What happened to you?" Jackie said. "Were you there?"

Mishka walked inside and told her story.

"Have you heard from your father?"

"I lost my phone."

"I've been calling him at work but it's useless, the line's been busy. He won't answer his cell."

"What about Nicki? Have you talked to her?"

"She's catching a ride home with a friend."

Sitting close to the TV, Mishka watched the breaking news, replays of the planes going through the towers. By now, the towers had collapsed. She still couldn't believe she was there.

"Why is America under attack?" she said.

"I have no clue. What I do know it that it's no accident. A plane hit the Pentagon too."

Mishka feared that a missile would come storming into their neighborhood at any moment. When Niki walked in, Mishka told her story again. Soon she went into the bathroom to clean up. Under the shower she heard the doorbell ring repeatedly. She turned off the shower.

"Mishka!" Jackie said. "Gordon's here."

Wrapped in a bathrobe, she hurried out and saw Gordon standing there, her bag hanging from his wrist. He looked tired, but his eyes lit up when he saw her. They held each other.

"What happen to your face?" he said.

"Oh, I fell. How'd you make it back?"

"Me walk the whole way, pick up me car at home and drive here."

"I had to walk here too."

"After the second plane everything went crazy. Me looked but didn't see you, so me start to run up the street."

Jackie invited Gordon to stay for supper. They watched TV and discussed what had happened. Jackie set Calvin's dinner aside and held on to her phone waiting for his call.

Chapter Seventeen

One week later…

No one had heard from Calvin. Mishka called his cellphone many times but was forwarded to his voicemail. She came home from work and saw Jackie sitting on the couch, her eyes glued to the television.

"Have you heard anything?" she said.

"The fire chief said that some men, including Calvin, went to assist at the towers and hasn't been seen since."

"Oh no."

She sat beside Jackie and increased the volume on the television. There were reports of mass deaths, missing firefighters, police officers. No mention of Calvin. Mishka picked up the phone and began dialing Sophia who was aware of the news, but Mishka had been holding out telling Sophia about Calvin.

Mishka prepared for bed, worried about what might've happened to her father. Tracy called and asked for updates.

"I am so sorry," she said. "All we can do now is pray." Her voice began to quiver. "I spoke with him about coming for Thanksgiving."

They were both silent.

Later that night, Mishka was startled out of a deep sleep by a loud scream. She hurried out of bed and met Nicki going up the hallway.

"What was that?" Mishka said. They both ran back to see. Jackie had collapsed on her bedroom floor, crying, her cellphone still in her hand.

"He's gone!" she said.

"No!" Mishka said.

Both girls got down on the floor and huddled with Jackie. They wept in each other's arms.

Mishka had been awake all night. She called Sophia when the sun came up.

"Me think you should come back home," Sophia said, crying.

Remembering Paul, Mishka's woe suddenly turned to fear. "It's too soon to make a decision, Mommy. Let me take some time to think about it."

Mishka thought about her and Calvin's conversation in the car the day he took her shopping, their first milestone toward building a relationship. Now this. She closed her drapes and lay in bed. After hearing the news, Tracy flew in. She spent her nights consoling the family. Mishka overheard Tracy and Jackie making funeral arrangements, and Tracy persuading Niki to talk Mishka out of isolation.

"Please," Nicki said, sitting on Mishka's bed. "Let's be here for each other."

Mishka rolled over. "How much did he mean to you?"

"As much as he means to you."

"What was he really like?"

"Oh, Mishka. He was my father too. I met him after my parent's divorced. He helped Mom take care of me, taught me things, took me places, and you know how would react whenever boys came around."

They smiled. Mishka sat up.

After the funeral, Jackie drove Tracy to the airport, Nicki and Mishka among them. She hugged Tracy and said goodbye.

"If ever you need anything," Tracy said, "I'm here for you, alright?"

Mishka nodded. Tracy kissed her forehead before waving goodbye.

Mishka managed to motivate herself to go back to work after taking a leave of absence. Nothing felt the same. She felt hollow inside. Her forehead healed, the scar still visible and her brows hadn't fully grown back yet. With Gordon's support, she was able to make it through the day. He treated her to lunch and gave her a lift home.

As time passed, she was still stuck on the day Calvin was laid to rest. There was so much more she wanted to know about him, so much she wanted to tell him about her life in Jamaica during his absence. Too late now. She began to think about Sophia's suggestion to return home. Perhaps the time had come for her to pack and go home. But what would she go back to? How will she survive? How will she fulfill her promise to Sophia?

Jackie was still mourning. She wandered around the house desolately, her face often filled with sorrow. Mishka didn't know what to say to make her feel better. One night, she knocked on Mishka's bedroom door.

"Hey," she said, sitting on the bed, a folder in her hand. "I need to talk to you about this."

Mishka sat up in bed as Jackie opened up a folder revealing sheets of paper.

"It's your father's will."

"What's a will?"

"He left you money. I'm going to let you have it."

"He never told me anything about having a will."

"Well, I'm sure he had plans to tell you about it someday."

She handed Mishka a sheet. "Here's his insurance policy. I'll handle it at a later time, but just so you know, he wanted you to have twenty-five percent of it, fifteen percent for your brother. There's other money available to you guys now, three-thousand each. I'll give it to you by the end of the week. You can wire Ricardo's portion to him."

Mishka was overwhelmed by all the information.

"I have something to say to you too, Jackie."

"Sure," Jackie said, putting away the papers.

"I appreciate everything you've done, but…"

She sighed.

Jackie waited. "But, what, Mishka?"

"It's hard being here anymore. Everything happened so fast and here I am in a country with a family I just met. Furthermore, I don't expect for you to take care of me now that dad's gone."

"I understand, but I don't mind if you stay here, Mishka. Calvin would do the same for Nicki. If you choose to move on that's fine. Do you have plans?"

"I've been thinking about moving to Florida with Aunt Tracy."

"If you have a change of heart I have absolutely no problem with you living here."

She packed her bags and made arrangements with Tracy to move in with her.

Going back home to Sophia was where she needed to be, but her plans weren't in place quite yet. The cash that Jackie gave her would only go so far in Jamaica. She had no plans to go back to work at Paradise. And Paul—she would be back in his domain. She'd have to go back stronger, with more resources in order to face him again. She would return home someday, but for now, she'd move to Florida.

She called Sophia and explained her decision not to return.

"You sure bout it?" Sophia said.

"You wanted me to come here to succeed. I still have a chance, Mommy. I miss dad but coming back to Jamaica isn't going to make me feel any better. I have to brush myself off and press on."

"Alright. You must know what's best. Remember that me still here and always love you."

She arrived at Palm Beach international. She picked up her luggage and saw Tracy waving outside the terminal. They rushed into each other's arms.

"Glad you made it," Tracy said.

Mishka sat in the front seat of the car and took in the lush palms along the streets—no brownstone buildings like New York, no one walking on the sidewalks, much cleaner. They drove along the lakes.

Jamaica Tough

Tracy arrived at a gated community. It was a tropical heaven for Mishka. She took in the nicely edged grass and palm trees.

"How're you doing emotionally?" Tracy said.

"I try not to think about it."

"I know that you and Calvin haven't spent a lot of time together, but if you ever feel down think about the good times you two had."

"We haven't had much, but I do miss him."

Tracy parked in front of her apartment and helped Mishka unload her luggage. Inside, Tracy gave her a tour and showed her where everything was.

"Nice place," Mishka said. "Very nice patio too."

"That's where I sit each evening, watch the birds eat from the feeder. Good way to wind down from work."

"Is the weather always warm here?"

"We have some cool days now and then. Not as cold as New York."

"I haven't seen any buses or trains here yet."

"Everyone drives."

"No wonder."

"Hey, I'm starving, would you like to go out and eat?"

"Sure, after I change into something more comfortable, like some shorts."

She sat forward as Tracy cruised through City Place, a lively scene with outdoor restaurants, bars, boutiques, people strolling along tidy sidewalks, art exhibitions. They parked and walked to an Italian Restaurant where they sat outside and waited to be served.

"So how does Jackie feel about your leaving?"

"I think she wish I'd stay."

"Keep in mind, Mishka, my contract is coming to an end and I'll have to go back to Jamaica. Have you thought about how to get your feet on the ground here, or will you go back home eventually?"

"I want to live here in America. Some day I'd like to bring mommy here too. For now I'm going to rent an apartment with the money that daddy left for me. I'm going to start looking for jobs first thing Monday morning."

"Calvin left you money?"

"Three-thousand. I used some of it to pay my way here. The rest is to get me into a place to live as soon as I find a job. Jackie said there's insurance money too, but she'll let me know about it later. I'm not going to sit around and wait for it."

"I'll do all that I can to help you while I'm here. Sounds like you have your head screwed on tightly to your shoulders, proud of you."

Monday morning, Tracy dropped off Mishka at the bus stop on her way to work. She sat and studied the bus schedule as she waited for the bus to arrive. Finally on the bus, she thought it only made sense to seek employment close to home, considering she didn't have a vehicle. Not far from where she lived, the bus stopped in front of a hospital. She exited the bus and walked onto the hospital compound. She followed the signs to the human resource department. A woman behind a desk greeted her.

"How may I help you?"

"Are you accepting applications for non-medical positions?"

"There's a list of openings posted on the board hanging on the wall. If you wish to do an application you're welcome to use our computer."

Mishka scanned the board carefully before completing an application for a full-time position, receptionist. After submitting the application, she looked at her bus schedule and hurried back to the bus stop.

She received a phone call from the hospital several days later to schedule an interview. Professionally attired, she met with the recruiter. She sat upright in a chair and spoke in an articulate manner.

"I see you've done some bookselling, and quit because…?"

"I relocated. It was a difficult decision, but I had to."

"New York," she said, still looking at Mishka's application. "Terrible what happened there."

"Yes, it was. As for the job I'm very trainable and always punctual for work."

She looked up at Mishka, "You have a positive energy."

She rode the bus to work each day. Tracy picked her up at nights. It wasn't the shift that she'd hope for, but she was satisfied having a job. She woke up early one morning and went to the leasing office to inquire about an apartment. After signing the lease and making the payment, she received the key to her apartment. Tracy later drove her to a thrift shop where she put some furniture on layaway, which she had delivered. Tracy helped her arrange the furniture and congratulated her.

"Good thing I found this job as soon as I did," Mishka said. "The money dad left is almost gone."

"Don't feel bad. You've used it wisely. Sure looks nice in here. I have to take you to work a little early today because I need to come back and work on a class project for the kids."

"When are you going back to Jamaica?"

"End of summer."

"I'll have no one here after you're gone," Mishka said sadly, sitting on her bed.

Tracy hugged her. "You'll be fine. You're doing all the right things to keep you occupied."

"Thanks for taking me back and forth to work, Auntie."

"Oh stop. I'm not leaving yet. I'll still pick you up. I'll just drop you off here."

They laughed.

Chapter Eighteen

One year later…

Tracy's return to Jamaica caused Mishka to change her shift from nine to five. The bus was her only source of transportation. While working one afternoon, a nice-looking gentleman dressed in a black tailored suit, maybe thirties, walked up to her desk. His hair was cut short, neatly edged, giving it a slick finish. He placed his leather briefcase on top of the counter and reached for his wallet. He smiled at her and flashed an identification card.

"Hi, where can I find Room 3230?" he said.

She smiled at him. No doubt, he was New Yorker. The word *where* pronounced "*whea.*" She took the ID card, wrote his name on a visitor's pass and gave him direction.

"Have a good day," she said, handing him the pass.

Before walking away, he stopped, studied her.

"Something wrong?"

"No, no. Thanks."

He walked toward the elevator.

On his way back from his visit, he stopped at her desk again.

"Have we met before?"

"I don't think so. I've only been here in Florida a short time."

She tried to backtrack in her memory to where she'd met a good-looking Caucasian man. At the nightclub where she'd danced maybe? She hoped that wasn't the case. He looked at her nametag. She looked at the pass on the front of his suit jacket, the streaks of gray at his temple. She rose slowly.

"You're Brad, Manhattan."

"How did we…"

She shook his hand tragically. "You're a medic, the bombing."

"What's your name again?"

"It's Mishka."

"Ah, Mishka. Your accent, when I heard it I couldn't help but ask myself where have we met. Anyway it's good to know I'm not losing my mind. How're you doing?"

She sat back in her chair, shrugged her shoulder. “I’m alive, can’t complain.”

“Right. Quite obvious.”

“What’re you doing here? She said. “Vacation?”

“Still feels like a vacation, but no, I had plans to move here after taking the Bar exam up north.”

“In that nice suit, you don’t look like a bartender.”

He laughed almost hysterically. “Sorry, it’s an exam for lawyers. When we met I was fresh out of law school, still working as an EMT.”

Mishka cringed at her own ignorance. “I am so sorry, Mr. Brad.”

“It’s fine.”

“I guess that explains why you look so sharp.”

“Sharp really isn’t my style. If it were up to me I’d be wearing shorts and T-shirt.”

“Why’re you at the hospital? Is a friend sick?”

“I am here to visit a client. Medical malpractice.”

“Malpractice, I see.”

He glanced at his watch. “Hey, nice running into you, small world.”

He put on his sunglasses and headed for the door.

Tongue-in-cheek, she wondered, of all the people he must've rescued, he remembered her. Of course, he had a close look into her eyes.

When he came to visit his client again the following day, he smiled at Mishka as entered the lobby.

"Know where you're going today?" she said, smiling back.

He tapped his temple as though he had it stored in his magnificent brain. On his way out, he stopped at her desk and reached inside of his suit pocket.

"Here's my card," he said, handing it across the desk. "We should have lunch sometime."

"Thanks, but I don't drive."

"If you'll be kind enough to accept the invitation I'd be entirely pleased to pick you up."

"Okay, I accept."

She took the card, wrote her number on a piece of paper and handed it toward him.

"Here," she said. "In case I lose yours."

Saturday morning, she rolled out of bed happy to have had the day off. She'd been putting in many hours at work and didn't know what to do with herself today. She began her day with a cup of tea, when she heard he phone ring. She picked it up and answered.

"It's Brad," the voice said. "Callahan."

"Hey, morning, Brad."

"Did I catch you at a bad time?"

"No, not at all."

"Are you available for lunch today?"

"Lunch, sure."

"Great."

"Where to?"

"The Old Key Lime House, on the waterfront. They're famous for their corn fritters, and seafood of course."

She moved her curtain and saw his car pulling into her driveway. She picked up her purse and walked outside. He was waiting to open the passenger door. Casually attired, he greeted her with a glowing smile.

"You look normal today."

"Why do you say that?"

"The shorts and T-shirt."

"I get hot in those silly suits."

They took off.

"It's quite nice around here," he said.

"Too bad I'm hardly ever here to enjoy it."

"Must be difficult getting around without a car."

"The bus is just fine for now."

"Where are you from, Mishka?"

"Jamaica. Ever been?"

"No but I've heard you guys are *irie*."

She laughed. "I haven't heard that word in a long time."

"Why would you leave such paradise to come here?"

"What gives you the idea Jamaica's paradise?"

"My parents went there years ago to celebrate their anniversary, Montego Bay. They told me how beautiful it was."

"Well I'm not from Montego Bay. In answer to your question my mother wanted me to
come here for a better opportunity."

At the restaurant, they waited to be seated. When the waitress finally greeted them Mishka followed her to a booth on the terrace. She sat and examined the menu, Brad across from her. The waitress left the two to decide what to order.

"What brought you to Florida?" Brad said, looking down at his menu.

"I lost my father the day we met. I decided to move here with my aunt right after. She worked here as a school teacher, and went back to Jamaica in the summer."

"I'm really sorry to hear about dad."

"Thanks."

"Do you have other family here, Mishka?"

"My stepmother and her daughter. They're still in New York. My mother and brother are back in Jamaica."

They waitress came back and politely interrupted them.

The luncheon hour had past and the two had the terrace to themselves. Brad wiped his hands on his napkin and took a sip of his drink. Signing to the waitress across the way, he began to fumble for his wallet. Mishka noticed and reached for her bag.

"I'll take care of my part of the bill," she told him.

"No need," he said, handing the waitress his card. "I'm the one who invited you to lunch, remember?"

The waitress walked away.

"Brad," Mishka said. "I appreciate your kindness but I don't like for people to pick up my tab."

He looked at her as though confused.

"It's common courtesy for a gentleman to pick up the tab whenever he takes a lady out to a restaurant."

She reached into her handbag, took out some cash and handed it toward him.

"Thank you, but here, I want to pay you back."

He took it and smiled. "I suppose, if it makes you feel better."

"The corn fritters were delicious by the way."

"Glad you like it."

She glanced out at the water, a yacht sailing by. "What about you, any family here?"

"My parents retired in Phoenix, near my brother. My sister lives on Long Island with her husband and three daughters. I'm here alone."

"Why did you move here? Why Florida?"

"I've always wanted to live near the ocean where the weather's warm."

"Do you live in Palm Beach?"

"Jupiter, half hour north."

"I assume you're single?"

"Actually, I'm sort of seeing someone."

Her eyes rested on him with a deep stare. "What do you mean by *sort of*?"

"Well, Pam and I aren't exactly a couple."

"What are you then?"

"Incompatible. The more we get to know each other, turns out we're very different. She also hates my job and thinks it consumes me."

"You two live together?"

"She lives with her parents."

"How old is she, if you don't mind my asking?"

"Thirty-six."

Mishka laughed almost insultingly.

"Look, I know what you're thinking. She is an only child and her parents enjoy having her. I don't necessarily think that's the norm for a person her age, but hey, I'm not an only child so I wouldn't know. It works for them, and me."

They rose and walked to the end of the terrace. Mishka leaned against the parapet and watched a school of fish swam together.

"Where's Pam at the moment, as we're here in each other's company?"

"She flew out to California to spend the holidays with her sister."

"Why aren't you with her?"

"She didn't ask me to go and I didn't offer."

"It mustn't be that great if you two are in separate places at this time of year. Christmas is a special time of year for people to be together."

"Well there's your answer. Let's talk about you for a moment, are you in a relationship?"

"I had a boyfriend when I lived in New York, it didn't work out. We 'sort-of' ended up as friends."

"Do you mind if I ask what happened?"

"I'll tell you some other time, that's *if* I get to know you better."

"Okay. What're your plans for the holidays?"

"No plans. I miss my family a ton."

"You must feel like an island here all by yourself."

"Sometimes, but I manage."

"You're an interesting character, Mishka, a breath of fresh air I must say. I'm glad I ran into you again."

She found herself naturally attracted to him, odd, because attraction was a long lost feeling, and never before for a white guy. Just when she felt something for Gordon, she went cold. There was something special about Brad that delighted her. Perhaps it was his confidence, the way he spoke. She admired how articulate he was. But what would he want with a Jamaican girl, even though quite good-looking, who worked as a receptionist, took the bus, and lived in an apartment? She thought that he might've had something up his sleeve with the absence of his estranged girlfriend.

On the night of Christmas, she sat up in bed and called home. She talked to Sophia and Ricardo. There was something soothing in knowing she was loved, even from far away. After saying goodbye, she lay in bed and reflected on the times when happiness was all she felt. Going to block parties and soccer games with Roxanne were things girls did growing up in Jamaica. She longed for Sophia's fruit cake, and words of encouragement. So much had happened since. How blissful life had been until Paul attacked her. She wondered if he still terrorized Roxanne or how many other girls. She still felt scarred and questioned whether or not life would ever return to normal. It felt as though many years had flown by, and so quickly. She climbed out of bed and stood before the mirror. She hadn't felt any connection to her body for some time. She undressed slowly and admired herself. For the first time since her attack, she confronted the fear of looking at herself again in an assertive manner. She gazed at herself, banished the mental scar that lingered. There was nothing physically wrong with her body, but inside, she had always felt unclean, damaged. She convinced herself that in order to move on she had to finally feel like the person she saw looking back—a young woman with dreams beyond what was expected of girls of Jones Town. Her lack of self-esteem was one reality she refused to accept or to cope with anymore. Still gazing at herself, she touched her sensitive points, pleased to feel a tingle.

Tired from work, she went home and took a long bath. She later saw Brad calling and readily picked up.

"I'm inviting you out again," he said.

"Hm, are you sure that's a good idea?"

"Why don't you join me and decide at the end of the evening?"

"Where are you inviting me to?"

Jamaica Tough

"My colleague Jason is having a New Year's party at his home. Starts at seven."

"That's quite an invitation."

"I'd like for you to be my Cinderella for the evening."

"Well in that case I should go and find my glass slippers."

Thrilled, she wore a red dress and a pair of high heels. When Brad arrived, once again, he stepped out and opened the door for her, not wearing a suit, but still dashing in a red crew-neck sweater and khakis.

"You look stunning," he said.

"You did ask for a Cinderella," she said, fastening her seatbelt.

"A Jamaican one even," he said, laughing.

"You know, Brad, I didn't expect to hear from you again."

"I expected a *hell no* for asking you out again."

"Why'd you ask then?"

"I pictured you sitting alone pining for the beautiful shores of Jamaica. So I figured why not give it a try."

"What would Pam think about you taking me out, Brad?"

"My best guess is she'd be more concerned whether you were better looking than she."

She flashed him a mischievously smile. "Am I?"

"If I give you my honest opinion you'll accuse me of aiming to get laid."

"Does that mean Pam isn't beautiful?"

"She was, very beautiful, until she went under the knife."

Mishka laughed even harder.

"Nose job?"

"And boobs. I don't know why women do that. I greatly prefer naturals."

"How do you know that I don't have something unnatural?"

"I figured a young woman who rides the bus can't afford plastic surgery."

Mishka found this line a bit smug, but he was right.

"Hey," he said. "I work the same hours you do during the week and my office is across the street from the hospital. I can take you to and from work, no big deal."

She crossed her legs. "Riding those lovely buses will be hard to give up, plus, I don't want to put you out of your way."

"It's not out of my way, Mishka, it's *on* my way. I don't mind, my pleasure."

"I have to think about it."

They rode in silence for a moment.

"I have to ask you," she said. "What made you want to become a lawyer? You were such an excellent medic, and sure-handed."

"You sound like my old man. He was a surgeon and did everything to convince me to follow his foot step. My EMT experience was wonderful but I'm better at what I do now."

"Gosh I felt so stupid assuming that the bar exam was for bartenders."

"I don't think you're stupid. You'll look back on it and laugh at yourself one day."

At Jason's, there were already vehicles parked in the circular driveway. The property was fully landscaped, surrounded by high hedges. Brad walked up a graveled pathway to the house and rang the doorbell. A tall, blonde woman opened the door. Brad introduced Mishka.

"This is Lynda," he said. "Jason's wife."

She shook Mishka's hand. "Oh I love your dress!"

Mishka thanked her and stepped inside. The house was huge, three stories. Christmas decorations were everywhere, festivity in the air. Brad greeted friends and introduced Mishka all around, mostly to couples. A musical ensemble in the corner of the room played soft, classical tunes. Servers dressed in crisp, white shirts served hors d'oeuvres—sliced blue cheese on crackers drizzled with rosemary-infused honey, garnished with thinly sliced scallions. The champagne glasses glistened under little hanging white lights. Everyone appeared comfortable mingling. On one side of the house was a nicely decorated room filled with children's toys. Mishka felt like going in there and playing with them, but instead, she accepted the glass of champagne offered by a waitress.

Everyone was standing. The women avidly spoke about home decorating and children's activities. From where Mishka stood, it wasn't a mystery that Lynda's lips were surgically enhanced. They were so plump, it looked painful. The men stood in circles with champagne glasses in their hand, discussing politics, stocks, and sports. Mishka turned her attention to the center of the room, where couples did ballroom moves. Brad walked up behind her.

"Would you like to dance?"

"Not like that," she said, pointing at the couples on the dance floor.

"I know it's not the jammin' you Jamaicans do but this can be fun." He took her by the hand. "C'mon, follow me."

"How would you know about what Jamaicans dance like anyway?"

"I've listened to reggae. I don't imagine you can move slowly to it."

She put an arm around his shoulder.

"Oh my gosh, everyone's looking at us. My moves must be terrible."

He pulled her closer. "It's because you're beautiful."

Her hip parallel to his, she followed along.

"See," he said. "You're not doing so badly. Look up at me, improve your posture. Try sliding your feet instead of picking them up. That way you're less likely to pierce my toes with those fancy heels."

Although she was wearing stilettos, he stood a few inches taller. He changed to lighter conversation, allowing her to float freely with him. Her chest brushed against his, but she didn't apologize. For her, it wasn't at all an unpleasant sensation.

After a polite applause Brad excused himself to another glass of champagne. Lynda came across to Mishka.

"Doing okay?" she said. "Anything you need?"

"Oh, no. Thanks for asking."

"If you happen to change your mind, ask Brad, he knows his way around here."

"Sure, thanks."

"He hadn't told us about his new companion, *Mesha*, is it?"

"It's Mishka, and we're friends."

She lifted an eyebrow and took a sip of her Champagne. "Ah, friends."

"Yes, friends."

"Are you in the law field as well?"

"No, are you in law?"

"Heavens, no! I'm a wife and mother of three. Before meeting my husband I was a wedding coordinator, for the upper crust if you know what I mean. The children keep me much, much happier."

"I'm sure."

She took Mishka's hand and shook it. "Thanks for coming. It's nice meeting you."

She walked away and muttered, "Pamela will be gnashing her teeth when she hears this."

Everyone gathered around and counted down to the stroke of midnight, Mishka standing beside Brad. The other couples kissed. Mishka and Brad looked at each other. He closed the distant between them, held her cheeks and leaned in. Her arms around his shoulder, she closed her eyes and parted her lips allowing him to push his tongue deep into her mouth. His touch was warm, his cologne alluring, and the sweet taste of Champagne on his breath. The sound of music and Champagne glasses touching around the room broke their moment. Brad raised his glass to Mishka and smiled. She smiled back, feeling an emotional connection.

They later said their goodbyes and left together.

"Did you have a good time?" Brad said.

"Different I'd say."

"You're a good sport. Thanks for coming. Otherwise, I'd have been the only single person there."

"Oh, so that's why you asked me out, and there I am thinking it was my… *naturals*."

He howled. "Maybe subconsciously that was it, but I rationalized it by thinking I might give your New Year's Eve a lift."

"Kind of public service, is that it?"

"Well, yours and mine. I can't entirely deny your, ah, naturals being far in the background. I'm glad I went with my impulse to call you. I've enjoyed your company, and thanks for the dance."

"What did your friends think about you showing up with me?

"The guys asked who you were and I said you're my date. They don't take me seriously. They think I'm whipped by Pam."

"What's whipped?"

He laughed. "It's an expression. I'd tell you the whole phrase but you might be offended."

"No, I'd like to know."

"It means hen-pecked. Do you know that expression?"

"I don't, but what's whipped?"

"I think you better Google it."

"I have to wait to get near a computer? C'mon! I want to learn how Americans say things."

"Okay. I'll tell you, but only for the sake of your cultural enrichment. Please understand I'm not the one who invented it."

"Okay. What does it mean?"

"Pussy-whipped."

It was her turn to howl.

"Pussy-whipped! Your friends think you're pussy-whipped?"

"That's how guys talk sometimes. I don't think I'm whipped. They try to hook me up with different women and I decline. I'm more than capable of meeting someone on my own."

"So I take it they don't think Pam's the one for you?"

"Precisely, and they're right, but I don't need dating agents."

Mishka took it all in as they drove through the sparkly night.

Jamaica Tough

"They think it's cool you're from Jamaica. They say you look exotic."

"Me? I think you guys are exotic."

"Why in heaven's name do you think that?"

"Let's see, out of twenty or so people I was the only black person."

"I think I like being exotic."

"I was way outside of my element."

"Guess there's a first for everything, for both of us."

"Are you saying I'm the first black woman you've gone out with in public, or private?"

"Yes, you are. Beauty lies within, Mishka."

"Are there people here who judge other's based on race here in America?"

"Sure."

"Well, in Jamaica, it isn't black versus white, most of us are black—it's black versus brown. A person of brown complexion will have an easier time getting their way through life."

"You're pretty dark. Did you have a rough time?"

"Not really because I mostly stayed to myself, only had one friend, Roxanne. When I was in school, though, there were times when students as dark as me got picked more than others. They were seen as underachievers. They have a saying in Jamaica; *anything that's too black is no good.*"

He glanced at her. "Did you consider yourself an underachiever, Mishka?"

"Good question. Back then I wasn't so sure. I just did my best. My mother told me at a young age that education is the only thing that can save a poor black woman and I always keep it in mind."

"Well, that's the case anywhere you go, unless you're from a family of wealth."

They arrived at her apartment complex.

"This conversation is getting pretty heavy," he said.

"Yes, let's lighten it up." She cleared her throat. "The kiss, was it…"

"Oh, that! Hey, just to say Happy New Year, an America tradition."

"Right, a tradition," she said, a little let down.

"That wasn't quite honest, Mishka. It was more than just tradition. It was nice, actually. Thanks."

She was tempted to kiss him like he had her, but instead she ended the date respectfully and gracefully by leaning over and kissing him on the cheek.

"Happy New Year to you too," she said. "No need to open my door."

She stepped out, and hoping Brad was watching, she accentuated the sway of her hips as she walked away.

Chapter Nineteen

Three days later…

Mishka's evening with Brad made her feel like a teenager with a crush all over again. He was a gentleman, and more mature than any man she'd ever met. She was disappointed he hadn't called. She supposed he must've forgotten his offer to take her to work. Of course, that was a big commitment, but she hoped he would keep his promise. When she didn't hear from him for several days, she picked up his card, stored his number in her contacts, and then called.

"Nice to hear from you," he said. "I thought I might've scared you off the other night."

"You should've asked me."

"I can be shy when it comes to women, especially when they're as beautiful as you are."

"That's nice of you to say."

"I was also hoping you'd call. Glad you did."

"I called to say hello but I also have a request."

"Anything."

"Are you sure?"

"Just ask."

"I'll think of a few things, but for now, I'd like to ask if you happen to know anyone who would teach me how to drive at a moderate fee. I've checked into driving schools but they are too costly for a girl who rides the bus."

"Driving lessons, hmm, let's see. Brad Callahan's Driving Academy. I hear they're quite good, and really cheap."

She paused, confused. "Oh! You. Are you sure?"

"Why else would I offer?"

"You're a busy man and I wouldn't want to take up all your time."

"True. But I can do some pro bono work."

"Did you say pro-*boner*?"

He cackled.

"*Pro bono* is what I said, and it means to work at a reduced fee or for nothing. I'll teach you at no charge."

"Awesome. When can we start?"

"What's on your docket for Saturday?"

"I'll make myself available."

He called her Saturday morning. She threw on a pair of jeans shorts and sandals. She peeked through the window and saw him moving to the passenger seat, reserving the wheel for her. Rather than keep him waiting, she let her shoulder-length hair flow and went out.

They hugged.

"Did you have breakfast?" he said.

"A cup of tea. That'll hold me over until lunchtime. I'm not big on breakfast anyway."

"Let's roll. We should practice around here first, and then we'll head out to the beach, enjoy this great weather with a walk on the sand."

"How should I start?"

"Adjust the seat, mirrors, and put on your seat belt."

She knew where the gas and brake pedals were from watching Calvin and Tracy drive. She drove slowly around the apartment grounds while Brad patiently explained simple traffic rules to her.

"You're doing great for your first time."

"Thanks. Nice car, it feels new. The brakes are very sharp."

"It's nearly a year old."

"You must be a simple guy, are you?"

"How can you tell?"

"People who have successful careers as you do most likely would prefer a BMW or Mercedes. You have a Camry."

He laughed. "That's quite an observation, but you're right. I am a simple guy."

"Simple says a lot about who you really are. I'm simple too."

"I've sacrificed driving a flashy car for having a boat. I enjoy being out on the water."

"You have a boat?"

"I do."

"Must be peaceful boating."

"Very much."

"Is Pam still in California?"

"She sent an email to say she's back, and asked about you and me at the party."

"She must have talk to Linda, huh?"

"Yup. Their buddies."

"Do you think it was inappropriate to take me there?"

"Absolutely not. I was invited. There were no restrictions on who I should take along. And beside what goes on with my personal life is my business."

"I know you said things between you two aren't great, but I feel guilty, as if I'm condoning cheating."

"You forgot to put your turn signal on. They'll flunk you for that. Otherwise you're doing great. After this turn, speed up a little. Have you noticed everyone passing us?"

"Are you avoiding the topic?"

"Let's focus on driving for the moment. We can talk at the beach."

They walked down some steps to the beach where she took off her sandals. Brad took off his shirt. She admired him through the corner of her eyes. He was solid, tight, strong arms, some dark fuzz on his chest. He held her hand as they waded along the shore.

"About my cheating on Pam."

"Yes."

"First, you shouldn't feel guilty."

"Why not?"

"We're at the point where all we ever do is exchange phone calls and occasional emails. If I decide to meet someone that's my decision. I don't tell her that she can't go out and meet people. If she decides to, hey, I'd give her my blessing."

A Frisbee landed near their feet. He picked it out of the surf and flung it back to a teenaged girl who waved.

"What did you tell her in the email when she asked about us?"

"The truth—we met—I asked you out—you're a lovely person."

"You told her that?"

"Sure."

She squeezed his hand and kicked some water. They walked without speaking.

"I like you Mishka," he finally said. "You're a beautiful woman, but that's not all that matters to me. I want to know more about you."

"You do, huh?"

"But there's more to it. Something about our meeting again, sharing that awful day up there, and here we are walking on the sand. Like kismet or something."

"What's *kismet*?"

"Fate. Destiny."

"Oh."

"About your driving, you did okay getting us here in one peace. I'll pick up a handbook for you to study for the road test. We can practice until you're ready to get your license."

Holding hands, they strolled along the beach until they found an umbrella and chair concession.

"Pretty here," Mishka said. "Reminds me so much of home. This is my first time at the beach in America. I haven't gone since fifteen years old with my first boyfriend."

After mentioning Nathan, she had a sudden flashback of Paul, but she immediately rejected it.

"So long ago."

"Too bad you didn't bring your suit. We could go for a swim."

"I can't swim."

"You're from Jamaica by beautiful water and can't swim?"

She smiled, lying back on her lounge chair. "No one ever taught me."

"I have a pool at home. I'll have to teach you sometime."

"Good luck."

"I'm thirsty, want something?"

"Sure."

He hopped up and went to get them cold drinks. Looking out at the ocean, she felt a wave of jubilance. Her life suddenly looked as bright as the sun sparkling on the water. She took a deep breath. It felt great getting to know someone outside of her culture. Perhaps one day she'd have a chance to share it with him.

He came back and handed her a bottle of water and took his seat.

"How do you like working at the hospital?"

"It's okay, but certainly not my dream job."

"What is your dream, Mishka?"

"Why don't you take a guess? Let's see how much you pay attention."

"I can see you doing anything you put your mind to. You have a strong mind for a young woman. If I had to take a guess I could see you on a runway."

"Oh stop."

"You have what it takes. If you have the opportunity you should take it."

"I'll keep it that in mind but I want to become a pediatric nurse. I want to start school as soon I have a car."

"Not a bad career choice. I'm sure you'll be great at it. So, now that you're almost a licensed driver, have you any plans for a car?"

"I want to find a used one, that's after I have enough to actually buy one. I'm working on it."

"Car shopping, that's something I can help you with. For a first-time buyer you can use a male's expertise."

"You're right. I know nothing about cars, but I'm already taking up a lot of your time."

"I don't mind if you take up my time."

"It's down the road from now anyway. We'll see."

"Damn!"

"What?"

"I forgot to give you a lift to work. Can we start on Monday?"

"You don't have to if it's too much."

"It isn't. Monday, okay?"

"Fine."

"Thanks for not calling me out for breaking my promise."

Gazing toward the horizon, they sipped their drinks. Some wind-surfers were doing stunts, their bright sails matching Mishka's spirit.

Chapter Twenty

Two days later…

Monday morning she began to think he would forget to pick her up again. Though she hoped that he wouldn't forget, she was prepared to take the bus in case he failed to show, and she certainly wouldn't call to remind him. She waited a while longer until he called from the gate. She buzzed him in and hastily gathered her things. When he saw her coming, he stepped out and opened her door.

"Are you always this punctual?" she said, looking at her watch.

"I'm making up for last week." He reached into the cup holder. "I stopped and bought tea, chamomile, just for you."

She took it. "Thank you. It sure smells good."

"What time do you get off work?"

"Little after five."

"I typically leave my office at four-thirty, but I can stick around and do some work until it's time to come and get you."

"I can take the bus if…"

"I said I'll be there."

They rode mostly in silence, but she felt the air alive between them. When they arrived at the hospital, he gripped her hand as she got out of the car, as though they had an unspoken understanding.

When he arrived to pick her up from work that evening, he stepped out, reserving the wheel for her.

He handed her a booklet. "Study for the road test."

"You really meant business, huh?"

"Wouldn't you think I'm a jerk for breaking yet another promise?"

"Maybe." She glanced at him and smiled. "You should stay for dinner this evening."

"You forgot your turn signal again."

"Is that a yes?"

"Yes."

She showed him around her apartment, not much to see. He made himself comfortable by sprawling on her bed. She felt good seeing a man in a business suit lying on her comforter. She opened the blinds and headed for the kitchen.

"You've made this place cozy. What're we having for dinner?"

"My newly discovered shrimp fettuccine alfredo. Quick and easy. I'd make a Jamaican meal but it's time consuming. Next time, maybe."

"Sounds yummy."

He sat up and removed his coat, placed a pillow behind his head, and turned on the television. Reaching up into the cabinet, she turned and smiled at how quickly he was adjusting.

"I'm going to take a shower while this simmers," she told him.

"Should I keep an eye on it?"

"I'm setting the timer. If it goes off please turn off the burner."

She came out in a white bath robe and ushered him to the table. He loosened his tie and pulled it off, put it in his pocket. She brought their plates and sat across from him.

"I don't have Champagne," she said. "I hope lemonade is fine for you."

"Lemonade's fine. Dinner looks and smells terrific."

In the midst of their meal, his phone rang. He ignored it. It rang again. He reached into his pocket, looked at it, and then put it back.

"Is it Pam?" Mishka said.

He nodded. Their mood broken, he continued eating as if the call was unimportant. Mishka didn't ask any more questions.

After their meal, she brought their dishes to the sink. He downed his lemonade and settled on the couch, scanning the TV guide. She came back and sat next to him.

"What're you looking for?"

"Checking to see what time the basketball game comes on tonight."

He raised his arm and touched his shoulder. "I think I pulled a muscle bench-pressing this morning. Still hurts like hell."

"Want me to rub it for you?"

"Please, if you don't mind."

He removed his shirt and tossed it on the bed. She rose and walked to the dresser, where she picked up a bottle of lotion. She squeezed some into her palm and rubbed her hands together, making them soft and warm, gently kneading his shoulder.

"Can you do the back of my neck?" he said.

"My knees hurt from kneeling. Come on the bed where I can get comfortable."

She sat behind him with her back against the headboard. She wrapped her legs around him baring them from her robe. She began rubbing his shoulder, his back. His eyes were closed. His fingers teased her toes, sending a tingle up her thighs. She admired his strong arms, and wanted to lay in them.

Finished, he reached for his shirt and put it on. She buttoned his shirt for him, fixed his tie.

"There you go," she said, patting his chest.

When she reached for his coat, he caught her hand.

"What's wrong?"

"Thanks for the massage."

"The pleasure's all mine."

He held her close and kissed her lips. She closed her eyes and kissed him deeply. Her body tingled again. She gently pulled away and reached for his coat. He put it on. She walked with him to the door.

She waited for him to take her to work. She'd fallen asleep thinking about him—the touch of his skin, the scent of his cologne, his kiss. When he finally arrived, she hurried outside and saw him smiling as she approached. He stepped out and hugged her.

"Let's stop for coffee on the way," he said.

They took off.

"How's your shoulder?"

"I used Bengay before bed. Doesn't hurt as much."

"Glad to know it feels better."

"Thanks for the invite last evening. I'm not a good cook, but maybe we should do dinner at my place next time."

"I can teach you if you're willing to learn."

"Back to practical matters. If you can get out of work a little early before the end of the week, I'll pick you up for the driving test. Think you're ready?"

Mid-week, she took a sick day off from work and rode the bus to the community college where she enrolled. She later called Brad to take her to the driving test as planned. She used his car to do the road test. He stood by and watched.

"Congratulations," he said. "You even remembered the turn signals. Now you're official."

She kissed him on the cheek. "That's because I had such a great teacher."

"How much do you have for a car?"

"Fifteen-hundred. Not enough but I'll get there."

"Here's what we'll do—an old friend of mine owns a car dealership here in Palm Beach. I'll pick you up over the weekend and we'll take a look and pick something out, cool?"

"I won't have enough."

"How bout I offer you a loan? I'm excited to help you pick out a car. Guys like doing that. And now that you're a licensed drive there's no point in having me drive you around anymore."

"Thanks but I should wait and do it when I have enough."

"Oh, c'mon. It's no skin off my nose. Let's make it fun."

"I'll think about it."

She mused about it all week. She struggled with the thought of accepting his loan. She'd learned to work for what she wanted. Although he seemed to care about her, she didn't want him to see her as someone who needed a handout. Saturday morning, he called her from the gate. She buzzed him. She saw him parking his car, and opened her front door. He later stepped inside and pecked her on the cheek.

"Did I miss your call?" she said, looking at her cell.

"I said I'd be here. We're going to pick out a car today."

"I haven't decided yet, Brad."

"Why don't you get dressed? We'll take a ride over there and see what he has."

He introduced her to the owner of the dealership. Brad stood and spoke with the owner. Mishka wandered off and looked around at all the cars on the lot. Brad later found her and asked her to follow him.

"What do you think about this one? It's an eight-year-old Accord."

She examined it. "Looks good for an older car."

"It's in great shape. Low mileage, no dings. I have the keys. We can take it for a spin."

He drove it around the block, even on the freeway.

"It's perfect," he said. "The engine purrs."

She turned and looked at the back seat. "Clean too."

"It's a deal for four grand. I'll offer him thirty-five hundred. He doesn't want cars this old sitting there. He might go for it. I'll make him an offer he can't refuse."

"I think you're way too worked up about this. Why don't we wait a while to get it?"

"Don't argue. We're getting it now."

Back at the lot Brad and the owner conferred in the sales office. Mishka signed a plethora of papers, and they both wrote checks. She left the men alone and walk back to the lot. She sat behind the wheel of her car, trying out the stereo, her mind reeling with joy.

Brad came out and handed her the keys. "Congratulations."

She took the wheel.

"Why do I get the feeling we won't see each other again for some time?"

"I have a busier than usual week ahead. I have a meeting next Saturday at the golf course with my buddy. We have business to discuss. If there's a change in plan I'll drop by to see you."

They drove away in their separate direction.

She began to miss him terribly, and hoped he was truthful about his schedule. She had doubts, and thought there was something behind his kindness. Perhaps it was a nice of saying he was tired of taking her around. She kept busy at work and drove herself to classes in the evenings. Days went by and Brad hadn't called. She hoped that something would interfere with his meeting so he'd come over and see her instead.

Saturday morning, sure enough, he called her from the gate. She was already awake having her tea, but she left it on the counter and hurried outside to meet him. Casually dressed in shorts and T-shirt, he was halfway at her doorstep. She rushed into his arms.

"Man!" he said, smiling. "What a week."

"Feels like I haven't seen you in ages."

They went in and shut the door.

"How was your week?" he said, lying across the bed. She curled up next to him.

"The usual."

"Sorry for not calling. It's been a rough work week. I drove home each night drooling on myself."

"You were supposed to discuss business with your friends today, what happened?"

"Jason had to leave town on short notice."

"I see."

"How's the car running?"

"It's running great. Monday after work, I forgot and walked out to where you normally pick me up. Then I remembered I no longer have a personal driver."

He laughed. "What do you feel like doing today?"

"The beach?"

"Bring your suit this time."

"We'll have to stop on the way and pick one up."

"Let's run into Target. I need to get more tanning oil."

"Am I driving?" she said, fixing her hair.

"I'll drive. I have a few things I'd like to show you later."

At the store, Brad gave his opinion as she modeled the swim suits. She finally decided on a one piece suit cut high on the hips. When they went to check out at the register, he reached for his wallet.

"I'll pay for my suit," Mishka said. "You don't have to always pick up my tab."

"Sorry, it's a habit.

At the beach, Brad stepped out of the car, allowing Mishka to put on her new suit. Holding hands, they went to their usual spot. He took off his T-shirt and sat on a chair. She took the tanning oil out of her bag.

"Roll over. I'll help you."

She applied the oil to his upper body.

"Those hands of yours," he said.

"What about them?"

"They work magic."

She took her time applying it.

After she was finished she pressed down on his chest. Their lips met.

They waded into the water waist deep, their passion turned to hilarity. She rode him piggyback. They had a splash battle. They relaxed on the sand letting the waves wash over their feet. Mishka watched a pod of dolphins swim by.

He looked at his watch. “We should go.”

Their day was going well. But she was uncertain about how it might turn out. So far, she felt comfortable around him, but she didn’t know if her feeling would clamp down again. If the horror of Paul returned as it had with Gordon, her ability for that kind of pleasure might never be restored. This could be her last attempt with any man for the rest of her life.

The ride to Jupiter was scenic—rural, quiet. His home sat at the end of a street, a cul-de-sac. He parked in the driveway. She waited for him to open her door, admiring the rows of palm trees leading up to the walkway. She stepped out and followed him. He took out his keys and opened the front door. The walls were yellow, decorated with framed ocean photos. In one corner of the room sat an office desk piled with papers. He opened some double doors and led her out back. The pool was surrounded by a spacious sun deck and landscaped gardens. They walked back inside.

“Who keeps it so tidy around here?”

"My housekeeper, Maria. She does a beautiful job."

"How often is she here?"

"Once a week. She shops for groceries and cleans."

"Look at all the kitchen space. You should learn how to cook."

"I'll take a lesson from you sometime."

"You've turned this room into a gym. Cool. What type of machine is that?"

"Bowflex. I use in the mornings before work. I'm turning forty, need to stay in shape."

"I want to look like you when I get older."

"God, I hope not. You'll have to get a sex change operation."

She smiled. "You know what I mean."

"Twenty-one, you have a way to go, but make good use of it. Soon you'll wonder where the hell time went."

She tested the different equipment while Brad explained their functions.

"Why do you have a punching bag hanging from the ceiling? You box?"

"I'm no Tyson but I use it as a part of my workout."

She tested it. "Ouch. My knuckle."

"That's why I have gloves. That thing is filled with sand and weighs a ton."

She looked at her hand. He took and examined. "A little red. Want me to ice it?"

"It's okay. I'll survive."

"Are you sure?"

"I've had worse happen."

"Let's go down to the marina for lunch. I'm getting hungry."

They arrived at the marina and parked in front of a sandwich shop. Behind the counter, an older couple brightened when they saw Brad approaching.

"Hey there, Sir Brad!" the man said.

"Hey!" Brad said shaking the man's hand. "Good to see ya."

"Who's your compadre?"

"This is Mishka, a Jamaican lady with a Russian name."

"Yeh, mon!" the man said, his arms covered with tattoos. "I know it well. Me and my honey cruise to Mobay every Easter."

When the man bagged the sandwiches Brad reached for his wallet.

"You have a bad habit of not letting me pay my bill," Mishka whispered.

"I'm pleased to have met someone who thinks it's a bad habit."

She followed him down the boardwalk where yachts were moored. Some of them were inhabited. A lady wearing bikini was painting the hull of one named *Sun Dance*. The marina was more of a small community, more than what she'd expected to see.

Brad stopped. "There she is." He pointed ahead toward a white boat with the name *Lolita* written in blue across its side. "I'll use the winch to pull her closer. It's high tide."

He climbed aboard, took the food and helped Mishka across a narrow plank.

"Everything on a boat has a different name than stuff on land," he said. "For instance, this isn't a floor, it's a deck. The rope over there is a line. This door I'm unlocking is a hatch."

"What's her measurement?"

"Fifty feet."

He disappeared down some steps and came back with plastic cups, napkins and such.

“Can we eat here on this bench or whatever the correct name is on a boat?”

He laughed. “Sure.”

They finished their meal and chatted a while.

“Let me show you the cabin,” he said.

She descended to the confines below deck.

“Sorry about the stuffiness,” he said. “I haven’t been here in weeks. Maria comes here more than I do.”

“To clean?”

“And to replace stuff.”

The color scheme was navy blue and white, with varnished mahogany, a small living area, a galley and a master bedroom. She touched the surfaces.

“Much nicer than my apartment.”

They sat on the deck and looked out at the water, boaters going by, some waved.

“What would you be doing today had we not met again?”

“Golf with my buddies till late afternoon, go out to eat, sometimes go fishing.”

"Everything sounds fun, except golf."

He looked at her and smiled. "As long as we know each other I'll switch out golf for a day with you anytime."

He locked up Lolita. With the water red and pink from the evening sky, they strolled, arms around each other to the car, and drove back to his Jupiter.

When she came out of the bathroom he was occupied at his desk sorting through papers.

"What're you doing?"

He wheeled the chair around facing her. "My other bad habit, to mess around with my job every chance I get."

"That is a bad habit."

"I'll work on it," he said, getting up. "So, are you staying overnight?"

She hesitated.

"Ah, sure we're not getting ahead of ourselves?"

"Please, don't take it the wrong way. I'm only offering companion."

His words were a relief, but she felt as though she insulted him.

"I'm sorry for taking it the wrong way. Actually I'd love to stay. I'm enjoying your company."

"Don't feel pressured. It's okay with me either way."

"I want to stay, but only if I can take a shower."

"Of course you can. Should I leave while you do so?"

She cackled.

The spray of water on her body enlivened all her nerve endings. It seemed Brad was a genius at allowing the moment to build. After a long shower, she went out with a towel wrapped around her. Brad lounged on the recliner watching a game of basketball.

She stood before him putting her wet hair in a ponytail. "Is there a blow dryer around here somewhere and something for me to sleep in?"

He rose. Her towel came loose and fell to the floor. She picked it up and wrapped it around her.

"I'll take the shirt," she said, hustling toward the bathroom.

He knocked on the door. "Here's the shirt. There's a hair-dryer under the sink."

After drying her hair she put on his oversized T-shirt and went back out. He was in the kitchen putting away the dishes. She went in to help.

"I saw you looking," she said.

"How could I not?" he chuckled. "They're perfectly formed, and they're real for Christ's sake."

"Like 'em?"

"Yes, I do."

She reached up in the cupboard to put away a glass. "What else do you like about a woman besides her boobs?"

"The quality of her mind."

She smiled at his simplicity. "That's a broad statement."

"Shall I spell it out?"

"Yes. Please."

"Her interests, hobbies, books she might like to read, people she associates with, the things she dreams about. There are other things too, but I rather not offend you."

"Go ahead, say it."

"I'll tell you some other time."

"I'm getting to know you, let's hear it."

"Next time, I promise."

"It can't be that bad."

He closed the kitchen cabinet and went back to his game. She followed.

"Please, tell me."

"I see you won't take no for an answer."

She plopped down beside him. "One thing you'll get to learn about Jamaican women, we're determined."

"There's no winning here tonight. So here goes—I like a woman who's hands on and affectionate, has sexy feet. Eyes are nice to admire too. I like yours by the way. I prefer a woman with plush lips, a round ass, long legs, and as you know, breasts that are real. Sound like someone you might know?"

"Want to touch them?"

"Are you trying to tease me?"

She lifted her shirt. His eyes grew wide. He held them.

"My gosh they're awesome."

She suddenly felt the power she had at Paradise, one that comes from turning a man on.

She let the shirt fall back. He backed away, still ogling.

"Well?" she said.

"Fan-tastic. I can look at them for a living."

They sat quietly for a moment, both paying attention to the game.

"I was a little surprise to learn you were single at our first lunch date," he said. "You're beautiful, funny, sexy."

"I had too much going on, my father, finding a job."

"Yeah, that's right."

"I had a boyfriend in Jamaica, but I came here and that was that."

"But you'd mentioned one in New York that didn't work out so well. Do you know me well enough now to share what happened?"

"We worked together, started out having a good time. Things went south … I guess he found someone else."

"He must've been a real idiot."

She didn't want to broach the topic of turning to ice with Gordon. She was unable to muster up the courage to talk about it.

She changed the topic.

"Why don't you have any children, Brad?"

"It's not as casual as it sounds."

"What do you mean?"

"It's about meeting the right person, get to know them beyond the surface, fall in love, tie the knot, and then start a family. I've spent the last ten years of my life building my career, and I haven't found the right woman yet."

"Say, things turn out perfect between us, we're compatible. Would you marry me and want to have children?"

"Why do you sound so unsure?"

"Well, you know, a Jamaican woman for a wife. What would your family think?"

He smiled. "Growing up in our household my parents believed that every man is created equally. That's what they taught us. In the event of marriage they'd support my decision and welcome you to our family."

She suddenly felt out of place.

"We really shouldn't be talking about this. Sorry I brought it up."

"There's nothing wrong with having an open conversation, Mish. That's what adults do."

"Yeah, I guess."

"Tell me about growing up in Jamaica. What was it like? What's your family like?

She answered only with generalities.

"I had a unique upbringing, very different from here."

"It seems you're a long way away from home. You do pretty well for a person who hasn't been here for long."

She looked at him. "I've been feeling better these last few weeks,"

He winked. "Ditto."

She rested her head on his shoulder. His company conversations appeared to have satisfied her for the moment.

The urge to release her bladder woke her from of a deep sleep. Feeling the warmth of skin against her legs, she opened her eyes. She sat up and looked around the dim room, recalling Brad waking her up off the sofa after the game. She turned around and looked at him. He was fast asleep. Not wanting to wake him, she quietly walked to the restroom. She came back and cuddled with him. As she lay there, she watched him sleep, ran her fingers through his hair, wondering what it would feel like if he made love to her.

Chapter Twenty-one

Two weeks later...

Balancing work and classes became a challenge for Mishka. She sometimes had to remind herself that hard work would pay off. The college campus felt much like Manhattan during rush hour, but she managed to get around. She looked forward to her visits with Brad. She cooked Jamaican dishes and became skilled with a winch, even mastered swimming. His haircut was as conservative as his views on American politics. Nestling in his arms became something special for Mishka. He was her security blanket.

She called him on her way home.

"Sorry you're caught in such nasty weather," he said.

"No need to start worrying, Brad. I am driving carefully."

"So how was your day?"

"Was good. I'm glad it's over."

"I'm sure."

"What're you doing?"

"Sorting my suits for drop off at the cleaners. Are you coming over tomorrow?"

"I feel bad about taking you away from your friends. It's been a long time since you've seen them."

"They make fun of me for not getting out, but I tell them my weekends are brighter being with you."

"You told them that?"

"Sure."

"Lord I hope they don't hate me."

"Why don't you start your weekend a little early, come on over tonight."

"I'd have to go home and get some things first."

"You left your body wash and some clothes here. I washed them for you."

"How sweet. Thank you. In that case I'll see you shortly."

When she arrived the outside lights were on. He must've heard when she pulled up because before she rang the doorbell, wearing only a pajama bottom, he opened the door. They hugged.

"Are you hungry?"

"I could eat a crocodile."

"I ordered Thai. There's plenty in there that I haven't touched."

He took her books and bag to the living room and went into the kitchen with her. She helped herself to the microwave, went back into the dining room, and gobbled down the *Pad See Ew*.

"So your friends mock you for my taking up your time. They think you're *whipped*?"

"They both laughed really hard.

"Funny you remembered that. No, they haven't said that, and I wouldn't give a shit anyway."

"They know we're in a relationship?"

"Yes but I don't go into detail about us. It's not their business."

She rose and brought her plate to the kitchen. "I'm going to take a shower. Where's the stuff that you washed?"

"I folded and put them away. I'll get it for you."

Jamaica Tough

Rain pounded the rooftop. It turned out to be a stormy night. She came out and saw him on the sofa watching the game. The moment he sensed her presence, he shifted his attention from the game and onto her, his eyes filled with lust. During their time spent together, they'd been teetering on the edge. Tonight, she detected they were a step closer. She sat beside him, her legs crossed and bared from her lingerie. His eyes pierced her thighs.

"What's that gleam in your eyes?"

He drew closer to her ear. "You really wanna know?"

"That's why I ask."

"You're turning me on. You look and smell amazing."

She flashed him a flattering smile, and glanced at the front of his pants. Her smile turned into a mischievous grin. Her eyes drifted over his abs, sending shivers down her spine. They leaned in for a kiss. He held her in place. She was prepared when his mouth captured hers. His hand slipped up her dress, lightly caressing her cleavage. His touch was tender, teasing. Still kissing her, his fingers crept lower. She'd forgotten what it felt like being touched there. He broke off his kiss, picked her up, and brought her into bed. The scent of strawberry candles indicated that he'd arranged the setting prior to her arrival. They held and kissed each other again passionately. He reached around her back in search of her bra clasp. He found and released it. With a slight shrug of her shoulder, her bra fell to the floor. He gently pulled her closer by her hips, and buried his face between her breasts. Her body was electrified. She was gradually loosening up, and it felt right. She tipped him onto the bed. He leaned back on his elbows and watched as she slowly pulled her thong down to her ankles, stepping out of it. She extended her arms out sideways and turned around, still feeling self-conscious. His eyes roamed up and down her body. Her fingers ventured through the opening of his pants, taking him into her hands. She stopped. He stepped out of his pants. She wet her palm with her tongue and reached for him.

She fell back on the bed. He raised her knees and descended. Her body squirmed. She rotated her hips, guiding him to where it felt best. She felt a sense of resurrection. Her body came alive. Perhaps sensing that she wanted control, he gave in and rolled onto his back. She straddled his hips and raised her head up from his chest, looked down at him, a teasing smile on her face. She made love to him.

The fire she'd been feeling was now raging, so much so, she was unable to prolong the excitement. She inhaled and exhaled deeply, until suddenly, there was an intense surge throughout her body. She felt lost from the world for a moment. She collapsed on his chest. He held her. With her thighs still trembling, she realized that this time she hadn't been overcome by her secret. There was no horror, no grim images. She felt a wave of freedom.

Chapter Twenty-two

One month later...

In the central Atlantic, a powerful storm headed for the coast of Florida. Before long, it was upgraded to a Category Three hurricane. Warnings and mandatory evacuation orders were now in full effect for Mishka's area. She called Brad.

"Hey honey," he said. "I just walked in from work and picked up the phone to call you. The office closed a little early because of the storm."

"What do you think about it?"

"It's possible we'll see some devastation. We should get away until it passes. I've reserved a hotel room for us up in North Florida, roughly three hours away."

"Sounds adventurous. Let's make it a vacation and pretend it's Jamaica."

"We'll have to be quite imaginative for that, but let's give it a try. Be sure you bring any important documents or photos you might have in case your place gets flooded."

"Think it'll be that bad?"

"Better safe than sorry."

"Are you coming to pick me up?"

"You should bring your car with you."

She took her suitcase from her closet and packed everything that fit. She lifted it into the trunk of her car and went on her way. The sky was cloudy, winds fierce.

Brad was in the garage changing his oil. She greeted him and proceeded to assist with preparation for their journey.

"I'm going in to separate my things," she said. "Only taking what I'll need."

Inside, her phone rang—Sophia. She stepped outside to answer.

Brad walked by. "I'm going to lock up."

"Okay."

"Hi, darlin'," Sophia said. "How you makin' out in the storm?"

"I'm going out of town with Brad. Everything alright there?"

"We hopin' the storm don't come here. You know our houses can't manage it. Who is Brad?"

"My boyfriend. I'll tell you more about him another time. How's Ricardo and Aunt Tracy doing?"

"Tracy alright. Ricardo in police trainin' now. Im almost have the badge."

They laughed.

"Tell them I say hello."

"Mishka," Sophia said. "Me want to ask you something."

"What?"

"Why Paul ask me if you soon come back from America? You and im have dealings?" Mishka hesitated.

"We don't have any dealing. What did he say?"

"Im ride past me outside an' ask why me send away Roxanne's friend, an' if you soon come back. Strange to me that im would ask for you."

"What did you tell him?"

"Nothing. Me jus' smile."

"I'm sure it was only a joke, Mommy, that's all. He knows me and Roxanne were good friends."

"Me hope that's all it is, a joke."

"Have you seen Roxanne lately?"

"She come to see her sisters Christmas, and stop over here for a piece of me fruit-cake. She asked bout you. Say she miss you. Me don't see her since." Her voice lowered. "Yesterday, Marlene come here an' cry to me, say Paul tell her something bout Roxanne work as whore over back-road."

Mishka was shocked! How did he find out where she went?

She saw Brad walking out the door.

"Mommy, I have to run. Whenever you see Roxanne, please give her my number and ask her to call me, as soon as possible. I'm going to call you back later."

She walked over to the car where Brad was loading up.

"Everything okay?" he said.

"Yeah, that was my mother. She called to see how I'm doing."

"Is she worried?"

"A little. I miss her so much. You'll have to meet her someday."

"I'd love to."

Brad leading the way, they took off in separate vehicles. Mishka was very concerned about Paul speaking to Sophia. She knew what he was capable of. She thought, what if Paul thinks that Sophia knew what he'd done and intentionally sent her away? She recalled the hateful glare he gave her the day Calvin drove her to the airport. She began to worry about Roxanne, and was reminded of how he terrorized her before leaving. She wondered what caused him to tell on Roxanne. Something must've gone horribly wrong. She wished she could get Sophia away from there.

She turned on the car stereo and tried to keep up with Brad in the evacuation traffic. The wind and rain were dying down as it got dark and they were farther away. She saw Brad calling.

"Let's get off at the next exit." he said.

"Good, I need to stretch my legs."

"Let's grab a bite while we're at it."

It was dark. They walked into the restaurant together, and followed the waitress to a window booth.

"Everything alright, Hon?" she said.

"I need to talk to you whenever we're settled."

"About what?"

"Not now."

"Please don't do this. Is it something I did?"

"You haven't done anything wrong. Let's eat for now."

They finally arrived at their hotel. A harried-looking brunette welcomed them.

"Mr. and Mrs. Callahan?"

"Yes," Brad said. "We're storm refugees."

"Almost everyone is tonight. Thanks for calling about being late. We held the Honeymoon Suite as per you request."

Mishka stood next to Brad and smiled sheepishly at the desk clerk. Brad took the room keys, politely thanked the clerk, and then hauled their luggage toward the elevator.

In their room, Mishka shifted the drapes and walked onto the balcony. She sat and listened to the waves, people talking as they walked along the beach. She went back in and saw Brad standing over the nightstand, reading the hotel information card, his hands in his pockets.

"Nice place," she said.

After noticing that he hadn't acknowledged her, she turned on the television and lay on the bed.

"Room service is still open," he said. "I'm going to order a bottle of Zinfandel. Want something?"

"No thanks."

She rose and released her halter dress to the floor and stepped out of it.

In the shower, she heard a knock at the door. Brad opened it and took care of room service. When she came out he was still reserved at the table, pouring his wine into a glass and watching the weather updates.

She sat on his lap. "What is it you wanted to talk about?"

"I found your diary."

Her cheeks flushed with the heat of shame. Her throat tightened with the words that formed in her mind.

"Why'd he do that to you, honey?"

She looked up at him. "Where'd you find it?"

"At the house. It must've fallen out of you bags."

"You shouldn't have read it."

"I didn't know what it was. I opened it to where you left your pen."

She rushed into the bathroom and slammed the door. He followed.

"I'm sorry, hon. Please open the door."

She finally came out and climbed into bed, covered her body with the sheet. He gently pulled the sheet from her head.

"Who is he?"

"My neighbor's boyfriend. You don't have to keep seeing me if this will change the way you feel about me."

He held her in his arms.

"I love you."

She let out a gasp as if something deep inside her had flown out. She sobbed into his chest as he held her.

He dried her face with the sheet.

"Does your mother know about it?"

She told him what had happened, everything.

"That son of a bitch. Why didn't the police arrest him?"

"Everyone's afraid of him. Ghettos in Jamaica are operated by men like him."

"What the hell kind of place is that?"

"I know it's hard for you to understand. Maybe there are places in Jamaica where these things don't happen. The ghetto is where I lived. My family was about as poor as can be."

"You're right. It is hard for me to understand. What a way to live."

He reached for the wine and chugged it down.

She realized that she changed his notion of the paradise he imagined in Jamaica.

He lifted her chin and kissed her softly, looked into her eyes. "This won't change the way that I feel about you. In fact I've been feeling closer to you more and more each day."

He took her into his arms and kept her there.

"Ever thought about moving in together, hon?"

"You mean you have?"

"I think we should."

She rolled away from him.

"It would take some time to think about it."

"Why?"

She took a long pause.

"What's wrong?"

“I can’t see myself living with a man, Brad. I am afraid to.”

“What’s your fear, honey?”

“It’s not you, Brad. I love being with you. It’s me. The way I was raised, I’ve never felt comfortable with men until we met.”

“Well there are obvious reasons.”

“And my father, he wasn’t around until I moved here.”

“Oh, honey.

She wrapped herself in a white robe and walked onto the balcony, Brad beside her. He sat in a chair. Mishka settled in his lap, her back against his chest and his arms around her. It was late, and a cool, quiet night.

“I think we should do it,” she said softly.

“Do what, sweetie?”

“Move in together.”

She waited for a response.

“Did you hear me, Brad?”

“If you have fears then you should think about it some more.”

“We can try it for a month or so, see what happens.”

“Are you sure that’s what you want to do?”

"I'm sure."

"Well, should we get you to see a therapist first, maybe?

"I've made it this far without one. I don't want to talk about it with anyone else."

"You sure are a tough cookie. This is what I meant when I told you a while back that there's something special about you. You are pretty tough, Mishka."

He carried her inside. She lay in the dim light while he went to the restroom. Something filled her heart as she realized his presence in her life. She felt that a guardian angel must be looking out for her.

She woke up and dragged Brad downstairs for breakfast. They ate and watched the weather update in the dining area. About to make landfall, Hurricane Frances was the headline of the day. The seas were wickedly rough, waves seven feet, and raining hard.

"Now that we've decided to move in together," he said, "I hope we'll have a home to go to."

She picked up a brochure. "Let's find something to do and not sit here and fret."

"What do you have in mind?"

"There's an art museum near here." She handed over the brochure. "There's a map too."

When they arrived, Mishka gallivanted around like a little girl and asked Brad questions about the various artistic items. Not taking her seriously, he answered with jokes. They stopped in a room filled with paintings.

"This is so beautiful!" she said.

"Do you know the artist who did this flower?"

"Georgia O'Keefe."

"Wow, smart."

"Think I go to school to warm chairs?"

He laughed.

"Who's your favorite artist?" she said.

"I have a few. Michelangelo, Donatello, Da Vinci. Who's yours?"

"Vincent Van Gogh. I love his work, the one called Starry Night. Such a beautiful piece. I learned about him in art class. He was a different kind of guy, though."

"You mean bizarre?"

"Well, yes. That's a better way of putting it."

"Didn't he cut off his ear and send it to his girlfriend?"

"He only had prostitutes."

"Ah-ha! So that explains the syphilis."

"Besides that I think it's tragic such a genius felt all alone."

"You know the wall picture in the den at home?"

"Yeah."

"After retirement my grandfather painted a replica of Diego Rivera's, Peasants. I've kept it over the years. I only hope it's still intact when we get home."

Back in Florida, Mishka rushed out of the car, stunned to see a boat leaning against the side of Brad's house. Trees were down, pools of water everywhere. Curious to see what the inside looked like, they opened the door, only to discover the place was flooded. The house had a rank odor. They left their shoes at the doorway, and sloshed about inside, trying to salvage all they could.

"There's no way we can stay here tonight," he said.

He locked up, left his car in the driveway, and drove with Mishka to the marina.

His boat was beaten up, one of the masts snapped in two. He re-tied it. They headed to Mishka's apartment. Nervous about what she would see, she held Brad's hand. Only a mile away, the damage was worse. Approaching her gate, she saw National Guardsmen. She flashed driver license.

"What's going on?" she said.

"No one's allowed to stay."

She looked at Brad in dismay. As she got closer, many buildings had been flattened, only a few still standing. She couldn't believe how extensive the damages were. No one was able to drive past a certain point, debris spread everywhere. She parked on someone's lawn. They walked to where her building once stood. Everything was strewn about. No roof. She'd lost everything, except for what she'd packed before leaving. People were here and there rummaging through the mess. She took a deep breath and examined the damage, nothing salvageable. She and Brad walked back to her car. Too stunned for tears, she sat quietly in the car.

"Where do we begin?" she said.

"We can start by finding a hotel until the insurance company comes and assess the damage at my house.

"How does it work?"

"They'll send someone out to see the damage, and then they'll cover repairs. Don't worry. We'll make it through."

"I'll help best I can."

"That's what I call teamwork. We better check into a room for the time being, until we can move back home."

"You should drive. I need a moment to get myself together."

"Aren't you glad we decided to leave?"

"After what I just saw, sure. How long do we have to stay at a hotel?"

"At least two weeks. I can't imagine having our place in any livable condition before then."

After hours of hotel hunting they finally found vacancy at a Holiday Inn.

"You guys lucked out," the clerk said. "We have one suite left.

Mishka reached for her purse to pay. Brad stopped her. She looked up, her eyes rested on him.

"Fine," he said, placing his wallet back into his pocket.

She handed the clerk her card and smiled. They later walk to the parking lot for their bags.

"Honey," he said. "You didn't have to pay for our suite."

"Part of the settlement for my car. And you don't have to pay for everything."

Chapter Twenty-three

Five hours later…

She went to bed second guessing herself, whether or not it was a wise idea to move in with Brad temporarily. They seem to do well together so far, but if living under the same roof changed their relationship in any way Mishka would have to make other plans. She knows that he cares about her and hoped for the best. She had seen relationships fall apart quickly, like her relationship with Nathan. Sophia spoke about how in love she was with Calvin when they first met. He later left her. Mishka knew how broken hearted Sophia felt even years after Calvin left.

Mishka recalled Sophia's phone call the day she and Brad left town. She needed to speak with Roxanne to find out what happened between her and Paul but the moment wasn't right. She'd have to do it when Brad wasn't around. She snuggled in his arms and tried to forget about it.

Jamaica Tough

She finds herself in Jamaica at her old house, alone. She hears a knock at the door and opens it, only to see Paul standing there. Horrified, she slams the door shut and runs back inside. He opens it and chases her to her bedroom. She unlocks her window, pushes it open, and attempts to climb out. He catches her by her blouse and yanks her to the floor. She pleads with him not to harm her. He helps her to her feet, sits beside her on her bed, and calmly tells her to be there later when he returns. She agrees to meet him after dark, at the soccer field. That night, she watches him through a hole in the fence. He says goodbye to Marlene, opens the gate, and pushes his bicycle up the street. Wearing all black, Mishka's face is hidden under a hat. She follows him close without being noticed. As he rides slowly across the dark field, she runs up behind him. He hears her coming, looks back, and reaches for his machete. She removes her hat and points her pistol at him. She sees a red dot on his forehead. The feeling of revenge reminds her of an orgasm, so sweet she can taste it. No sense of pity, only to make him pay. She closes her eyes and fires, but hears nothing from the pistol. She opens her eyes and sees him still standing there, holding up his machete, chuckling, horns on his head. She kicks him in the groin, but not hard enough. His hands are around her neck, squeezing it, her feet dangles from the ground. She tries to fights back but she losing air, unable to scream. She gasps and then falls at his feet.

Brad shook her awake.

"Honey, are you okay?"

Heart still racing, her eyes glanced around the room.

"Why're you moaning," Brad said.

"I had a bad dream."

She rose and walked to the bathroom, sweating.

Next day, her phone vibrated in class. She looked at it and didn't recognize the number. The only person who called her from Jamaica was Sophia. She stepped outside to answer. The voice sounded familiar.

"Hey, Roxanne!" she said. "How you do?"

"I'm doing fine. How're you?"

"Good. Me see Miss Sophia downtown today an' she give me your number. Why you never tell me when you leavin' here? After all we been through together."

"I'm so sorry, Roxanne. It's a long story. We'll have to talk about it some other time."

"Alright. So you like it there?"

"Yes, thank you for talking me into coming. How bout you, what're you up to these days?"

"Oh Lord me have so much to tell you, but first let me tell you bout dirty Paul."

Mishka listened carefully.

"Christmas night, me go look for Mommy an' me sister them. After me leave an' walk back home, guess who stop me at ball field?"

"I already know, and what happened?"

"Im force me to go sleep with im, at this house im have near where me father live. Me tell im no. Im beat me up bad, tear off me clothes! Mishka, me put up a fight. After im let me go, im threaten me, say im know me an' you sell front roun Back Road, an' im go to tell Mommy bout it. She call me one day an' ask if it's true. Me tell her dancin' is all me do an' Paul is a fuckin liar."

"Did she believe you?"

"No, cause it come from her God, Paul."

"Do you know if he told Miss Marlene that I worked there too?"

"She don't say anything bout you workin' there, only me."

"I only ask because Mommy thinks I was only a bartender there, remember?"

"Yeh. After you leave here with Calvin, Paul see me one night an' ask where you gone with a man in a car. Me know you never comin' back so me tell im you gone to America. Why Paul ask bout you, Mishka? You sleep with im too?"

"Didn't have a choice."

"You don't have to say more. Me know how wicked im is. Im have to kill me first before me sleep with im again. Im do enough when me younger. If me have to die over it now, so be it."

"Roxanne, if you can avoid im, please, do it."

A beep interrupted the call.

"Me only have one minute left," Roxanne said.

"I'll see you again soon. I'm coming back to visit Mommy."

"Really? When?"

"After I graduate. I'll save your number and call back so we can talk more, okay?"

"Yeh, me keep yours too."

The line went dead.

She ran back to class. She sat in her seat, thinking. She grabbed her books and walked out. The more she heard about Paul, the more she wanted Sophia to get away from Jones Town. She wished she could speak with Brad about it, he always had answers, but he'd heard enough about Jamaica, where she grew up. She sat in her car in the parking lot and called Sophia.

"Hi, darlin'," Sophia said. "How you made out in the storm?"

"Lost everything from the first one. Another hurricane is on the way. It's supposed to hit tonight."

"Oh dear, you okay?"

"Yes, Mommy, fine. I want to tell you something, a confession."

"What kind of confession?"

"Remember when I was there and said I worked at the club as a bartender?"

"Yeh."

"I lied."

"Why?"

"Because I was a stripper."

"What you say to me!"

"I'm sorry."

Mishka sensed Sophia's sorrow.

"You there, Mommy?"

"See why me tell you to go to America with Calvin? Those are the things me didn't want you to do, because of needs and wants. Yeh, times did hard, but you know me wouldn't want you to do something like that. Any mother would feel bad to know that her daughter involve with go-go business."

"You shouldn't feel bad, Mommy. I didn't see anything wrong with helping my family. I'm glad I did."

"Me still proud of you," Sophia said. "It already happen, nothing me can do to change it now. You still me daughter, an' me glad you don't do it no more, right?"

"Right, Mommy."

Mishka went home, hiding her feelings. She felt horrible about having to confess to Sophia, but she felt better telling her now than to have her find out later. She asked Brad for a massage to relax her until she fell asleep.

They hunkered down and rode out the hurricane in their suite.

Not enough daylight around their schedule, Brad suggested they meet the appraiser over the weekend. Mishka rose at dawn on Saturday, prepared to help. The anonymous boat and tree were now gone, allowing them to labor freely. While Brad showed the insurer around, Mishka cleaned up the yard, picked up branches and leaves. Brad later came out to mow the lawn.

They went shopping for new carpet, paint, and furniture. Brad hired a crew of workers to do major repairs on the inside since he and Mishka were busy at their jobs during the week. Brad stopped by after work each day to see how things were going, and told Mishka about the progress.

"Things are slowly looking great at the house again,"

"Can't wait to see it."

"How're your classes coming along?"

"Glad you ask. I'm starting clinical during the week from eight to four, which means I'll only work on the weekends."

"Okay."

"It won't be for long."

"I'll support you."

She kissed him. "Thanks for understanding."

"You're evolving. I'm fine with it."

"The good part about it is, during the week, I'll get home before you do. We'll have a little more time together."

"Great."

"Oh, and guess what."

"What?"

"My dad's wife, Jackie, she left me a message today. She wants to know where to send a check, from my father's will."

"Did you give her your new address?"

"It was a busy day. I'll call her first thing in the morning."

"Do you mind if I ask how much?"

"Ten-thousand."

"Quite a bit."

"I'm going to send it to my mom to buy a house."

"I'm sure she'll be happy to get out of that dreadful place."

Jamaica Tough

They packed and checked out of the hotel. Mishka waved goodbye at the desk clerk on their way out. At the house, Brad handed her a key.

"Go ahead," he said. "Open it."

She took it and opened the door. Brad closed it behind them.

"Are you sure we're at the right address?"

"Yup."

She kicked off her sandals and walked into the living room where she noticed something on the wall.

"The painting—Starry Night!"

"For you."

She walked over and touched it.

"Brushstrokes and all. I can't believe you did that."

"A little house warming gift."

"I love the frame. Where'd you find it?"

"Let's just say through a friend, special ordered. C'mon, check out the bedroom."

She walked in and turned on the light.

"Three words: elegant, inviting, and warm."

"You picked it all out. Excellent taste."

"The carpet feels so soft under my feet."

She continued the tour, satisfied with her choice in style.

Chapter Twenty-four

One month later...

As the days and weeks went by, she developed an even stronger attraction for him. The sentiment of watching him go off to work in his suits, walking around in her underwear, brushing against him, seeing his soap in the shower, his shaving kit, cologne, seeing his body, the smells, the sounds, the constant closeness—it was quietly arousing.

Home early during the week, she spent her evening sweating in Brad's gym. It was her way to wind down after a tiring day. On the weekends, he went back to golfing with his mates. She grew tired of waiting around for him to return from his links. She picked up the phone and called Sophia.

"You soun' tired today," Sophia said.

"Just got in from work. Did you find a house yet?"

"Me go out to look at one this morning. Me like it."

"Is it the one?"

"It reasonable for the price, look good too."

"Location?"

"Portmore, Saint Catherine. It really nice. You an' Brad can stay here when you come to Jamaica."

"Good. How's my brother? Did he turn police chief yet?"

"Yes me dear, im finish police trainin' an' is workin' on the road, station right here in Jones Town. Im move out, live uptown with im girlfrien'. As a matter of fact she pregnant."

"I can't believe Ricardo grew up so fast, Mommy. I'm going to be an aunt."

"An' me a granny."

"How time flies."

"Me all alone here now but me proud of im."

"How often do you see him?"

"Not too often but im come her for food sometimes. Say im miss me cookin'."

"I haven't spoken to him in so long."

"Me tell im whenever you and I talk. Im know you doin' well."

When Brad walked in Mishka was lying on the sofa reading. He leaned over and kissed her.

"How was your day, hon?"

"Fine."

"Doesn't sound very exciting."

"Where've you been?"

"With my buddies."

"Did you have a good time?"

"Yes. It was good seeing them again."

"What'd you guys do all day?"

"Golf, talk, had a bite, I had a drink beer. Does that bother you?"

"Wish you were here when I got home."

"Oh, honey," he said walking away. "I'm here all day on Sundays. I make a point of it."

Next day, she came out of the shower and saw that she'd missed some calls from Sophia. She called back immediately.

"Me have some really bad news, Mishka."

"What?"

"Ricardo wake up Marlene early this morning, tell her say Roxanne dead."

She was unable to speak. The phone hit the floor. She heard Sophia's voice yelling through the receiver and picked it up.

"What happen to you, Mishka?"

"The phone fell. What happened to Roxanne?"

"Nobody know."

"Where was her body found?"

"Some children walkin' to school across the ball ground see the body an' call police."

"Where's Marlene?"

"She ask me to go with her to the morgue. We jus' now come back. She not so well at all.

Hard to lose a child."

"I want to talk to her."

"She gone home. Paul with her now."

"Did he go to the morgue?"

"No, only me an' Marlene."

"Did you see Roxanne's body?"

"Look like she fight off whoever kill her. Her fingernails break off an' her throat cut."

"Oh, no!"

"Something smell fishy, but it's police business now, not mine. Marlene an' me been friends now for plenty years. Me feel for what she go through. Me watch you an' Roxanne grow together. Now me will have to go to her funeral. Me feel it to me heart."

Brad walked in from work and changed out of his suit, waiting for Mishka to acknowledge his presence. She lay in bed facing the wall.

"Why so cold?" Brad said.

"Don't want to talk about it."

"Still upset about last weekend?"

"No."

"Come on let's talk about it."

She rolled over and faced him. "Remember my friend I told you about, Roxanne?"

"Yeah."

"She's dead."

He sat on the bed. "I'm sorry, Honey. Was she sick?"

"The asshole who raped me, I think he killed her."

"Why would you think that?"

"He's evil."

“Any rapist is evil but why do you think he killed her?”

“When we were in grade school she poisoned him after he fondled her. He raped her when we were in high school.”

“Wait a minute. He did it to her too, and neither one of you said anything?”

“I told you how things are in Jamaica, Brad.”

Chapter Twenty-five

One week later...

She had nightmares of her beloved friend, and about Paul coming after her too. She desperately wanted to attend Roxanne's funeral but to leave the country seemed impossible. She was almost finished with her degree and couldn't afford to miss a day of class. She wanted to believe that Paul wasn't the one who might've killed Roxanne, but how else would her body have ended up in No Man's Land? She wanted to speak with Ricardo to see how much he knew. She dreaded their conversation but he was her best source of information.

"Are you a part of the investigation, Ricardo?"

"Yeh."

"Who do you think did it?"

"Can't say yet, don't have enough evidence."

"How much longer before you'll know anything?"

"No tellin'. Things like this happen here every day, Sis. To tell you that we will find out who do it would be a lie."

"Was she raped?"

"Not as far as me know. Why you ask me that?"

"She's a female isn't she?"

"Yeh, but it sound to me like there's more to it why you ask that."

"Please don't start the police psyche now. I only want to know why someone would kill her."

"Me can't tell you that yet, still workin' on all the evidence."

"Hope you're doing all that you can to find out who did it."

"Homicides take a longer time to solve here. We have plenty of it to deal with, some still unsolved from years ago. Catching a murderer red-handed is what works in Jamaica an' we have to catch im good."

"Let's not talk about it anymore. Mommy tells me you're going to be a father, when is the baby due?"

"Supposed to be next few weeks."

"You might see me before the baby gets here."

Jamaica Tough

Saturday evening, Brad's car wasn't in the driveway when she arrived home. Inside, she dropped her bags at the door, opened up the house, and ordered pizza. She changed her clothes and took a bottle of water from the refrigerator before exercising.

Tired, she ate and then showered, still waiting for Brad to come home. She sat on the sofa and looked down at her feet—a pedicure was long overdue. She went for her kit and polished her toenails. Not long after, her cell phone rang. She answered—Brad.

"Honey," he said, his speech slurred. "I'm outside of the gentleman's club. Can you pick me up?"

"Are you kidding me? why the hell should I pick you up?"

"I don't want to get a ticket."

"Ask one of your great buddies to drive you home."

She ended the call. Her phone rang again.

"What?"

"They're not ready to leave yet."

"Then call a damn taxi."

"Honey, please, I'm tired. I want to come home."

"Where is it?"

"It's called Rachel's."

She fired up the computer and searched for Rachel's, after which she grabbed her keys and took off.

She found it, an off white building with palm trees out front, golden pillars at the entrance. Written in gold, the word *Rachel's* above the doorway. She circled the lot and found Brad's car. She parked next to it and honked. Startled, he sat up, climbed out, and opened the passenger door of her car. They took off.

"Thanks for coming, Honey."

"I'm really pissed at you." Her accent grew strong. "Wha' the hell you doin' in there? Is that where you've been playin' golf?"

"The guys wanted to watch the game there and have some steak and a beer."

"You mean to watch tits an' ass?"

"I didn't go there for that."

She parked in the driveway and left him in the car. He walked in behind her and sat on the sofa, took off his shoes.

"Try not to hate me, okay?"

"You didn't have the decency to call and say where you were or what you were doing. Guess it wasn't meant for me to find out."

He walked to the bedroom shedding his clothes. "I said I'm sorry."

She heard him climbing into bed.

"Are you coming in?"

She ignored him and walked to the kitchen for a Snicker bar. Before she finished eating it, she heard him snoring. She went for a blanket and pillow, and go comfortable on the sofa.

Next morning, she was awakened by the sound of the shower. She changed into her robe and made a cup of tea. Brad walked into the kitchen and kissed her on the cheek.

"Good morning," he said.

She walked passed him to the bedroom with her tea in her hand. He followed.

"Honey, I know I was wrong and I'm really sorry."

"You were disrespectful."

"Yes, you're right, and I'm sorry."

She turned and looked at him. "I don't know about other woman you've been with but it's not okay with me for you to go out to some bar or whatever that place is, to look at tits and ass. I take this relationship seriously and I won't tolerate that."

"The only tits and ass I give a damn about is yours. You know that."

"But did you think I'd be happy about you going there?"

"The guys and I are members there. Yesterday was my first time back since you and I met. I know it was wrong, I should've come home sooner, and again, I'm sorry."

"Is that a fetish for you men, to go out and look at other women's body?"

"Don't be silly. You know me better than that."

"I worked at a place like that back home. The men would come in every single night if they could."

"Wait a minute, you never told me that."

"Well now you know, and I hated it. I'm not saying you shouldn't see your friends, Brad, but I'm not at all comfortable with you going back to that place. You need to promise me you won't ever go back."

He held her cheeks and looked in her eyes. "I promise."

They sat together on the bed.

"When you were off on the weekends," he said, "We were always together. Now that you're doing this training thing I get a little bored watching you study all the time. I won't go back to Rachael's, I promise."

"The only thing you did right last night was not drive home but I'm not going to congratulate you for it."

She removed her robe and walked into the bathroom. Brad stood at doorway and watched her adjust the showerhead. She noticed him standing there, leaning against the door with his arms folded.

"Not now, if that's what you're thinking," she said, closing the curtain.

She dried herself and stepped out to see him lying on the bed, waiting for her to come out. She walked over to the dresser, stood before the mirror, and gently applied lotion to her bare skin. He leaned back on his elbows and watched with envy. She knew what was going through his mind.

Fully clothed, she gave him a lift to pick up his car, still a bit of tension lingering between them.

"Just so you know I won't be doing anything today except review for my exam tomorrow morning."

"Is that it for your program?"

"Yes."

"You know, Honey, you are pretty tough. I'd better be careful from now on."

"Tough for the right reasons."

"Look, don't worry about doing anything today. I'll whip something up for dinner and wash whatever laundry we might have. How about I quiz you later in preparation for your big exam?"

"That'll help. Thank you."

Chapter Twenty-six

Three day later…

She rose long before Brad's alarm sounded. She sweetened her tea and turned on the television before beginning her morning exercise. Her mind was finally free from her studies. Jogging on the treadmill, she thought about the possibility of ever seeing justice for Roxanne. Paul was crafty. He wouldn't have left behind any evidence to connect him to the murder. If anyone saw or heard anything in Jones Town they'd never tell.

Brad walked in with his coffee suited for his morning workout.

"You're full of energy today," he said.

They kissed.

"Thank you for last night," she said.

"No, thank you."

She picked up the boxing gloves and asked Brad to secure them around her wrists. She stood firmly before the punching bag and threw some blows.

"I'm taking a vacation from work to go to Jamaica."

"When?" he said, clunking the machine.

"As soon as I purchase the ticket."

"Do you need some money?"

"No, I have some. I'm going to look for tickets later."

"I'd love to go with you but I have a trial coming up."

"It's fine. We can go together another time."

"Sophia will be happy to see you again."

They stopped to rest. "Do you think I should tell Ricardo about the last time Roxanne and I spoke?"

"Absolutely. It's the right thing to do. Look at it this way, Hon—if there's no witness or real evidence that Paul committed the murder, he'll walk scot-free, right?"

"I guess."

"So if you do say something and all else fails, then at least you tried."

"Should I tell Ricardo what Paul did to me?"

"Would it help you? "

"Who knows."

"You hardly have a case. It would be your word against his. I don't know the statute of limitation in Jamaica. You should ask Ricardo. Be careful what you say, it might cause him do something he'll regret. I'd wanna kill the bastard."

"I doubt I'll want to press charges at this point, but I need to tell Ricardo what I know about Roxanne."

"He'd have to report it. It will put him in an awkward position if the law's the same as here. I guess what I'm saying is think carefully about that issue before saying anything. I'll see what I can find out about the laws there."

They showered together before Mishka watched him go off to work.

Chapter Twenty–seven

One week later…

When Mishka learned she passed her exam, she wasn't in the frame of mind to celebrate. She felt a sense of self-worth, but had a difficult time showing it. She was still boggled by Roxanne's death. When Brad walked in she told him about her exam results.

"You did good!" he said, hugging her. "The best nurse a patient will ever have."

"You're way too kind."

He gave her a big kiss. "Proud of you. Sophia will be too. Did you tell her yet?"

"Not yet."

"You should. It'll make her day."

"Pretty soon I'll have to start thinking about a new job. Can't wait."

"You shouldn't have a problem finding one now that you're in the medical field."

She called Sophia to get an update on the new house.

"Ricardo say im will help me move in this weekend."

"Are you satisfied with the place?"

"It need minor fixin', but me can take care of that later. You will see when you come. Me like the neighborhood, mostly workin' class people."

"Glad you like it."

"Me really thank you for help me, Mishka, an' me happy bout how you keep your head high. Me thank God every day that you listen to me an' leave here with Calvin, see now, you go back to school an' make something of yourself. Look how we used to laugh at Ricardo when im say that im would turn police. Im really do it an' make me proud too. Sometimes me can't believe it. Look where we come from."

After Brad went off to work next morning Mishka fired up the computer and researched rape statistics in Jamaica. *According to the police commissioner's office, at least one woman was raped every 12 hours—two per day. The numbers also revealed that for that year, there were 606 reported cases of rape.* She knew there were countless others lost in silence.

She knew that the day would come for her to return home, but the circumstances had suddenly changed. It was more than to fulfill her promise to Sophia, Mishka needed to know exactly what happened to Roxanne. If Paul was for sure the culprit, Mishka wanted him to pay. Besides her secret mission, she looked forward to hugging Sophia again.

Three days later, Brad drove her to the airport. They sat together in a restaurant until it was time to board her flight.

"This is our first time apart," she said, holding his hand.

"I'll miss having you home. I'll have to find a Jamaican restaurant while you're gone.

"No Rachel's."

He smiled. "That means you better get back here soon."

"Two weeks will go by before you know it."

He reached into his pocket and took out his wallet. "Here's some cash to take with you."

"You don't have to do that. I have enough cash."

"Extra cash might come in handy if you have an emergency and can't reach me right away."

She took it. "Let's hope I won't have an emergency."

He later kissed her and waved goodbye.

As the plane sat on the runway, she thought about how far she'd come, from such humble beginnings, the challenges she'd overcome, the man she'd fallen in love with. Then she remembered Paul. The plane took off, jolting her from her thought.

Finally in Kingston, she waited anxiously for her luggage. Watching the people move about, no doubt she was home—the dialect—the smiling faces of those who were returning home. Outside, the atmosphere was humid. The air still. People waited patiently, looking in to see if their loved ones were coming out. Sophia saw Mishka first, shouted her name, beaming, waving. Mishka waved back. Tracy, Ricardo, and his pregnant girlfriend were with Sophia. Mishka walked faster as a man pulled her luggage on a trolley. She took the handle of her suitcase and thanked him.

"Five dollah," he said, stretching out his hand.

She hesitated, and then pointed at his uniform. "Don't you work here to help passengers?"

He shrugged his shoulder. "You know how it go here."

She handed him a tip and rushed into Sophia's arms. Sophia squeezed her. It felt the same, still her mother's baby. Sophia held Mishka's shoulder and looked her over.

"You turn into a sweet young lady." She squeezed Mishka again. "Me so glad to see you!"

Tracy came over and hugged Mishka. "I heard you finished school, congrats."

Mishka noticed Ricardo and his girlfriend waiting to be greeted. She reached up and hugged her brother.

"When did you get so tall?" she said.

He introduced his girlfriend to Mishka. "Dalia," he said. "Me soon to be wife."

"Sure there's only one baby in there?" Mishka said.

Everyone laughed.

"Wouldn't be surprise if there's more," Dalia said.

They chattered and walked to where Mishka would pick up her rental car.

Inside, she saw her family through the glass door standing in the waiting area. Dalia sat on a chair and rested her swollen ankles. When Ricardo glanced in at Mishka, she used her hand to call him inside. He walked in and stood next to her.

"Problem gettin' the car?"

She drew closer to him. "Me know this isn't a good time, but we need to talk, in private."

"Me supposed to go to work later on, but me come by the house tomorrow, roun two o'clock."

She later said her goodbyes and departed with Sophia. Mishka began to focus on the traffic. She looked over and saw that Sophia's grin was still there.

"You drive good, though," Sophia said.

"Brad taught me."

"Maybe you can teach me one day."

"I will. Gosh, the roadways here look so narrow."

"Drive slow an' take your time. Pure mad people drive down here an' the road bad. Don't know what the government do with tax payer money, them need to use it to fix the pot hole."

Downtown Kingston, she drove slowly and cautiously. Buses and cars were stopping and going, people ambled across the street without looking, and sidewalks were lined with vendors.

"Wait here let me go buy patty," Sophia said.

"Beef for me."

"You want to call Brad meantime?"

"I'll call him later."

"No, call im now. Let im know you reach alright."

"It's okay Mom. I'll call later."

Approaching the causeway, Mishka saw a newly constructed toll booth. Different than what she remembered from her trips to the Back Road.

"When did they start collecting from people to come cross the bridge, Mommy?"

"Bout a year after you leave here. You have to pay every time you go through, back an' forth. Smaller vehicle pay less. Bus and truck pay more. From them start to collect everything raise—taxi fare, bus fare. Lord, them kill we poor people every which way we turn."

Sophia's new home sat on a quiet road, a green mountain ahead. Pleased, Mishka parked and observed the neighborhood.

"Let me open the gate for you," Sophia said, getting out of the car.

She waved at the neighbor across the street. Mishka drove in and parked the car next to an enclosed verandah. She dragged her luggage inside and walked through. It was clean and nicely furnished. The smell of paint still lingered in the air. Sophia showed Mishka to the room she'd prepared for her. Mishka opened the curtains and unpacked her things.

She rose early next morning to take Sophia to work, giving her a break from the packed buses and taxis. On her first day alone, Mishka visited sites she remembered—Hope Gardens—Devon House. She reminisced about her Sunday outings here with Roxanne. The memories became unbearable. She looked at her watch and recalled her meeting with Ricardo. She later hurried back across the causeway.

When she arrived home, she ate lunch and waited on the verandah. Minutes later, she saw Ricardo parking his car at the gate. He walked onto the verandah, removed his firearm from its holster, and sat on a chair. He greeted Mishka.

"Mommy have any food in there?"

"Leftovers. Hungry?"

"Didn't have time to stop for lunch today."

They walked inside.

"Take off your shoes," she said. "You know Mommy don't like boot marks in her house."

He took them off and sat down at the kitchen table. She proceeded toward the stove.

"Place quiet," he said, looking around. "So what you want to see me bout?"

"Roxanne."

"Wha' bout her?"

"Anything on the case yet?"

He scratched his head. "Well, the coroner say that im see a piece of skin residue under her fingernail. We're goin' to have it tested for DNA. That will take some time, if they even find anything at all."

She set the plate in front of him and took a seat at the table. "Found anything suspicious at the crime scene?"

"Went there twice but didn't find anything but blood."

"Why you think someone would kill her, Ricardo?"

"Your guess is as good as mine. Her throat cut deep, some kind of big blade. Why someone want her dead, me couldn't tell you."

"I think Paul did it."

He choked on his rice. She handed him a glass of water. He took a sip and cleared his throat.

"Me a police an' live here. How you know who kill Roxanne?"

"She told me that she had a fight with Paul, he wanted to rape her again. That was a short time before she died."

"Rape her again? Wha' you talk about?"

"When Roxanne and I were growing up Paul raped her. That's why she left and went to live with her father. My gut tells me he killed her. Everyone loved Roxanne, Ricardo, you know that!"

Ricardo stopped eating and wiped his mouth on a napkin.

"But we need more than gut feelin'." He leaned back in the chair and folded his arms. "You know, me used to like Roxanne. After you left here she an' I were together, but when me find out she was a go-go it change me mind. We remain friends, though."

"How'd you know she was a go-go?"

"Marlene come cry to Mommy bout it one night. Mommy say…" he paused. "You never see smoke without fire."

"What?"

"Mommy say something to me same night. She say Paul tell Marlene that Roxanne was a whore somewhere over the Back Road. You know anything bout it?"

"We danced. Me don't know anything bout her workin' as a prostitute."

"You used to dance too?"

"Yes."

He shook his head and stroked his beard. "When me hear that she die me couldn't believe it. The first thing that come to mind is that she either get caught-up in a cross fire or somebody rob her. When me look at the scene it didn't make sense. She still have plenty money in her purse, no sign of gun play. Me go back to the scene alone afterwards, look for condom, spent shell —couldn't find a pin. What me know though is that she really have it out with a man. She resist for some reason an im kill her."

"Paul killed her, Ricardo. He did it! He keeps a cutlass with him all the time, under im bicycle."

"How you know that?"

"Don't matter how. You know me wouldn't lie to you bout something like this. He killed her."

Ricardo was quiet, thinking.

"Me *can* see Paul doin' something like that yes, but not to Roxanne. Im there with Marlene the whole time, come to the funeral, hold on to Marlene when she couldn't let go off the casket."

"Where was she buried?"

"Calvary Cemetery."

"I want to go there."

She and Ricardo walked out to his car. He lit a cigarette.

"You smoke?" she said.

"If you have to do my job you would too."

"Let me have one."

She lit it and rolled down her window.

"I remember how badly you wanted to become a policeman," she said. "I get the feeling you aren't so happy about it after all."

"Frustrated. The crime is out of control an' the biggest problem we have out here is the corruption in the department."

"Maybe you went in there with your expectation too high."

He let out a sarcastic laugh. "That boy Paul."

"Wha'?"

"If im really kill Roxanne im deserve to hang from the highest tree."

"Stop here so I can get some flowers."

At the cemetery, Ricardo led Mishka where Roxanne was put to rest. Mishka replaced the withered flowers with fresh ones. Sensing Roxanne's spirit, she sat quietly on the grass and read the words inscribed on the headstone—*Roxanne Hope Mckenzie—February 26th 1984-July 4th 2007—R.I.P.* Under that: *My body lies peacefully, but my soul lives on.* In an instant Mishka drew in a startled breath. She remembered the scent, the perfume Roxanne wore when they worked at Paradise. She glanced around to make sure she wasn't losing her mind. Roxanne wasn't there.

Ricardo heard her sobbing and helped her to her feet. On their way to the airport Mishka asked Ricardo for another cigarette and lit it. Before travelling to Jamaica Roxanne's death felt surreal, but now that Mishka visited the cemetery, touched the headstone, she was more determined than before to make Paul pay.

"Paul's been messing around with children for a long time," she said. "Me sure it's not only me and Roxanne."

Ricardo jammed on the brakes. "Wha' you say!"

"That is how me know bout the cutlass. He put it to my neck like he would slice it, take me to a house and pull a gun on me when I try to run. Then he raped me."

Mishka's words were like a scar disfiguring Ricardo's face. His mouth was pursed shut, his jaw clenched tight. With his hands around the staring wheel tightly he sits forward, and through clenched teeth he said, "Me mus' kill im bomboclat."

Mishka was suddenly forced back in her seat. She fastened her seatbelt. "Slow down!"

"Im fuck with me family, im fuck with me. Me show that coward pussy something."

"No way, Ricardo. That's a way ticket to prison."

They were approaching a red light. Her safety belt saved her from hitting the windshield.

"You ever see police kill anybody here an' go to prison?"

She looked at him. "How you expect to use the government's gun to murder someone and not be investigated?"

"This is Jamaica. Plenty ways roun' that."

"Oh yeh? You mean to commit suicide before you get sentence?"

He chuckled. "Look like you been gone too long. This is not America. Things run different here."

"I'm sure there are a few policemen left with a little integrity."

"Yeh? Show me one."

"Oh, Lord, why didn't I listen to Brad and not tell you any of this?"

"Walk a day in my shoes, deal with mother-fuckers like Paul an' then tell me how much integrity you have left."

"If you've lost it because of what you do for a living it's time to consider a new career."

"Maybe you right. Me feel the same way when me partner take out a young youth, happen right in front me eyes."

"What you talkin' about?"

"Kill the youth dead. First week on the job."

"Why did he kill him?"

"Can't talk bout it."

"You think I'm goin' to tell someone? Or is it because it was a cold-blooded murder?"

He became serious. "Drop the subject."

"Did you have something to do with it, Ricardo?"

"Me say drop it."

"If you did nothing wrong why is it such a mystery?"

"Police business."

"I'm no police, but I am your sister."

He hesitated. "Don't say a word to no one, hear me?"

She raised her right hand. "To me grave."

"The brother who train me is a veteran in the force. We go on the road one mornin', im tell me that a young youth, bout nineteen, was involve in a shootout and im goin' to arrest im. We track the youth, go to three different location, couldn't find im. Me partner make a call an' find out where the youth rest, a house in Spanish Town. Me take up the radio to call the Spanish Town division to let them go an' arrest the youth. Me partner stop me, say im want to go an' get the youth. When we reach there an' park the jeep outside, im tell me to take out me gun an' get ready, cause the youth might be strap. When we go inside the house, the youth lie cross the bed, talk on a phone. Me partner ask im to hang it up an' show im hands. Im get up, show im hands, an' ask what im do wrong. Me partner ask bout the shootout an' the youth admit to it, say it was self-defense, even tell we where to find the gun. Me partner find the gun, tell im to sit on the floor, an' shot im—three to the chest.

"Are you serious?"

"After the youth fall to the floor me partner check im pulse, say im dead. Me get fraid now, cause me think we have to cover the scene."

"So what else you do then?"

"When me ask im wha' we do im say nothing, procedure say we mus' carry the body to the nearest hospital so doctor can pronounce it. Me start to vomit when we pick up the body, drop it on the ground."

"I've heard enough, and please tell me you didn't let im get away with it."

"I was under the premise that as police we must cover for each other no matter what. After we back to the station an' write up the report, im tell the squad at the station what happen, it was like a celebration, fist bump and all. One of the corporal say to me, "You train with the best. Hope you learn something today." Me go home that night an' ask meself if me should jus' forget bout goin' back."

"Where's your partner now?"

"America, im left bout two weeks after it happen."

"What was his motive for killing the young man? I'm sure he had to report to someone."

"The usual, the youth had a gun an' point it, so he had to protect us."

"What a damn shame, an' shame on you too! How can you see that happen and not tell the truth? That's someone's child."

"That's something me still struggle with internally. Me get to understan' say me can't change the corruption that inoculate the force. The horse done gone through the gate. Every man who work as police in Jamaica know how things work. If you “upset the apple cart”, as you Americans would say, your life is in jeopardy. Protect yourself is the motto here, it also mean to keep your stripes, at all cost.”

“Wait, so the police kill the young man, fabricate the report, and then migrate to America. Was the case under investigation?”

“Supposed to, but people here don’t rely on investigation. Once a person die here that’s it, after the funeral life go back to normal for everybody. Investigation take years an’ nothing will come of it anyway.”

“But how can your partner leave the island after killin’ someone without a proper and complete investigation?”

“Im can leave once there is no charge at the time. But the investigators tip im off, tell im it was best if im leave the island because the dead man relative come here from America, them threaten to hire lawyer for independent investigation.”

“I knew all along that the system here is fucked up, but not to this extent.”

“Back to Paul now.”

"I can't condone what you want to do to im. You don't want anyone's blood on your hands. The best way to get im back is to make his life miserable, like he did mine, Roxanne. Jamaica doesn't have the death penalty anymore, does it?"

"Not since 1988. The chamber rusty."

"Good. So he'll rot in prison if we can find a way to get him there."

They made it to the airport in time to see Sophia walking through the door.

"Mommy knows what Paul do to you?"

"No."

Sophia sat in the back seat of the car and looked at Ricardo and Mishka.

"Why you two together? Where you come from?"

"Calvary," Mishka said.

"Lord have mercy!" She glared at Ricardo. "You couldn't wait till she settle here before you take her there?"

"I wanted to go, Mommy," Mishka said. "Ricardo does a better job drivin' here, so I asked him to take me."

They took off.

Mishka began to miss Brad dearly. She and Sophia lay awake catching up on their time apart. Mishka talked about her new life in the States and told Sophia all about Brad.

"Me like how im treat you," Sophia said. "You don't deserve nothing less."

"You're right, but let me tell you, he isn't perfect."

When Mishka told the story of Brad's night at Rachel's, they both had a good laugh.

"Show me someone perfect," Sophia said, "Me show you the good Lord Himself. After Calvin die me worry bout you till me sick. Me glad you meet somebody who love an' care bout you. Hope you get married soon an' give me some pretty grandchildren."

"We haven't talked about marriage yet, Mom."

"What if im ask you?"

"After I make sure he's the one there should be no reason not to say yes."

"You think im will ever cheat on you, Mishka?"

"I don't believe so, but sometimes men don't need a reason to cheat."

"Me glad you know. Take your time with the relationship before im get you pregnant, though."

"Am I too young for him, Mommy?"

"My honest advise is that if you two love each other an' see a future, happiness should be all that matter. If you happy, don't fret bout what anyone else think. Live your life and be happy. Me see the good Lord behind it. Im soon marry you."

"Mom," she said, firmly. "If it's meant to be it'll happen in due time."

"Me pray bout it."

"Never knew I would ever love or trust again."

"Somebody break your heart before?"

"No, not really."

Sunday morning, Ricardo and Dalia accompanied Mishka and Sophia to the famous Dunn's River Falls. When they arrived, Mishka looked around and realized there were only a church group of Jamaicans, everyone else were tourists. There seemed to be an enormous gap between the ritzy attraction and the inner cities. Sophia and Dalia were checking out the craft vendors. Mishka looked across the way and saw Ricardo sitting alone on a rock at the bottom of the falls. She persuaded him to go for a climb. He gave in and took her hand. The tourists were already well on their way to the pinnacle of the falls. Not long on their climb Ricardo began to speak.

"Me have Paul in custody at the station."

Mishka stopped. "You find something on im?"

"Me lock im up for possession of ganja, have im bicycle at the station."

"You find the cutlass?"

"No, but me see some type of home-made case under the seat. Im wash it clean."

"Im carry a cutlass, Ricardo. Me tell you, a cut-off one."

"Me believe you, but me hands tie now cause me don't have nothing else yet."

"Wha' we do now?"

"Me goin' to stall the paperwork, but me can't keep im at the lock-up for more than a week before im see judge."

"Then what?"

"Im will pay a fine and walk."

"That's it?"

"It was only half-ounce. When we go back to Town me goin' to interrogate im bout Roxanne."

"Don't count on a confession. Make sure you have a plan B."

They resumed their steep trek up the rocky falls.

"Me talk to Marlene last night," he said, "Ask if she know why Roxanne move to live with her father. She claim she don't know but me don't believe her."

"If she know why is it she stay with Paul?"

"Fear. Anyway, me think you should tell her bout what you an' Roxanne talk bout over the phone recently."

"You mad! You tell her. You're the police."

"She'll take it better from you. Maybe she will remember something Paul do or say right after the murder."

"No. Don't think me can do it, Ricardo. Next thing you know she tell Paul I'm here. Sorry, can't do that."

"Let's climb this mountain and then find something to eat. Me let you know what me find out after me talk to Paul later."

On their way home, Mishka sat in the back seat of the car with Dalia, thinking about her conversation with Ricardo. She would've done anything to help him solve the murder, but talking to Marlene wasn't a part of the plan.

Marlene was too close to Paul and Mishka didn't want him to know that she was on the island.

Dalia asked Ricardo to stop the car. "Me pee-pee on myself," she said.

Everyone laughed. Mishka turned on the light and looked down at the seat. "Good, you didn't get any on me."

"Pull over here, Ricardo," Dalia said.

She stepped out and soon realized it wasn't urine. Her water broke!

They rushed back inside. Ricardo sped off. Dahlia held her tummy and began to holler.

"Mishka!" Sophia said. "Take care of her back there. You're a big nurse now."

"Everything will be fine, Dalia," Mishka said, hoping desperately she wouldn't have to help deliver a baby in back seat of the car.

Chapter Twenty–eight

Three days later…

Honored to have named Ricardo's baby girl, Mishka thought that Chelsea was absolutely adorable. She looked forward to meeting her niece during her visit but witnessing the birth was special. After taking Sophia to work Mishka visited with Dalia, taking over the household chores while Dalia caught up on sleep. Rocking and feeding Chelsea was the most peaceful moment she'd ever had. She thought about what Chelsea might become, and was confident that Ricardo would do everything to protect his daughter. But would it be enough to shelter her from the Pauls of the world.

Dalia woke up and walked into the nursery.

"Ricardo say you mus' meet im right now, New Kingston."

Mishka handed over Chelsea and hurried out the door.

At a restaurant, she sipped a Ting and waited for Ricardo to arrive. He later walked in found her. They sat in a corner of the restaurant. She studied his eyes from across the table. He removed his hat and placed it on his lap.

"Paul deny everything but me have some good news."

"What's the good news?"

"Me go back an' talk to Marlene this mornin'. She take me inside the house an' show me something."

"What?"

"Blood stains on her white rug, from the bottom of Paul's shoes."

She leaned closer. "Really?"

"Me take the shoes to the lab to get it tested."

"When did she first see it?"

"She say the day after Roxanne die."

"So she know the whole time?"

"Yeh, but she hide it from Paul. Me ask her if she believe im have anything to do with it."

"And?"

"She say deep in her belly she believe it."

"Same thing me tell you."

A waitress came over and took Ricardo's order.

"You want anything?" he asked Mishka.

"No, thanks."

They were alone again.

"Now that we don't have a confession what good is it to question Paul after all?"

"Me know as well as you that im would lie. The body language is what me want to see. Im look frighten when me ask point blank if im kill Roxanne."

"Wait, educate me a little bout this interrogation process. What you look for in body language?"

"Im stammer when me ask bout im whereabouts the night of the murder, im couldn't sit still, palms close an' turn down on the table. A person who innocent don't act guilty."

"You ask Marlene where Paul was the night Roxanne die?"

"She say im show up at her house close to 2am, but im tell me 9pm."

"Im kill Roxanne, Ricardo. Me can bet me life on it."

"Me do all me can mon, don't worry. Im beg me for a cigarette when me question im. Me keep the butt to send to the lab."

"I have to admit, Ricardo. I am a little worried about you now that he knows you're on to him. He's a fuckin snake, and he'll be back on the street in no time."

"Don't fret, Sis. Me watch im like a hawk. A hawk can kill a snake, have im for lunch."

"What you think will happen when he finds out Marlene talk to you."

"If im got nothing to hide there shouldn't be a problem if Marlene talk to the police bout who might murder her daughter."

She glanced at her watch. "Shit! I have to go pick up Mommy."

At a stoplight, through the corner of her eye, Mishka caught a glimpse of a black car next to her. She turned her head. It was the car that brought her home the night she was raped. She saw Paul's friend behind the wheel. Their eyes met. She looked away, reached for her sunglasses, and rolled up her window. The light turned green. She sped down the boulevard. Through her rare view, the car turned slowly onto a street. She hurried to the airport.

Chapter Twenty-nine

Two days later…

She overheard Sophia on the phone giving Marlene direction to where she lived. Rather than showing any concern, Mishka analyzed Sophia's behavior and waited to see if she'd say something about Marlene. Before dusk, Mishka heard a knock at the front door and peeked through the curtain. Surprised to see Marlene with her two daughters, Mishka hurried to the door. Marlene stood in the doorway, one side of her face swollen. Sophia led her inside to the settee, her pre-teen daughters just behind her. Sophia sat next to them.

"Why Paul beat you up so bad, Marlene?"

"Im vex cause Ricardo come talk to me again bout Roxanne."

"Wha' you mean Ricardo come talk to you again?"

"Im think Paul kill Roxanne."

"Oh Lord!" Sophia said. "Mishka, get Ricardo on the phone for me now."

"For what?"

"Me don't want no trouble between im an' Paul, me want to talk to im now!"

"Ricardo is a grown man, Mommy, he's doin' his job."

"Paul come home from jail this morning vex'," Marlene said. "Somebody tell im that Ricardo talk to me. Im beat me over it, call me informer. Im say if me talk to Ricardo again im kill me. Me don't have nowhere else to go, Sophia."

She wept into her hands.

Sophia looked at Mishka in disbelief. Mishka looked back at her as if she, too, was stunned. Marlene's daughters held her but they didn't shed a tear. It broke Mishka's heart for the girls to see Marlene in such sorrow. She wanted to take them for a ride but she didn't want to miss any of the information.

"Paul?" Sophia said, "Kill Roxanne?"

"Me confuse," Marlene said, wiping her eyes. "Me can't understan' why Paul want to hurt me baby."

Sophia folded her arms and gazed across the room. "Me don't know what to think, Marlene."

Mishka sat quietly. She needed to tell Ricardo what was happening. She contemplated meeting with him but the thought of going out alone brought her fear.

"I'm goin' to talk to Brad, Mommy," she said, opening the front door.

She sat in her car and called Ricardo instead. "Marlene jus' show up here all black and blue!"

"Me see when she walk past the police station. Didn't think she come back anytime soon with that bag over her shoulder."

"Paul beat her for talkin' to you, and now that she's here we all in danger!"

"Keep cool, Sis. Me can't talk bout it right now. Me come see you in the morn."

Peeved, Mishka sat in the car pondering. She picked up the phone to call Brad. No, she thought, better to let him enjoy life with his buddies. What he doesn't know won't hurt him. She became paranoid—she'd seen Paul's friend at the stoplight, now Marlene was at Sophia's. Perhaps by now Paul knew that Mishka was in town. The thought of hiding in a hotel room seemed to be the ideal solution, at least until the dust settles, but what about her mother? Should she uproot Sophia from the comfort of her home to hide from Paul?

After thinking it through, Mishka decided that the time had come for her to fight. She wouldn't run and hide anymore, not now. Then a thought hit her—the firearm she'd hidden before leaving Jamaica. But what if someone found it or a mongrel dog dug it up? Maybe it was still there wrapped in the plastic sack just the way she'd left it.

Sophia startled Mishka with a knock on the window. Mishka climbed out of the car and walked inside. Marlene was still sitting on the settee, frozen and traumatized. The girls were at the table eating. Mishka sat beside Marlene and hugged her.

"You should try an' get some sleep, Miss Marlene. You look tired."

"Weeks now me can't sleep, Mishka. Roxanne is all me think bout."

Mishka rubbed Marlene's back. "Please don't start cryin' again, Miss Marlene. It's goin' to be okay."

Marlene raised her hands toward the ceiling and cried harder. "Help me, God!"

Sophia brought blankets from her bedroom and made a cot on the carpet for the girls.

"You can sleep in my room tonight, Miss Marlene," Mishka said. "Me stay out here with the children."

Later, with everyone in bed, Mishka place a bottle of water and a large metal spoon into her handbag. She picked up her keys and walked back to Sophia's bedroom.

"Soon come back, Mommy."

"It's eleven o'clock now. Where you goin' so late?"

"Eleven o'clock isn't late on a Friday night in Jamaica."

"Mishka, me know you a grown woman now, you haven't been here in a long time, careful drivin' out there. Don't pick up no one in your car, lock your doors."

"I won't be long. Wait up for me."

Driving back across the bridge, Mishka saw a full moon ahead. If the pistol was gone she'd have to come up with another plan. Perhaps she could pay Norman a visit. Closer to Jones Town and into Paul's territory, her heart palpitated. She rolled up her windows and turned off the stereo. She drove past Nathan's house. He stood on the corner talking to a young lady. Mishka didn't stop. As she drove onto other streets, residents glared at the strange car driving through their neighborhood. No sign of Paul yet.

At her old house, she parked out front and checked her rear view before slinging her bag over her shoulder. She locked up the car, peered up and down the street, and went inside. She closed the gate behind her. Everything looked the same. It was dark, but the street light was bright enough to help her see where she was going. It was really quiet. She heard the water dripping in the outdoor shower. The property appeared vacant. She headed for the tree. She recalled burying the pistol between the tree and the fence that bordered Marlene's yard. She looked for the rock that marked the spot. It was still there! She took a step back and surveyed the area carefully before rolling away the rock. From across the fence she heard the dim sound of a TV. Paul must be there watching it. She stooped, removed the water bottle from her bag and poured it on the packed ground. She then reached for the spoon and began digging. She felt a fingernail snap, a sharp pain. Not much deeper to go, she touched something smooth, there it was, the plastic bag. She gasped in relief, yanked it out, and shook off the dirt. Her hands were muddied, her finger hurting.

She covered the shallow hole and looked around to make sure the coast was still clear. The sack felt light. She opened it and looked, catching a glint of silver in the moonlight. When she got up from the hole, she heard the gate open. A man walked in. Paul! No, wait. He didn't move like Paul. Her heart settled. She'd been scared almost out of her shorts. The man began to sing. He hadn't noticed her. She waited quietly behind the tree until he walked by. The faint sound of the TV was still there. The new tenant didn't go inside. He sat on the stoop and lit a cigarette. She waited. It seemed hours until he flicked the glowing butt away. He stood, stretched, and walked toward the fence. Had he seen her? She shifted away from where she stood. At the fence, he opened his pants, pulled out his thing, and began to pee. Her eyes were closed. It took him a long time to finish. She heard his zipper. In a moment she opened her eyes. He was gone. She heard the house door creak open and slam shut. A light came on inside. Time for her to make her break. She hurried through the gate and to her car. As she searched her bag for her keys, she turned and saw the man standing at the gate, bearded, about middle-age.

"So you the driver of this vehicle, with rental plate. Me wonder who park in front me place."

Mishka thought quickly. "Ah, sir, do you know a lady who lives inside there by the name Sophia?"

"She move, mon. Me live here now."

"Oh. I lost her number and since I'm in the area I wanted to stop and see her. Didn't know she moved."

"Yeh, mon, she gone, but where you were jus' now? Me look roun, don't see no one."

"I parked here and walked to the shop to buy something."

"You talk like American. What's your name?"

She had unlocked the door and opened it. "Grace," she said, getting in.

She took a deep breath, felt sweat under her arms. When she drove past the police station where Ricardo worked, her heart settled.

Across the causeway, she wanted to ensure that the pistol was still in operating order, and needed to test it. She veered left toward the Back Road and parked at the beach.

No one there, only the sound of waves. Bag in hand, she kicked off her sandals and walked onto the sand. Cautiously, she removed the pistol from her handbag, and felt for the safety. It was still on. With the tail of her blouse, she wiped it clean, released the magazine. The rounds were still there. She put the magazine back in place, disengaged the safety, and located the trigger. She raised her hand above her head and fired. Needing no more confirmation, she engaged the safety and placed the pistol into her handbag. She ran across the sand to the car and drove home.

The girls were fast asleep. In the kitchen, she cleaned Sophia's spoon and put it back in its place. She washed the grit off her hands and wrists, noticing some on her blouse, she dabbed it with the kitchen towel. After examining her ruined fingernail, she splashed water on her face, wiped it dry, and walked back to her bedroom. Marlene lay wide awake.

"Need anything?" Mishka said.

"The only thing me need is Roxanne."

Mishka walked over to her suitcase and reached into the pocket.

"This is Benadryl," she said, handing it to Marlene. "I took one on the plane. It'll help you sleep."

Marlene sat up. "How long it make me sleep for?"

"Roughly eight hours. It won't knock you unconscious or anything. You'll feel drowsy at first, but it will help you sleep. Let me go and get you some water."

Marlene swallowed them and lay back down. Mishka pulled the covers over Marlene's shoulder and shut the door behind her.

Checking the doors to make sure they were locked, she thought of a place to hide the pistol. There were too many people around. The safest place was in her bag. She went to Sophia's bedroom for a blanket.

"You come back quick," Sophia said.

"I told you so."

Mishka kissed Sophia on the forehead. "Night, Mom."

She turned off the lights and checked the doors again.

Before lying down, she placed the bag on the floor beside her, edging it slightly under the settee. Feeling safer, she covered up and looked down at Roxanne's sisters sleeping, beautiful girls. She wondered if Paul had already corrupted them.

Chapter Thirty

Hours later...

Mishka woke up to the sound of utensils and voices in the kitchen. She slid her hand under the settee and felt her handbag, brought it with her to the restroom to wash up before having breakfast. Marlene had slept, but still looked weary. After breakfast, Mishka drove Sophia to the airport. In the car, Mishka looked over at her mother, a woman who'd worked hard over the years just to stay afloat. Mishka saw the years of hardship on Sophia's face, bags under her eyes.

"Do you have someone in your life, Mom?"

"Me children."

"What about a gentleman?"

"Don't have time for that."

"Everyone likes to have a companion. I don't remember ever seeing a man around."

"You know, it's funny you ask."

"Why?"

"Before you born, me leave home early to live with Calvin because my father used to molest me."

Mishka glanced at her. "Oh, Mommy."

"You're a grown woman now so me can tell you. My father was the first man for me. After me move out, me get pregnant with you, an' then Ricardo. When Calvin left, me vow say me want to be alone. Me don't have good luck with men. It don't bother me at all. The only thing me wish for is that you an' me live closer, an' you give me some pretty grandchildren."

"Is that why you never talk about your father?"

"Yes."

Mishka found it sad that Sophia had little hope of finding love. She hugged Sophia goodbye and watched her walk in to work.

Back at the house, Mishka saw Marlene waiting on the verandah with her daughters and her bags. Mishka reached for her handbag and stepped out of the car.

"You can give me a ride home?"

"Why're you leaving, Miss Marlene?"

"Im call me, say im sorry an' im don't hurt Roxanne. Im want me back."

"Look at your face! You can't go back to him."

"We can't stay here forever. Me kids need to go to school."

"But he'll beat you again, Miss Marlene, maybe worse."

"Me whole life is in Jones Town. Please, me beg you a ride."

"I don't want to go there. I don't want to be responsible if something happen to you. I'm sorry, Miss Marlene, you're goin' to have to take a taxi."

"But me broke, don't have money for taxi."

Mishka reached into her bag. "Here's some money. I'll take you to the bus terminal. You can catch a taxi from there."

As she drove the depressed little family to the bus terminal, Mishka wondered why Marlene would ever go back to Paul.

Nothing was said when they got out of the car. Mishka stooped at the beach. She felt guilty about turning down Marlene, but there was no way she'd go back to Jones Town now. Last night was a risk worth taking. Luckily Paul didn't see her. She picked up her handbag and locked up the car. On the beach, she found a chair. Looking out at the clear blue sea, she recalled her trip here with Roxanne.

Too edgy to relax, she stretched her body and went for a jog along the sand. Going past a hutted restaurant, the smell of fried fish lead her inside. As soon as she began to order, her phone rang. She looked at it.

"Just a minute, mam," Mishka told the chef.

"You want me to start fry the fish?"

"Yes."

She stepped away to answer. "What's up, Ricardo?"

"Meet me at the gas station near Mommy house."

"I'm getting something to eat. I'll leave when I'm done."

"Leave now."

"But the lady fryin' the fish."

"Now!"

When she arrived at the gas station, Ricardo leaned against his car in the shade, smoking. He flicked his cigarette away and opened the passenger door of Mishka's car. She lifted her handbag to the back seat.

"What is it?" she said.

"Marlene jus' left the station. Paul broke her hand."

"I told her this would happen! Where is she now?"

"Me drop her off at the hospital."

"She told me earlier that Paul apologize and say he didn't hurt Roxanne. Why would he do this to her again?"

"She say im vex cause im can't find im shoes. Im beat her so bad she had to tell im where it is."

"She tell im that she gave it to you?"

"Yeh. An' she tell me that im left there mad, strap with a gun."

"So why don't you arrest him now, Ricardo! You know im strap."

"No rush. The DNA result soon come back. Me ask the superintendent to push the lab to work faster. If it come back negative then me will catch Paul an' lock im up for illegal possession of a firearm. It might be link to something. In the meantime me watch im close."

Mishka suddenly realized she too was going around strapped, but Norman had told her that the serial number was erased and that it was clean.

"If im vex bout you havin' the shoe, you think im know there's blood on it?"

"Don't know, but me hope im come for it. Im know me on to im. Im probably think Marlene try to set im up. For all me know she might already tell im everything."

"Aren't you scared, Ricardo?"

He laughed aloud. "Don't forget who have the license to kill. Me well want im confront me bout the shoe, so we can put this whole thing to rest."

"You think Marlene tell im I'm here? You think im vex cause Mommy take her in?"

"Marlene will tell im anything im want to know. Don't you see how bad im mash her up? An' if she tell im you're here im might know where you stay too. You need to watch your back, Mishka. Keep the doors lock at all times, curtains close, phone handy. Any sign of trouble call me first! When is your flight to Florida?"

"Day after tomorrow."

"Me can't provide you twenty-four hour security without concrete evidence that Paul is a threat." He looked at his watch. "Me have to go back to work now. You should change your flight to tomorrow. Maybe today, next flight. You have your visit, tell me what you know. Don't stick aroun' any longer. Me can take it from here. Me will get Paul, somehow, some way. You're jus' an extra burden right now."

"Me an' Mommy can hideout in the country till it's time for me to go back. Me have some extra cash, maybe rent somewhere for two days."

"No. Best if you go now. If anything me talk to Mommy an' take her to my house. Me go back and eyes Paul now, see what im up to. Me don't think you should even go back to the house until me call with Paul's location."

Her head spinning, she drove aimlessly, ending up at Devon House. On a bench in the shade, she used her cell phone to change her travel plans. She later called Brad. No answer. She called his office and reached his secretary.

"He's in court at the moment, may I take a message?"

Mishka gave the secretary the flight information. "Please ask him to call me as soon as possible, it's urgent."

Pacing, she saw people walking by and looking at her as though she'd lost it. She sat on the grass staring at her phone. She didn't want to leave Jamaica this way, but she had faith in Ricardo. He would take care of Paul and maybe justice would take its course. Her phone vibrated in her hand. She answered it.

"Go back to Mom's now. Me jus' spot Paul in a *black* car comin' into Jones Town."

Mishka packed her bags and sat on the verandah thinking about what to do with the firearm. She decided to stop on the way to the airport and toss out at sea. It was time to pick up Sophia. She headed to the airport. On the drive back, Mishka told Sophia that on Ricardo's advice she'd changed her travel schedule.

"What's the problem?" Sophia said.

She told Sophia about Marlene returning home, Paul attacking her again, and Ricardo's concerns.

"Wha' the hell goin' on, Mishka? Why is Paul after you?"

"Cause my brother wants to arrest him for killing Roxanne, and he raped me before I moved to America."

Struck, Sophia sat speechless, tears streaming down her cheeks.

"Me feel like a bad parent," she said, wiping away her tears.

“Don’t say that, Mommy. I didn’t tell you because there was nothing you could do bout it.”

“How can something like that happen right under me nose an’ me don’t know it?”

“Let’s not get into it now.”

“Me hope Ricardo lock up im bomboclat an’ through away the key.”

“Don’t worry, Ricardo will get im. Let’s go home and cook something for our last dinner before I have to leave.”

In the midst of dinner Mishka’s phone rang. She answered quickly.

“You at the house?” Ricardo said.

“Yes but me have a flight tonight,” Mishka said. “Ten o’clock.”

“Leave now!”

“What happen now?”

“Me lose Paul. Im slip away in a black car, Toyota Corolla.”

“Go to the airport. Me don’t know where im gone an’ me don’t like the smell of it. Hurry! Take Mommy! Me catch you at the airport.”

Mishka hang up. “Come, Mommy, Ricardo say we mus’ leave here quick. Me suitcase already in the car.”

Mishka grabbed her handbag and ran to the car. As she drove away from Sophia’s house, she saw the black car Ricardo described coming in her direction. She sped up.

“Mommy.”

“What?”

“Call Ricardo an’ tell im Paul behind us, and get the gun in me bag.”

“Where you get gun from!”

“Never mind, Mommy. Get it.”

Sophia called Ricardo. “Paul drive behind we now.” She looked at Mishka. “Im say to go fast, im will catch up.”

“Can’t go any faster. The traffic!”

In the rear view mirror, she saw the black car trailing close behind.

Sophia reached into Mishka’s bag and took out the pistol. “This small thing?” This for kill mouse.”

“Take off the safety,” Mishka said, pointing.

When they arrived in downtown Kingston, Mishka sped around a curve and lost control of the car. People leapt out of the way before the car smashed into a fruit stand. Fruits flew everywhere, mangos hit the windshield. Almost on its side, the car was wedged between a block wall and a pile of rice bags, steam coming from the hood. People gathered around.

"You alright, Mommy?"

"Yeh but me can't budge the door."

"Climb out this side. Me make a run for it."

Mishka unfastened her seat belt and kicked the door up and open. Not paying attention to the vendor yelling about his fruits, she struggled to climb out, horns sounding, traffic snared. She saw Paul stuck a few cars behind. Once out, she waded her way through the angry crowd and ran. She was fast, but there was no clear path. She looked behind her and saw that Paul had parked on the sidewalk. She ran faster. He began to chase her. She turned into an alley and saw it was a dead end. She stopped, turned. Paul ran in from the street. There was nowhere to go. He stopped running and walked toward her, drew a handgun from the back of his waist. He had the same look in his eyes as the day she left Jamaica with Calvin.

"So you the informer," he said. "Now me know why your brother try to lock me up!"

"What you want from me?"

"Me think you know, that's why you run." He moved closer, but not close enough. "Merica change you, eh? For a Jamaican gal you know to keep your fuckin' mouth shut."

He moved just close enough. She raised her leg at his pistol. It fired. The shot hit her upper arm, knocked her to the ground. He was on her, fuming, his gun at her forehead. She knew that it was over. He leered at her, his eyes filled with confidence, showing victory.

"Straight to hell me send you with Roxanne."

A shot sounded. He gasped. Blood spurted from his abdomen. Another shot fired, another, and another. He fell on top of her like a sack of yams. Her vision blurred, but not enough to keep her from seeing Sophia standing there, holding the little smoking pistol.

Chapter Thirty-one

Hours later…

Mishka woke up in bed surrounded by bright lights and white walls. She didn't know where she was the moment her eyes were open, but when she looked around the room and saw Ricardo, Sophia, and Brad at her bedside, she recalled Paul falling on top of her, and being rushed to the hospital in Ricardo's patrol jeep. She tried to sit up but her arm throbbed. It was bandaged and in a sling.

Brad kissed her on the cheek. "Are you in pain, Honey?"

There was a knock at the door. The nurse walked in.

"I brought your pain medicine and antibiotics, Mishka,"

"Perfect timing," Brad said.

Brad and Ricardo slid Mishka up in bed while Sophia rearranged her pillows. She took her medicine.

"I'll come in and change your bandage later," the nurse said.

Ricardo handed Mishka a newspaper. She took it and read the headline—*Female Security Guard Shoots Man Downtown Kingston.*

"Ricardo," she said. "Can I talk to you alone?"

Everyone else left the room.

"The gun," she said. "The one Mommy use, where is it?"

"Me already take care of it."

"Is he dead?"

"Them have im downstairs in intensive care."

"Really?"

"In a coma, under police guard."

"Is he goin' to make it?"

"Hope so. Mommy get im good, three shot, three hit. An' you want to hear something else?"

"What?"

"Me get a call bout the DNA result. It match."

She asked Ricardo to send Brad in. When he sat beside her she squeezed his hand.

"I'm really sorry," she said.

"What're you sorry about?"

"Taking you away from your job to come all the way here."

"Thought I'd never get here."

"How'd you know?"

"I got your message after court. When I called you back and didn't get an answer I had a weirdest feeling. That's when I searched the caller ID at home and found Sophia's number."

"I see you're still dressed in work clothes," she said.

"Didn't have time to change. I landed and came straight here, only left the hospital once with Ricardo to find a room somewhere in New Kingston."

She tried to smile. "I'm happy you're here."

"How's your pain?"

"Still hurts."

"Give the drug a little time to work. Wanna hear something positive?"

"What's that?"

"Your nurses' license came in the mail, thought you might be happy to know that."

When she was released from the hospital, Brad packed her things to take her to New Kingston but Ricardo insisted they finish their stay at his house.

"Thanks, man" Brad said, "But I haven't checked out of my room yet."

"It's cool, mon. I have an extra room at my place. No problem."

Brad looked at Mishka for her approval. She nodded.

Mishka's shoulder was still bandaged. Brad assisted her with baths and getting dressed.

"If it were any lower and ruined your lovely breasts I would've gone downstairs and finished off Paul myself."

She laughed for the first time.

Sophia made meals for everyone, and held her granddaughter every chance she had. Mishka lay in bed as directed by the doctor. The pain medicine kept her asleep most of the time.

One day, half between waking and sleeping, she overheard Brad and Sophia talking.

"Look like you really care about Mishka," Sophia said. "You come here quick."

"That was the most chilling news I've ever received over a telephone, but sure, Mishka's very special to me. I love her."

"Me happy to hear that. Me really sorry we have to meet this way."

"It's fine. I'm glad we finally met, and I'm thankful that Mishka is alive. It was a long flight here."

"Think you will ever come back to Jamaica after all of this?"

He laughed. "Mishka will come back to visit you I'm sure, but I don't think I'll feel comfortable about her traveling alone. So if she'll have me, yes, you'll see me again."

"Lord, me miss her already."

"She wants you to move to the U.S., but I told her she'll have to become an American citizen first."

"She say she want me to come there?"

"She did."

"Me love her so much."

"You know. besides driving, Jamaica isn't as bad as I thought. The hospital staff was very nice, and knowledgeable about what they were doing. Before coming here, from what Mishka told me about Paul, it led me to believe that Kingston wasn't a place for a guy like me."

"Certain parts of Kingston is not for a white man with nice suit. People look at you and know you're not from here, an' if you talk them think you rich."

He laughed. "Thanks for the tip."

"The North Coast is where most foreigner stay, but where me live now in Saint Catherine is safe. You and Mishka can come an' stay there next time. Ricardo will take you to see the countryside. Im a good driver."

He smiled. "I can see where Mishka got her lovely ways from. Thanks for the invitation and all you've done to accommodate us."

The day of Mishka's departure, Sophia went with them to the airport. Brad returned his rental car and left Mishka outside to say goodbye to her mother. They hugged.

"Thanks for saving my life, Mom."

"No need to thank me. I bring you into this world an' me wasn't going to bury you."

Sophia saw Brad coming and released her hug.

"Brad really love you. You mus' be good to im. Im goin' to marry you one day."

"And God forbid you miss the wedding," Mishka said, smiling.

"Take good care of yourself."

Sophia smiled and waved goodbye to Brad.

The End

Made in the USA
San Bernardino, CA
25 September 2015